Dream a Little Dream of Me

I0537316

The Dream Series

Book No. 1

Cobie Daniels

ISBN: 0692689737
ISBN-13: 978-0692689738

DEDICATION

To Sam
My knight in shining armor

To Mom and Dad
Who always believe in me

To Walter Elias Disney
For being the ultimate dreamer

"IT'S KIND OF FUN TO DO THE IMPOSSIBLE."

— WALT DISNEY

ACKNOWLEDGMENTS

This is the part I try not to forget the important people.

To my editor Jessa Sexton. I don't believe for one second our meeting was happenstance. You are simply the best.

To Courtney of The Designing Women at Formatting Fairies, thank you for an outstanding cover.

To my beta readers - Beth Aigner, Brittany Brown, Helen Dunn, Donna Magrini, Carrie McCord, Kim Mullins, Joshua Phelps, and Christine Surh for taking the time to read this when it was full of holes and mistakes.
I am grateful for each and everyone of you.

To Zoe York for your continued support and answering all of my ridiculous newbie emails.

To Heather Melito-Dezan for answering my "suspicious" legal Facebook messages.

To Michelle Young for making sure all my "Englishisms" did the queen proud.

To Melissa Blue Photo thank you for the gorgeous head shots.

To Michael Malkin for being a friend and resource through this process. Don't forget the little people when *Complex* hits TV.
Mazel Mazel.

August 2014
12 Weeks After the Incident

Another mid-Atlantic afternoon thunderstorm rolled in; Kelsey watched her horse trot towards the shelter of the barn as the wind began to whip across the field. The soybean crops lifted parched leaves to the heavens, begging the rains to quench their thirst. *Heaven*...Kelsey huffed under her breath as she was jarred back to her reality. The heavy clouds, the vibrant lightning, and the low thunder reflected the continual storm in her heart as she knew she was walking back into an empty house. Her family and friends really wanted to help, but when they said things like "take comfort that he's in heaven and you will see him again," she wanted to respond in the nicest way possible with "Fuck Off."

At any given moment Kelsey would find herself angry. Angry at her new situation? Yes. Angry at him? Yes. Pissed at God? Absolutely. Though she had felt multiple emotions since the incident, lately anger took precedence. She flipped on the bathroom light switch, turned on the water, added soap, and proceeded to clean her hands of the day's barn work. She stared into the mirror and had no idea who was staring back. As far as she was concerned, she was unrecognizable. Her caramel, shoulder length hair that used to shine was lost to a dull shade of brown beginning to show the signs of gray at the roots. Hazel eyes with the flecks of green that Jason loved to get lost in were now hidden behind a shade of sadness. Her once finely manicured nails had been chewed away, as biting them became a new nervous habit. None of that seemed to matter.

Kelsey continued to stare and then murmured, "Thirty-seven, and I look like I'm about to celebrate my fiftieth." Then she remembered she'd just recently locked herself in the house and tried her best to ignore her birthday. "Oh right…I'm thirty-eight now. Perfect." With a sufficient eye roll, she turned to dry her hands as the lights began to flicker. Quickly rounding up some candles, she lit the last one and placed it in the living room just as the power was gone. "Shit, seriously?" She grabbed the extra candle and made her way back to the living room. The coffee table looked like a shrink had vomited on it in the form of pamphlets. Titles like "Dealing with Grief," "Processing the Pain," and her particular favorite "Personal Grief Assessment." All were displayed in hopes Kelsey would talk about the incident. She scooped up all the pamphlets, walked them to the kitchen, and filed them in the garbage can. On the kitchen table were letters and cards. Most unopened. She couldn't bring herself to open them. Her eyes would just see letters forming words. Their messages of condolence were surely sincere, but her brain could not process when nothing computed in this situation. Her thoughts stayed in a perpetual cycle of sadness. Kelsey's heart was broken, shattered into a million microscopic pieces. So much so, that she was convinced no one would ever be worthy of making her whole again.

The power eventually came back on, which allowed her to take a hot shower and crawl into bed. The coolness of the sheets and the softness of the duvet hugged her body. Just when she had gained a moment of clarity, the empty void beside her in bed once again reduced her to a sob. The kind of cry that comes from deep within, leaving every joint and bone aching in the body. Reaching over to turn off the lamp, she let the darkness inside the room consume her. She lay in bed, asking the same questions that she asked every night for the past twelve weeks. "Why?"

At 3 AM, Kelsey woke with a jolt as another round of storms flared up. Her head pounding from all of the crying, she made her way to the kitchen for a glass of milk and Advil.

Heading back to work in only five hours after twelve weeks of bereavement, she was overwhelmed by the feeling of dread. She knew she had to try and find normalcy again, and maybe a routine would do that. She didn't need the money. Jason had taken out a very robust life insurance policy when they got married that paid off everything and left her a healthy savings account. However, Kelsey loved her job; more importantly she loved the people she worked with and the technology she worked with and knew that going back would hopefully help in this journey she never wanted to take to begin with.

As she walked back to her room, she stopped by the pictures hanging in the hallway. Staring at each photo, she felt her mind flooded with memories, and her eyes quickly filled with the only release they were familiar with. She made her way back to her room and began to talk out loud as if Jason were with her. "Jason, do you know how scared and tired I am? How am I going to survive this? Why did you leave me?"

She collapsed in her bed and lay in fetal position only to eventually fall into a deep sleep and dream vividly of the day her whole world spiraled out of control. In the dream, just as she did in real life, she found Jason slumped over the seat in his truck, head bleeding and not breathing. She erupted into screams, begging him not to leave her.

Before she knew it, the five forty-five alarm was already going off. Kelsey's eyes shot open. The drive one-way to downtown Norfolk was thirty-five minutes. Rush hour traffic added a good fifteen minutes, and if it was raining, then leaving at seven a.m. was a must. Thankful for an extremely simple dress code at work, which consisted of a polo shirt and her favorite jeans, she hayed her horse, fed the dogs, let them out one last time before crating them, then made her way to the car.

She could see her dad standing on his back porch forty yards or so from the driveway, coffee in one hand while using his other hand to send a faint wave. He knew today was a big first step. For some inexplicable reason, Kelsey felt like he was watching his little girl again, off to her first day of school. Kelsey closed her eyes and wished it were that simple and sweet. She gave a wave back and slid into the car. She could feel her heart start to sink and eyes fill with liquid therapy.

"No time for this! I need to beat that damn school bus, or else I'll never make it to work on time." She put the key in the ignition, adjusted her seat and mirrors, and put the car in reverse.

Having no idea how she would hold up once she got there, she put the car in drive and headed to the last place she was when she got the call.

August 1994
First Date

As Jason Bauer came around to open the passenger door, Kelsey recognized that this was the man she wanted to spend the rest of her life with. She'd just turned eighteen; most people would argue she couldn't possibly know, but Kelsey knew, and that was all that mattered. Standing at six feet to Kelsey's five foot seven stature, he had dark brown hair that accentuated his deep, piercing blue eyes. When he looked at Kelsey, it simply took her breath away.

One of the things that Kelsey immediately noticed about Jason was his chiseled chin and strong arms. When he held her, Kelsey felt safer there than she had ever felt anywhere. As he opened the door, Kelsey thought of how she was going to deal with her parents about all this. She was raised in a loving albeit very conservative home. Love was fine, but only if she did it the way her parents (in particular the way her mother) thought it should be done. Her mom would be okay if Kelsey married young to one of the nice boys from church. Especially one of those Brandon boys. While Kelsey thought they were a very nice family, she had absolutely no regard for either of those boys. She had read enough Jane Austen to know that she wanted to fall in love in the most unconventional way.

After a very nice dinner with Jason and some of the easiest conversation she'd ever had with any male, let alone this handsome twenty-two-year old, they played a round of miniature golf, laughing at each other as the competition to see who was going to win grew more intense with each putt. Once Kelsey secured the victory, they decided since it was a beautiful night, the moon at its fullest, a walk on the beach would be a great way to end a perfect date.

As they strolled, Kelsey pointed out the halo around the moon, which impressed Jason, as he had never seen one or even cared enough to see one. They continued to walk down the beach; the humidity reminded them that they were still in the middle of one of the hottest summers on record. They kicked off their shoes and socks and allowed their bare feet to be hit by the cool waves. Just as Kelsey was catching her breath from the feel of his hand over hers, Jason grabbed both of her hands, catching Kelsey by surprise, and pulled her to him. Eye to eye, Jason put his hands on either side of her face and placed a chaste kiss on her lips. It was all Kelsey could do to remain standing. He pulled away but didn't release her face.

"I'm sorry. I should've asked you first; you're just so beautiful…" and before he could finish, Kelsey kissed him back and this time surrendered her lips and tongue so that there was no question that he need not apologize. As they came up for air, he placed his forehead on hers. "Is this for real? We've known each other for a little over two weeks." His tone was of hopeful disbelief.

Over the early part of summer, Jason's parents had moved in down the street to Kelsey's family. Jason had come over to visit and saw Kelsey out back heading to the barn. She was wearing her hair in a long ponytail pulled back in a hat with a pink, short sleeve polo and brown riding britches and paddock boots. *Sexy* and *adorable* were the only words he could come up with. After one conversation over their fence that afternoon where he desperately tried to introduce himself and not sound like an ass, Jason asked if she would like to come into town to grab some lunch. From that moment, they had become inseparable, and Kelsey's mother watched with a raised eyebrow at their blossoming friendship.

"Kels? Can this really be happening this fast?" Jason asked again in a breathless moan. Kelsey's equally breathless response, "I don't even know what 'this' is, but I know I want more of it, and I want it to last forever." They both sat down in the sand, trying to figure out how to go forward. Jason had heard how conservative Kelsey's parents were, so "dating" was going to be tricky. Kelsey sat between his legs, her back to his chest. Their fingers entwined, Jason leaned in and gently kissed her neck, awakening Kelsey to her very core.

As they continued to sit there, Jason asked her about her hopes, dreams, and what she really wanted in life. He was enthralled listening to her passionately talk about her love of art and her desire to become a teacher so she could share that love with others; about her dreams of having her own land, horses and dogs, and a barn with a romantic loft; about the importance of family, faith, and helping others. He wanted to be the one to give it all to her, and he would jump through whatever hoops in order to make that happen.

They agreed that, no matter what, the obstacles they faced, they would face together. Regardless of her parents, high school graduation, and the next summer she was due to spend in England, they would get through it. He kissed her temple and said, "Let's get you home —don't want to get on your parents' bad side after our first official date."

As they stood, Jason grabbed her, pulled her in, and wrapped his arms around her. She laid her head on his chest. He breathed sweetly into her hair and said, "I love you, Kelsey Jane Chapman. I don't know how I already know this, but I do. I don't expect you to respond; I just need you to know." Kelsey pulled away from his chest; her eyes filled with tears. Putting her hands on his face, she quietly and passionately declared, "I love you, Jason Holden Bauer."

August 2014
Back to Work

At 7:53 AM, Kelsey pulled into the parking garage, her heart in her throat. She unbuckled her seatbelt and gathered her purse and lunch satchel. After she took two big cleansing breaths, she opened the car door, made sure she had all she needed, closed the door, and locked it. She made her way through the side door. Upon entering, she was greeted by several co-workers who very wisely welcomed her back with hugs and smiles and no words. For that she was grateful.

She walked into the break room to put her bag in a locker and lunch in the fridge. As she was heading back to gather her tools needed on the floor, her store leader Michael approached her. "Hey, Kelsey, got a minute?" Kelsey looked up, nodding her head yes. He led her into the office and closed the door behind them. He was a gentle guy, who loved his family and loved working for the greatest technology company in the world. His leadership and enthusiasm for both were endearing and inspiring.

"You ready for this, Kelsey?" His question caught her off guard, and she didn't answer back immediately. "I'm as ready as I'm going to be," she eventually said as she focused on the computer screen in fear that looking at him would cause the tears to come back.

"If you need anything at all during your shift, just say the word. We all know that you're just trying to get your feet wet again," he responded, making full eye contact. "We're here for you."

Before he could go on, Kelsey interrupted him, "I don't want to be coddled or to receive special treatment."

Michael looked perplexed. "I'm not suggesting that, Kelsey. I've been through a traumatic loss myself, and getting back into the game of life was tough. I just want you to know if something happens and you need to get off the floor, we have your back." Kelsey was touched and appreciated his concern. "Now get out there and have a good day and take it one minute and one hour at a time."

They both stood, and he gave her an encouraging hug that sent her out to the floor hopeful that the first day back wouldn't be the disaster she was expecting. By the time her lunch rolled around, Kelsey was beyond grateful that her morning contact with customers had been benign at best. Helping reset passwords for accounts and for Facebook were the norm before the incident, and thankfully that had not changed in the interim. Baby boomers who were encouraged by their children and grandchildren to own technology for Skype and FaceTime came in by the droves needing to reset passwords and security questions. It seemed all those couples gravitated to Kelsey, and she didn't mind one bit. She often thought that she and Jason would be the old hip couple their nieces and nephews would be proud of because they knew their devices inside and out.

Before she headed from the break room and back into the store, she checked her smartphone to see what she'd missed. There was a text from her sister with a short video of her nieces and nephew holding up a poster with the words "We Love You!" written on it. When she hit play she enjoyed twenty glorious seconds of the eight, five, and three-year-old declaring their adoration of their aunt.

Kelsey had experienced some of the darkest days and moments of her life over the past twelve weeks, but those kids were the perfect infusion of love and light that kept her going. All three had adored Jason, especially Sarah Jane. At age eight, she was a total princess and looked at her uncle Jason like the handsome prince that he was. They had a special bond, and she was having such a hard time processing that he was gone.

Kelsey watched the video three times then moved on to two voicemails. One was from her mom Melody, just calling to see how her day was and to let her know that she had walked over to the house to let the dogs out to play for a bit. Then one was from her doctor's office. When she played the message from Dr. Shepheard she began shaking her fist at the sky yelling, "DAMMIT." The message was a reminder that Kelsey was way overdue to come in for labs to check her iron levels. It dawned on her that, with all the bereavement and crying herself into oblivion, her exhaustion was just being exasperated by her anemia.

In 2012 what they initially thought was fatigue ended up leading them to discover that Kelsey was severely anemic and her body was not storing iron, which meant that her major organs were not getting enough oxygen. While they still didn't know why Kelsey's body started doing this, it put them on a path to finding out. The day the doctor told her, Kelsey's head was spinning with all the information that was being passed on to her. She reached out to her sister who worked in x-ray at the children's hospital. In her best reassuring voice, Ellie settled Kelsey's nerves and explained what to expect.
Dr. Shepheard put Kelsey on a special diet and scheduled iron infusions every ninety days. The

infusions had become the new normal, always scheduled at the infusion center at Norfolk General.

Looking back, Kelsey realized those Wednesdays in the center had become the best afternoon dates with Jason. They would last anywhere from four and half to five and a half hours. Jason would clear his schedule and pick up Kelsey as he insisted that they drive to the hospital together. They were a team in everything, no matter what. Once Kelsey was hooked up, he would sit in the chair opposite of her, take off her shoes, and use his lap as a footstool. While the iron dripped, they both read a good book or technology article on their smart devices, or napped. Sometimes he would slowly rub her feet and often times she would wake up and find him staring at her. Half awake she would reach for his hand and sleepily ask, "What are you staring at?" Jason would normally just smirk and say, "You, is that okay?" and then kiss her hand.

It was moments like that where she felt cherished and not like a burden. There were other people in the room who were hooked up and being treated for far worse things than severe anemia. Kelsey didn't take that for granted, and she knew they would figure all this out together as a team.

Before she went back out on the floor, she called the doctor back and made an appointment for an infusion for the following Wednesday. Another piece in setting up a routine again was now in place, and it would be nice to see and talk to Dr. Shepheard as they had become very good friends. It would also be helpful just to talk to someone who could give her some honest perspective about walking all this out without a counselor. Melody had been all over Kelsey about seeing their pastor for counseling, and while she understood her mom's concern, the last thing that Kelsey needed to hear from any pastor was to try and focus on the fact that she would see Jason again.

When five o'clock came, Kelsey inhaled deeply, pressed the *punch out* button, and then released her breath. The breathing techniques she had been learning in yoga before the incident had been beneficial the past several weeks. She made a mental checklist that she would need to sign up for another round of classes in the next few weeks. It would give her something else to do twice a week to make her physical body strong again as she rebuilt her emotional state.

Her first day back was officially over. As she climbed into her car, she buckled her seatbelt, grabbed the steering wheel, and let out a prayer of thanks. She decided not to focus on the fact that she was driving back to an empty home. There were still two and half hours of daylight left. She could get a quick ride in on Jedi and take the dogs out on the trails with her to get some exercise.

There were several places in life that Kelsey considered her favorite to be at any given time. Jason's arms were the first. She also loved to be with her nieces and nephew or with her horse, grooming him in the barn or out riding him on the trails. Kelsey spent the majority of her time doing the latter. Although seeing her nieces and nephews at least three times a week helped, spending her time in the barn dulled the sting of the fact that the first option of comfort was no longer available.

When she pulled up to the house, her horse Jedi greeted her at the fence. His head held high and proud, he let out a bit of a whinny. Kelsey walked over and greeted him with a cube of sugar and a big pat on his giant neck. "Hello, my handsome man." She always stashed cubes of sugar in her glove box as it had become a habit to greet her giant beauty when she got home. Reassuring him that she would be out momentarily with the dogs, Kelsey grabbed her keys and unlocked the door and walked into the side room that acted as a kennel and grooming room for her terriers Dodger and Rosie. They waited patiently in the kennels as Kelsey changed into her barn clothes and paddock boots.

"You guys ready for a short ride?!" The dogs bounced with joy, and in unison they headed out the side door for a couple hours of escape.

September 1994
Labor Day Weekend

At 8:30 AM, Kelsey came bounding down the stairs ready to head to the barn to groom her horse and get a ride in before lunch. She was expecting to spend late afternoon and early evening with her Jason but couldn't neglect her horse on such a beautiful Saturday morning.

Melody was sitting at the table reading her newspaper and sipping coffee when she saw Kelsey grabbing orange juice out of the fridge. "Off to the barn this morning?"

"Yeah, need to keep Triton in shape, and I love a good hack though the fields on a Saturday."

Before she could tell her mom what direction and which trails she planned on taking, Melody put the paper down and curtly announced, "Kelsey, we need to talk."

Kelsey knew that tone and stared straight at the cabinets in front of her. She knew this moment had been coming and was honestly surprised it was just now happening. She turned with her glass in hand and quipped lightly, "Okay. What's up?"

With steely eyes and a cool tone, Melody shot back, "Oh, I think you know what I want to discuss, young lady." Kelsey could feel the knot in her stomach tighten. She sat at the table and made direct eye contact with her mother. Melody kept the eye contact and started in. "While I am sure Jason Bauer is a very nice young man, and his parents seem very nice as well, your father and I do not approve of anything other than a friendship with him."

Kelsey's heart was in her throat as Melody continued her speech, "We've let you go off with him because we know that, although you are still yet to graduate, you are eighteen and legally an adult—but this is our house, and our rules have not changed. We feel very strongly that, if you are to start dating, your father and I could make arrangements with the Brandons and set up a date with one of their nice sons from church. Especially Joe, he's a sophomore in college this year and has plans to go into ministry. Your father and I raised you in the church for a reason, and as I said, while I'm sure Jason is a nice young man, he doesn't meet the Godly criteria that we've worked so hard to instill in you and your sister. Surely you don't want to disappoint God as well as us, now, do you?"

Melody Chapman was a master at undermining and manipulating to get what she wanted. The moment had finally arrived; Kelsey knew that her mother was going to throw down the preverbal gauntlet eventually, and she had done a masterful job this morning. Especially timing it before her morning ride, as her mother knew Kelsey would be alone with only her horse and her thoughts to keep her company. Melody knew that Kelsey was a thinker, and at times an over thinker.

Bravo Melody, Bravo were the only words that came to Kelsey's mind. Kelsey sat there in deafening silence but kept eye contact with her mother for several long, awkward moments. Moments that seemed to make even her mom uncomfortable. Melody looked at Kelsey and mumbled out, "Well? Do you have nothing to say?"

Kelsey took in a long, cleansing breath, blew the air out, and looked out the window to the barn to see the sun sparkling off the fish pond. She normally responded in calm respect to her mother's demands and manipulation, but the feelings she had for Jason had already made her stronger and bolder. It made no sense, she decided in that moment, to deliver anything other than the truth. Without taking her eyes off the pond, in a very calm, direct, and matter-of-fact tone, she unassumingly said, "Mom, I love him, and I'm going to marry him."

The room went from awkward and manipulative on Melody's side of the table to global thermal nuclear in a nanosecond. Melody, now standing and doing everything in her power not to lose control and scream, pointed her finger in Kelsey's face. "I forbid you to see him, Kelsey. If you think for one moment your father and I are going to let you throw away all that we have instilled in you, from your education to your faith, you are sadly…" before Melody could even finish, Kelsey stood up and calmly cut her off.

"My *faith*? Yes. Let's talk about *my faith* that you and Daddy *instilled* in me. When did it become *my* faith? For the last eighteen years I've been told what to believe, when to believe it, and how to believe it. When I asked questions that you didn't deem *worthy* of answering, you would shut down my thinking and manipulate me right back into your perfect box where you allowed your perfect faith and perfect family to reside. There I was, your perfect daughter 'honoring thy father and mother,' though not out of love and respect but out of guilt and desperately wanting your approval. I've never given either of you any reason to doubt how much I love you. God only knows I've always been the good girl, always in church, but what about life outside of church? The last time I read

29

my Bible, which, by the way, was just the other night, it dawned on me: Jesus wasn't in church all the time. Did you know that, Mom? He was actually out in the world hanging with those who needed him the most. I still have yet to find where Jesus ever said he would be disappointed in me if I had a drink or if I—god-forbid—if I kissed a man before my wedding day, Mom." Kelsey was slightly surprised at her own boldness, but her years of silence simply had to end.

"I let you go to parties!" Melody yelled.

Kelsey shot right back. "Yeah, but look at the grief you would give me before I even walked out the door! You would lecture me about whom I was representing, give a mini sermon from Galatians 5:6, and then back that up with Ephesians 6:2. It was never, *have a good time; we love you and trust you*. No, it was pound me with scripture before I even walked out the door. You may as well have pinned a scarlet letter to me to ensure that no one would come near me."

Melody hissed back, "If you thought for one-second I or your father were going to give you a pass to go out and party and have a good time with your friends when the Bible clearly says that debauchery is a sin then you, my dear, have lived in a fantasy."

Kelsey shot back, "No, Mom, I never wanted that. I just wanted you to stop using religion as your measuring stick to emotionally beat me with. Instead, I wanted you to show me that you trusted me as your daughter and as an adult. I've never given you a reason *not* to trust me!"

Melody could only stare and then shot off, "Kelsey, you don't have any idea how dangerous this world is and the evil that runs rampant."

Kelsey could no longer control her tone; her nerves were frayed, and she wasn't going to entertain this any further. "You know as well as I do NONE of us have control over any of it, good or bad! If there is ANYTHING that I learned in church it's that I have to trust God no matter what happens in this life." Kelsey just stared at her mother, remaining deadly quiet. Then she took one swig of her orange juice, swallowed hard, and set the glass on the table. As she turned to the back door to open it, she added, "Mom, I want to believe that raising us in church was what you thought best for our family, but right now I only see that it was the perfect tool that you needed so that you could always be in control. You always want control, and when you don't have it, you manipulate the situation until you get it. That is what being raised in the church has taught me."

In two steps Kelsey's mom was directly in front of her, and a heartbeat later, with a nearly unimaginable force, Melody smacked Kelsey across the face. "Don't you ever talk to me that way again—do you hear me?!" The intensity was hard enough to send Kelsey back two steps. Her face felt as if a thousand bee stings had made her cheek their target. Kelsey opened the back door and ran to the barn. In a flash, she saddled up Triton and took off across the fields. She didn't know where she was going, but with tears streaming down her face, she rode hard, and she rode fast.

* * *

Later That Afternoon

Coy Chapman worked two jobs so that his wife could stay at home and raise their girls. He wouldn't have had it any other way. He loved his girls more than anything. At times he did think Melody could be a bit hard on them. Especially Kelsey.

He loved that Kelsey and Ellie were very close as sisters and loved even more seeing them grown into bright, beautiful, smart girls who could think for themselves. What he couldn't wrap his mind around was that Kelsey was graduating from high school and heading off to England for the summer. Where time had gone, he had no idea; at one point in his life he thought he would never stop buying diapers, and now here he was about to send his daughter into the world. He knew that Melody had hoped to convince her to come back from England and take some time off before starting classes at ODU as she really hoped Kelsey would become interested in the eldest Brandon boy. Melody had it in her mind that it would be the perfect match. However, Coy knew what he saw, and Kelsey was not interested. She'd never even looked at the Brandon boys like the other girls around her did. In the end Coy just wanted his daughter healthy, happy, and always keeping her faith at the forefront of all she did. Though Melody was usually too worried about the bad that could happen to see it, Coy knew Kelsey was strong and faithful in her friendships, to her family, and to God. She was different from other teens and other girls because she was more concerned about those things than about fitting in or keeping up with the crowd. Because of this, Coy wasn't worried about her at all.

It was almost four in the afternoon on another sultry, summer day. Coy could taste the afternoon thunderstorms starting to roll in; the thick and heavy air was all the evidence anyone needed before even seeing the clouds. He was headed to his car from the warehouse where he worked part time on Saturdays when his supervisor ran out to grab him and tell him he had an urgent phone call from his wife.

Coy didn't panic much after years as a full-time fire fighter; panic did nothing for emergency situations. Big heavy raindrops started to fall out of the sky as he reached the back door; when he entered he could hear Melody screaming on the other end of the receiver. He grabbed the phone out of Jake's hand, "Melody, sweetheart, what's wrong?"

"I hit her, Coy. I hit her and now she is gone and it is starting to storm out here really bad and she hasn't come home yet! She's been gone for hours, and it'll be dark soon."

In a calm voice, Coy methodically breathed into the phone to his wife, "Melody, calm down. I don't understand what you're talking about."

"Kelsey. I smacked Kelsey across the face this morning and she rode off across the fields and now it's storming and she hasn't come home. What have I done, Coy?!"

"Melody, think, did she tell you what trails she was taking today?"

"No, Coy, didn't you just hear me?!"

"Melody, just stay there; call the neighbors and see if they've seen her. If not, then call emergency services. It's going to be okay. She is going to be okay. Just stay calm; I'm on my way home."

Just as Melody hung up the phone to start making other calls, Ellie came in from a friend's house where they had been working on a school project. "Mom! What's going on?" Ellie could see the panic in her mother's eyes and knew something downright awful had happened. Melody explained what was going on, and by the time she finished her story, Ellie was changed into her barn clothes and raincoat, and with a flashlight in one hand to help as it grew darker, she headed to the door to start searching.

The rain was pouring down in sheets; then there was the vivid lighting. The rain had dropped the temperature down twenty degrees, and the wind almost made it seem chilly. Ellie looked at her mother and asked her if Kelsey had taken a rain jacket with her. Melody's eyes were wide, and she could only shake her head no. Just as Ellie was about to run out the back door, the doorbell rang. Melody darted to answer it only to find Jason standing there with his raincoat on.

"Mrs. Chapman, I'm sorry to intrude, but I've been trying to reach Kelsey all afternoon, and your phone's been busy. I've been home all day, and she hasn't called at all even to confirm our dinner plans for tonight, and I got worried."

The only thing that Melody could do was stare at Jason, no words, just staring. By the time Ellie got to the front door, she all but pushed her mom out of the way and pulled Jason in. "Jason, Kelsey's been missing since nine this morning. She and mom had a falling out, and she ran to the barn and took off and hasn't been seen since!" Jason ran to the barn, with Ellie right behind him. By the time they both reached the gate to the paddock they heard galloping hooves and a whinny. They both turned at the same time to see Triton. And no Kelsey. Panic-stricken, Jason yanked the flashlight out of Ellie's hand and ran into the night calling Kelsey's name and praying that, when he found her, she would be all right.

October 1994
Homecoming Weekend

Courtney Freeman was the beautiful, vivacious ginger Kelsey was lucky to call her best friend. Courtney worked for the school newspaper and was the president of the Conservation Club. She collected trash in the local park and on the sides of the road once a month, and while her family went to church, they were, as Melody would say, "more liberal" with how they raised their children. Courtney was an animal lover like her best friend and planned on living in Jackson Hole, Wyoming, after graduation to take advantage of a non-profit internship that could turn into a permanent job with a world conservation group. Living in Wyoming would place her in the outdoors and mountains she loved, and not to mention she would be able to ski in the winter.

Their other bestie, Jasper Parker, was a looker himself. Dark hair, blue eyes, he had a love for Broadway and was a giant tech geek. He was the president of the Technology Club at school and had actually written code and algorithms for the software that the public school system was using citywide. He'd already been hired by FedEx Corporate to start working in their IT department right out of high school as one of their youngest employees in the history of the company. He would be leaving for Memphis, Tennessee, two weeks after graduation.

They'd all met in church and gravitated to each other. When Kelsey accompanied them to parties, she was always the "good girl" who made sure that, once drinking commenced, Courtney and Jasper got home. However, she also made sure that, if too much drinking happened, she would be toilet-side, holding Courtney's hair in her bathroom and providing a cool face towel to Jasper. She didn't even think about what her parents would say if they knew about this. Quite frankly she didn't care; these were her best friends, and she would not feel guilty for taking care of them. Especially when she always refrained from joining in the festivities. It's not like it would take much to get her drunk, but with her mother's voice in her ear constantly chirping "do the right thing," drinking at a party was never an option. Besides, someone in their friendship trio had to keep the level head, and Kelsey truly didn't mind being that someone.

By the time they arrived back at Courtney's house after one particular party, it was well after two a.m. Kelsey got everyone inside and made sure that Courtney and Jasper had changed before passing out: Courtney in her bed and Jasper on the small sofa in corner of the same room. Courtney's parents, again showing their more "liberal" side, were completely fine with all of them in the same room. They trusted the three of them, and that was that. On the other hand, if Kelsey's mom ever found out that she had stayed the night in the same bedroom as someone of the opposite sex, she would truly be grounded until the day of graduation.

Jasper had no intentions of pursuing anything with either of his best girl friends. He loved them too much, and while he had said nothing to anyone else, he'd already confided in them that he was attracted to the same sex. Courtney and Kelsey loved Jasper no matter what and regardless of what the church said in their small conservative town. Even as teenagers they knew the importance of true friendship not being defined by sexuality, religion, or politics.

Once she put them to bed, Kelsey kept her promise to Jason that she would call once she got back in from the party. She'd invited Jason to meet her there, but Jason was twenty-two and felt a little odd being at a party with a bunch of young high schoolers. He knew that the whole time he would want to figure out a way to sneak off with Kelsey, but she had friends to care for, so he said to call no matter how late it was.

Kelsey grabbed the phone on the nightstand, grateful the cord was long enough to let her crawl into the closet and close the door so she could talk to Jason without being interrupted by the incessant snoring that had started not five minutes after her friends both passed out. It took only a half a ring, and Jason picked up. "Hey, Beautiful," was the smiling voice that greeted her. "Well, hello yourself," was a smiling voice greeting him right back.

"How was your night?"

"It was good."

"Meet any handsome guys and fall in love?" Jason jokingly asked.

"Well, I will have you know that I was very busy keeping Courtney out of trouble with the quarterback of the football team."

"Trouble? Do you mean the kind of trouble that could lead to regrets the next morning?"

"Yep, that would be the kind," Kelsey responded with a quiet laugh. "The best part is that Courtney has never been interested in those kinds of guys, and if I had a video recorder to film what I saw, she would never leave her room again."

Jason laughed out loud, "I know I've only known her a short time, but Courtney doesn't strike me as the kind of gal who would be interested in the quarterback of the football team."

Kelsey loved that Jason already understood the personalities of her friends. "Well…" Kelsey responded, "Imagine my surprise when number seven, Ryan Landry, comes out of nowhere, sits next to Courtney at the bonfire, and starts chatting her up. Between the both of them they had only had about two beers, but as their conversation flowed, so did the alcohol. I could see them leaning into each other more; Ryan would whisper into Courtney's ear, and then she would giggle. I knew when I heard Ryan suggest that they go for a walk that it was time to round up the troops and get them home."

Jason laughed and loved how Kelsey was so unselfish in taking care of her friends and being the good girl. She wore it like a badge of honor. He did wonder, though, if that badge had become more of cross to bear. Would she ever allow herself to be free of it for her own sake? Jason sighed, "Well, I'm glad you made it back to Courtney's house and everyone is safe. How are you feeling?"

As Kelsey responded, she rubbed the entry point of the wound. "I actually feel pretty good. Now that they've removed the stitches, there's still pain, but it's getting better."

"Glad to hear it, Kels."

"I don't ever want to go through that again."

"I don't ever want to have to live that nightmare of finding you."

Before he could finish Kelsey interrupted, "Hey, stop. It's okay. I'm here, and that's all that matters, right?"

Jason let out a deep and unsteady breath. "I missed seeing you tonight," he said, sounding romantic and a tad bit pitiful to lighten the moment.

"I'm pretty sure I missed you more," Kelsey responded. "And I'm so ready to be alone with you. No distractions, no worrying about the time, my parents, just me and you."

Jason immediately felt himself aroused. "Kelsey, you have no idea how ready I am as well."

While kissing and touching had sufficed thus far, he was ready to take Kelsey with all the passion and love that had become bottled up inside him for three months. Kelsey was ready to finally feel the release of yearnings and desires that had collected in her heart and shot straight to her center. She and Jason had spent many a night on the phone talking about how they could plan a weekend away from everyone without her parents finding out. His place was perfect. He lived alone in a beautiful one-bedroom studio apartment on the twelfth floor of the tallest high-rise in Virginia Beach. His family owned a commercial construction company, and his pay allowed him the luxury, oceanfront apartment. Amazing views of the sunrise and amazing early morning runs on the boardwalk were what kept him there. Ever since Kelsey, he had dreamed every night about bringing her back to his place and touching her and worshiping her body in ways that she could never dream possible. To pour himself into her so that she knew that he was hers and she was his.

"Jason?"

"Mmhmm, yeah still here, Kels."

"I need to go, and so do you. I know you're working tomorrow."

"I am," he said, "but I'll call you when I get my first break and can get back in the office."

"That sounds great. I have a quiet Saturday planned, so I should be home from my ride by lunch. I'm sure mom and dad will have something for me to do after that."

"I love you, Kels. Get some rest."

"You as well, Jason. I love you too."

There was a brief silence when Kelsey finally said, "Jason, you have to hang up."

"I can't, babe," Jason snickered.

Kelsey laughed, "Wow, this love thing has really got us, doesn't it?"

"Yeah, looks that way, kiddo."

"Okay, well, we won't say goodbye; we'll just say goodnight!" Kelsey exclaimed. They both counted to three and said *I love you* and *goodnight* and quietly hung up the phone. Kelsey hugged the phone to her body and wondered how she would ever make it to graduation and even a summer in England without Jason. She wouldn't think about that right now. Since the accident on Labor Day weekend, she would take each day as a gift. Her heart was aflutter. November was upon them, and the holidays would be here before she knew it.

And only seven days later would be the weekend that changed her life in all the right ways.

September 1994
The Accident

When Coy pulled up to the house, the rain was coming down hard, and the lightning was flashing so bright that it lit up the fields like the afternoon sunlight. There were police cars, ambulances, a fire truck, and search and rescue. Besides the occasional lightning, complete darkness now covered the fields, and the rescue mission to find Kelsey was in full swing. Coy ran to the side door that led to the kitchen where he found his wife giving a police report. Melody jumped out of her chair and into her husband's arms where she sobbed. Coy just held her and let her cry it out until the officer interrupted.

"Ma'am, I have just a few more questions I must ask you."

Before Melody could respond, Coy spoke up and asked the officer if they had any updates. The officer nodded and filled Coy in on the search perimeter, showing him the map and all seven trails that led to Lassiter Lake. Each trail was a little different—some were windy, some were hilly, and some were both—but they all covered at least a fifty-mile radius. If she had made it to the lake, they would have to rely on ATVs and the rescue dogs to get them through the thick brush that could act as a canopy in these heavy rains.

Once the officer was done, Melody began whispering while her head rested on her husband's chest. With her eyes shut tight, she told Coy, "Triton is in the barn." He pulled her back and, looking confused, asked, "What?" Melody kept her eyes shut as the officer explained to Coy that the horse had returned rider less over an hour ago. Melody, again trying to find her voice, managed to say that Ellie was in the barn tending to the horse while Jason had run into the night looking for Kelsey.

"Jason doesn't know those trails!" Coy exclaimed. "He's going to end up becoming a part of the problem!"

The officer cleared his throat and tried to comfort them, "We have the best of the best in search and rescue out there. We're waiting for this band of storms to pass, as I can't send the team out into the lightning. The weather radar is saying this particular band should be past us in the next forty-five minutes.

"FORTY-FIVE MINUTES!" Melody screamed. "You can't wait! What if she's severely injured? What about black bear or coyote? You can't wait!"

Putting his hand up, the officer made eye contact and sternly boomed, "Ma'am, I'm going to step out and let you get yourself together as I know you're extremely upset, but when I come back in, I need you calm and ready to answer a few more questions for me. Do you understand?"

Melody wasn't used to that tone from anyone, but even Coy knew that it was the only way to get her to listen and calm down. The officer stepped out. Coy continued to hold Melody and prayed silently that this nightmare would be over soon.

Two hours later, Jason, soaked to the bone, had tromped through more mud than he had ever seen in his lifetime. The lightning was terrible, and the thunder was a constant reminder of the danger he was in. He just didn't care. Kelsey was alone and in just as much danger. Once he got through the soybean fields and came to the first trail, he rolled the dice that it was the one that Kelsey would have taken. Armed with only his rain jacket and flashlight, he called out to her every fifteen seconds, allowing himself to stop and listen—to try and hear her calling back over the wind and booming thunder. "Please, God, please let me find her alive," is all Jason could say over and over again.

Forty-five minutes later the lightning and thunder were gone, and the rain continued, but just as a drizzle. Using the flashlight to scan the ground, Jason jogged the trail, calling out her name and looking for any clues. He stopped when the light reflected something shiny. He slowly rotated the light back to the left and saw the buckle from Kelsey's paddock boot. Running towards it, he snatched it from the ground. His cry for her became more frantic. In desperation he took off at a dead sprint. He knew a lake was at the end of the trail; that much he had learned from his conversations with Kelsey. With his lungs burning in his chest, he ran as hard as he could until he found her. A lump on the trail, not moving, white as a sheet and with a large branch protruding into her side.

Jason fell to his knees. "Kelsey! No, no, no, Kels, kiddo, talk to me, please," Jason pushed her hair away from her face and started to scream, "Someone, anyone, help us!" He felt her wrist for a pulse, and relief shot though his body when he found it. Ripping off his jacket, he placed it over top of her. "Oh my god, Kelsey, you're so cold, baby. We've got to get you warm."

Just then he heard her moan slightly. "Oh, baby, oh god, just don't move. Help is coming, I promise. Help is coming. You have to stay with me, Kelsey; you can't leave me like this." Jason could hear the dogs and ATVs off in the distance.

"Do you hear that, Kels? That's for you. I'm going to run back down the trail and let them know that you're here."

Jason took off at a full run; he was screaming, flashing his light, anything to get the attention of anyone on the search and rescue team. Just when it seemed his efforts were going to be futile, one of the drivers saw Jason and immediately approached him. "I found her" was all he could manage to say breathlessly. "Get on, and show me where she is," the driver instructed.

Two minutes later they were at Kelsey's side; another search and rescue team member was now on site as they prepared to stabilize her body and have her airlifted out by the Nightingale. As Jason listened to him radio back to base that there was a clearing next to the lake where they could safely land the helicopter, the rescue team secured Kelsey's body and the foreign object sticking out of her side on the rescue board.

"I'm going with her," Jason declared to the rescue team.

One of the more senior team members walked up to Jason and put his hand on his shoulder, "Son, there isn't enough room for you on the helo. Let me get you back to the house so you can make your way to the hospital."

"Not until I see her in the air," Jason replied.

At this point they had connected Kelsey to an IV and were trying to get her body temperature back up as she was hypothermic. As he stood beside her, holding her hand, his forehead on her forehead, Jason started to talk to her, "I'll be there when you wake up, kiddo. Do you understand? I'm not leaving your side until you walk out of that hospital with me." The Nightingale was making her approach.

"Jason," said the familiar voice of the rescue member, "I need you to go get on the ATV and wait there; as soon as we load her, I'll get you back to the house." He rested his hand on Jason's shoulder. Jason kissed Kelsey's forehead and walked over to the ATV, where he watched as they loaded her and lifted her gracefully into the night sky. As the rescue member walked back over to Jason, he introduced himself, "My name is Jack Kenney. I'm sorry we had to meet under these circumstances, but let me get you back. Do you have someone who can drive you?" Unable to speak, Jason nodded his head yes. "Okay, then let's get you on your way."

By the time they got back to the house, Kelsey's family was already in route to the hospital. Jason's mom Regina was there to meet him; she threw her arms around him and just held him.

"Mom, can you please drive me to the hospital?"

"Absolutely, son, but do you want to shower first and change? You're soaked to the bone and a muddy mess."

"Mom, the only thing that matters is that you get me to Kelsey as quickly as you can."

Regina didn't even argue; she could see it in her son's eyes. "I'll bring you back some clean clothes. How about that?"

"That's fine, Mom. Just get me to her."

Though he was exhausted, he had the look of a desperate man in love and willing to fight anyone who tried to tell him *no* when it came to seeing Kelsey. It was eleven fifteen p.m. by the time they pulled up to the emergency room entrance. As soon as he walked in, Ellie came running up and threw her arms around him. "Are you okay?" is all Ellie could say and still try and keep it together.

"I need an update, Ellie, and now."

"They had to take her into surgery to remove that awful branch. It missed all her internal organs and major arteries. The doctor said it was a clean entry and that she lost a lot of blood. Oh my gosh, Jason! You're a mess," Ellie blurted out right in the middle of her update. He just stared at her, and then a small smile crept on his face.

Before he could respond, both Kelsey's parents came into the waiting area. Melody went straight to the chair and couldn't even look at Jason. Coy came right over and, before Jason could even react, embraced him and thanked him as his voice began to crack. Jason, who was not used to this kind of affection from his own father, was especially taken aback as he never expected it from Kelsey's dad. He finally accepted the embrace and hugged him back. The surgeon came out with an update, and every eye in the room was on him. He went to Melody. Coy was by her side in three strides.

"She is stable. We were able to remove the branch she landed on and clean out the wound of debris. It took two hundred stitches to close her up. She was extremely lucky that it was a clean entry, just a deep one. We did a blood transfusion because of the blood loss. We're going to keep her in ICU until I know she's stable enough."

"When can we see her?" Melody asked.

"She's in recovery right now. We hope to have her in a bed soon. As soon as we do, you'll be the first to know. I want you to know that if she hadn't been found when she was, I don't think she would have had this outcome. She was in shock, and, with all the blood loss, I'm not sure she would have lasted much longer. I'll send a nurse out shortly with an update."

Once the surgeon left, Coy and Ellie both looked over at Jason. Ellie could barely get the words out as she stared at Jason, "He saved her life, didn't he, Dad?" There was a brief pause to Coy's response, "It looks that way, sweetheart," his voice low as to not show his emotion.

Melody just stared out, not meeting the gaze of anyone. Jason excused himself and found the closest restroom. He locked the door behind him and slid down to the floor. With his knees up and his head back against the door, he took a moment to absorb all that had transpired over the past several hours and let the tears flow as the relief that Kelsey was going to be okay washed over him.

He spent thirty minutes sobbing into his hands giving his body permission to release the tension with heavy weeping. When he was finally able to stand up, he ran the cold water in the sink and splashed it on his very red face. He used one of the harsh paper towels to dry himself and headed back into the waiting room to wait with her family. His mom greeted him with a fresh set of clothes; he had just enough time to change and clean up when the nurse came out to the waiting room.

"Hi, folks; my name is Bernadette. Call me Bernie. I'm Kelsey's nurse and can escort two at a time to see Kelsey."

Melody stood right up, but Coy grabbed her shoulder. "Let him go to her first, Mel."

Like a caged animal, Melody responded with, "I certainly will not. She's my daughter, and he is the reason we're here in the first place!"

"Melody Chapman, that is a harsh and unfair thing to say in this moment," Coy ripped back. "I'll wait to go back with Ellie. I want Jason to go first."

Melody glared at Coy and continued to argue, but Jason was immediately at the side of the nurse who saw the urgency in his eyes and didn't quite care for the attitude of Kelsey's mom. "Follow me this way, son," Bernie said softly.

When he reached Kelsey's side, he couldn't believe how pale yet peaceful she looked. How she had gone from looking as if death would claim her at any moment just hours ago to this peaceful sleeping beauty before him. He was lost for words. With a half smile on his face, he held her hand and stroked her face as he leaned over and whispered, "Kels, baby, I'm here."

Bernie was checking her vitals when she looked at Jason. "She's on some pretty heavy drugs right now."

"When will she open her eyes?" Jason asked without trying to sound so desperate.

"She'll probably start to stir in a couple of hours when this first round of meds start to wear off. Just continue to hold her hand and talk to her. I'll be back to check on you in a bit."

As the nurse was leaving, Melody brushed by her, coming to the other side of the bed to grab Kelsey's hand. "Kelsey, Kelsey, it's Mom. I'm here, baby, as well. Jason and I both are, and we love you so much." Jason's head shot up, and he stared at Melody who had tears streaming down her cheeks but would look only at Kelsey. Kelsey offered no response except for her peaceful breathing as the sounds of beeping machines dominated the room.

Twenty minutes went by before Jason spoke up, "Let me go so Mr. Chapman and Ellie can come back here." Before he could release Kelsey's hand, Melody's voice cut the air like a knife, "No, no, let me go. I'll get Coy. She needs to see your face when she wakes up." Melody began to leave the room but stopped short of the door with her back to Jason. "I know I've been unfair to you, Jason. I know I've been unfair to

Kelsey, but that wasn't my intention. I just want the best for her; she deserves only the best."

"I only want to give her the best, Mrs. Chapman. I swear to you," Jason said with all the authority he could muster without sounding angry or hostile.

Melody finally looked up and made eye contact with him, "I know Jason, it's just, when you try to raise your kids a certain way, you want to protect them from this world and all the bad. I will never apologize for wanting to protect my kids, Jason, even if it seems extreme to others. I know that people think I have sheltered and used faith as a weapon. That was never my intent. Ever. I'll never apologize for wanting to ground my family in faith. However, after tonight, I've learned that my heart needs to open to a different plan. If that plan is to involve you, then I need to pay attention and let some things…change."

Jason let her finish all she had to say and simply said, "Thank you." By the time Coy and Ellie came in and spent some time with Kelsey, it was well after one in the morning. "I'm going to stay the night with her, Mr. Chapman. Why don't you guys get home and get a few hours of sleep. Then I can call you if anything changes." Coy looked over at Ellie who was sitting, dozing off while breaking the two visitors per room limit. He nodded to Jason and said he'd be back with Melody around eight a.m. With that, they left as nurse Bernie was coming in.

"Time to check her vitals again." This time when Bernie started the blood pressure cuff, Kelsey began to stir. "Her meds are wearing off," Bernie said. "She'll be due for more."

Jason noticed Kelsey tried to open her eyes but only managed a squint through which she barely saw Jason leaning over, his brow furrowed but also a half smile on his lips. "Hey, kiddo, I'm right here, just like I promised I would be." Kelsey was desperately trying to remember. "What.... what happened? Why am I here? Where is Tri..." before she could finish her eyes grew as large as saucers. "Where is Triton!?"

"Hey hey hey, it's okay. You're in the hospital. You took a nasty spill off your horse." Kelsey desperately tried to remember what happened. Even though she wore her riding helmet, she couldn't believe how bad her head hurt, not to mention the searing pain from her side. "Triton is safe in his stall; do you remember what happened out there?"

"Mom and I had fight. I wasn't ready to go home when the storm rolled in. I remember the wind got really bad, a large branch, and then something startled Triton, and he reared and I came off. That's all," Kelsey mostly whispered.

Jason placed his hand soothingly on her face. "I'm so glad we found you, Kelsey. You landed on a very large branch, lost a lot of blood. When I found you, you were hypothermic and non-responsive. You scared the hell out of me."

Bernie looked at Kelsey's chart to confirm dosages. "I'm going to go get your next round of meds, dear. Be right back."

Kelsey's eyes closed again, and Jason leaned over and placed his head on her forehead. "Hmmm, Jason, I'm so glad you're here right now. Where are my parents and Ellie?" Kelsey asked as she slowly reached her IV hand up to stroke Jason's hair. Jason brushed a gentle kiss over her lips. "They left a few minutes ago. They'll be back at eight, which is just a few hours from now."

"They let you stay with me?" Jason could only shake his head yes. They both stayed quiet for a few moments when Jason softly spoke, "Kels, I love you so much. Please don't ever do this to me ever again."

Nurse Bernie was back with round two of meds and a sleeping chair and blanket she rolled in for Jason. "I'm really getting uncomfortable, the pain in my head and side are so intense," Kelsey mumbled out. "Well, what I have will fix that for you in about one minute, sweetheart," Bernie assured her. "Now, Jason, when I give her these meds, it'll put her right back to sleep, and you, sir, will need to get some sleep as well." Jason looked at Kelsey and looked at the clock; he was beyond exhausted and decided after pushing the fold out chair next to Kelsey's bed that he could lay on his side and still hold her hand while they both slept. Five minutes later, Nurse Bernie switched the lights off and closed the door as both Kelsey and Jason fell into a deep sleep.

December 2014
Holiday Haze

After returning to work, the next several months flew by in a haze. Like the kind of haze, you find on the most humid summer nights in Virginia. It's almost as if a curtain was physically in front of Kelsey's face, and nothing was in focus. The holiday season was in full swing, and a typical day in her line of work offered total organized chaos. There were those who needed their devices fixed and workshops showing customers how to use their devices or reset tricky passwords and wall-to-wall people who wanted to purchase the hottest device to surprise their loved ones for Chanukah or Christmas.

Kelsey loved the chaos; it was something she thrived in, and with this being the first Christmas without Jason, she decided that throwing herself into the long and crazy hours would be the perfect way to help with the pain that seem to loom in her weakest moments. As she was about to take the next customer in the queue, she saw a man walk in carrying a computer almost like a serving tray. His face was ashen. Their eyes met, and Kelsey immediately knew she was supposed to help him.

As she approached him, she knew something was terribly wrong, "What brings you in today?" she asked carefully, not exactly sure of the response she would get. He stared at her in silence and held out the machine, almost as an offering. Kelsey instinctively reached to take it, but before she could ask what was wrong with it, she noticed a red residue on it. She immediately looked back at the customer, and, as if on cue, he told her, "That is my son's computer. He was killed twenty-four hours ago in a car accident coming home from college for Christmas. The only recent pictures of him are on this machine. It was in the front seat of the car with him. It chimes like it wants to turn on, but I can't get the screen to work. Can you help me... please?"

Tears were now rolling down the man's cheek, and Kelsey immediately took a deep breath, unable to react the way she wanted to in the situation. "I don't know what I can do for you, but I need you to have a seat and let me go talk to the technicians." He nodded, and Kelsey turned to walk to the back using every bit of her dignity to try and get this family a solution and keep her emotions out of it.

As she got to the tech room where the guys and girls certified to fix these things were diligently turning screws, Kelsey walked up to

Chris. He recognized that she was barely holding it together. "Kelsey, what's wrong?" He looked at the machine then at her and then back at the machine and noticed the red residue. In a robotic voice Kelsey murmured, "This computer was involved in a car accident twenty-four hours ago; the owner was killed, and this was up front in the car with him. His father is now here, and they need the pictures off the hard drive."

Before she could finish, Chris interrupted, "Kelsey we don't do data recovery, and if he doesn't have an appointment…."

Kelsey grew furious, completely appalled that her co-worker seemed to be so callous to the situation. "Are you fucking kidding me, Chris!? Did you not just hear a fucking word I said?"

All the other techs dropped their tools and began to shuffle out of the room, except for Jon, who slowly came up behind Kelsey and laid his hand on her shoulder. "Kelsey, let me help with this, can you hand me the machine?" Kelsey turned and made eye contact with Jon who saw that she was about to crumble to the floor. He carefully removed it from her hands and walked it to the bench and sat it down. As he began to remove the screws to get into the inside of the machine, he saw the trail left by the red residue; removing the back of the machine revealed fresh blood pooled over the fan and logic board.

Kelsey heard a quiet, "Oh wow, my god!" Jon jumped into action. "Okay, I need bio hazard bags, gloves, and safety goggles immediately," Jon yelled for his team as Kelsey walked closer to the bench where she saw the blood inside. Images and smells from that day immediately flooded her senses, and she ran to the bathroom where she began to cry and vomit. She collapsed on the floor in a heap where she spent the next forty-five minutes transported back to that day.

There was so much blood that day. The scene played over and over in her head. She was jarred back to reality with a knocking on the bathroom door, "Kelsey? Kelsey, it's Hannah. Are you okay in there?" Kelsey peeled herself off the floor and opened the door. Jon and Hannah waited for her. "Oh, honey," Hannah said as Kelsey collapsed into her embrace with a sob. "I'm going to call your dad to come and get you; just come into the office. We'll close the door to give you some privacy. You need to take the next couple of days off."

Kelsey wailed definitively, "NO! It's the holidays and you need coverage and I just came back!"

Hannah sighed, "Kelsey you've been working like a dog; we all see it, and this was bound to happen. You've been doing so awesome, but everyone has her wall, everyone."

Just as she finished saying that, Jon came in with the same advice. "Kelsey, we want you to take a couple days off. You need it, and god knows you have earned it."

"But what about the machine and that father I left out there?"

Jon responded, "I took care of the family; we got the pictures. The father was extremely grateful, and he told us a thousand times to thank you. Go home and take some time for yourself; you'll be back in here right before the big Christmas Eve rush."

"Maybe you're right." She relented and reached for her phone that had just received a text from her father that he was ten minutes away. They let her leave out the back door to avoid stares, and by the time she got to her dad's truck she was ready to be back in her home and her bed if only to cry it out and deal with this layer of sadness that the encounter had brought on. Would the magnitude of this pain and ache ever stop, she wondered? At this point, Kelsey was convinced it was here and here to stay.

November 1994
The Weekend that Changed Everything

"I'm so nervous, Jason," was all Kelsey could manage to say as she lay in a breathy heap on his bed. Jason lifted his head, "Tonight is about you, Kels." She loved when he called her that. Hovering above her, slowly kissing her forehead, her nose, "I need you to relax and trust me." He immediately felt the muscles in her neck relax in the hand he was using to support it. "That's my girl; you're completely safe with me." They'd fooled around a lot, but with Kelsey's parents wanting a play-by-play of her date nights with Jason, especially since the accident, being alone with him, at his apartment, was almost impossible. While Kelsey's parents had definitely turned a corner, to make this night happen there were many half-truths that had to be told to make it all come together. Including using Courtney and Jasper as alibis.

As their kisses became more intense, Kelsey could feel his desire pushing through his jeans. Jason slowly pulled Kelsey's white t-shirt above her head. Underneath was a cream-colored lace bra. "So beautiful, Kels." He slowly kissed her from her chin down, then to her collarbone where he focused on her neck. Kelsey had never understood what longing was until this very moment. As he continued the journey to the valley between her breasts, he began to lick and suck one nipple through the lace. Kelsey arched her back up, sucking in a deep breath and grabbing a handful of Jason's hair. He used his hand to gently but intensely roll the other nipple.

This powerful connection that was finally bringing them both together was more than either one of them was prepared for. Even though she was significantly less experienced than Jason, he was loving her and worshiping her as if she was the first girl he'd ever been with. As far as Jason was concerned, she was. He'd never loved so deeply. All the other times with the other girls, it was just about the sex. This was about experiencing her with a love that he didn't even know he was capable of. Her hands were in his hair, and she began to think about her mother finding out and how disappointed she would be.

"I'm not sure what you're thinking about, but please stop. This is about me and you," Jason whispered. She could only shake her head yes, blow out a jagged breath, and let all the distracting thoughts melt into the night. As his hand traveled down to her jeans, he began to unzip and tug them down. Suddenly he realized

that Kelsey wasn't wearing any panties.
"Kelsey!" Her eyes shot open, and she looked at him. "What's wrong? What did I do?" she asked.

"Oh, God, absolutely nothing, I just…I was *not* expecting you to have…nothing underneath."

"Oh," she said relieved.

"Kels, just when I think you cannot surprise me anymore, you completely undo me."

Kelsey smiled. His eyes grew very dark and his breathing more hitched, and he wouldn't stop looking at Kelsey in the eye. He pulled her to the edge of the bed where he continued to kiss her belly and remove her pants. He found the pink scar on her side and lingered there as he shuttered at the thought that this moment almost did not happen. He gently and lovingly pressed his lips to it. "I promise to be gentle," he whispered as he continued his trail of kisses all the way down one leg, down to her foot where he focused on the inside of her ankle, using his teeth and tongue before he switched over to the other leg, working his kisses up and up until he paused intensely on her inner thigh.

Kelsey thought briefly about how she should have been beyond embarrassed by what he was doing and where he was going. With all this pent up desire, she was too undone by his gentleness to feel inhibited by any self-consciousness not to mention the overwhelming throb between her legs was about to send her over the edge. The edge of where, she had no idea, but anything at this point to find release at the hands and the mouth of this beautiful man was completely welcome. He pushed her legs a little farther apart and then separated her lower lips where he began to suck on her clit with such force that it sent a bolt of heat through Kelsey's body.

He stopped briefly, "Kelsey, open your eyes, and look at me." When she did he, he caressed her cheek. A bead of sweat was tracing down Kelsey's brow, and she was now calling Jason's name and begging *please*. His hands traveled back down between her legs, pressing and kneading the inside of her thighs. With two of his fingers he went for her center as he carefully searched for the spot that would detonate her release. He watched her face as he tried to find different positions and locations, lightly and firmly, all the while using his other hand to roll her nipple. Kelsey was convinced she was having an out of body experience as the pressure began to build and build. She could only utter, "Please, Jason." Keeping his fingers inside her, stroking and massaging her carefully, he leaned up to her ear, "Come for me, Kels."

Kelsey could feel the throb of her core at an impasse. But as Jason continued to explore, it immediately caused Kelsey to moan and push her hips forward. Pleading from Kelsey became more desperate, hungrier. She clamped down hard around him and tumbled in a free fall as the muscles spasmed around Jason's fingers. Kelsey was so vocal as she came, Jason couldn't help but quietly chuckle. He quickly lay next to her as she continued to come down from a high she never dreamed possible.

He held her for a long time before a word was spoken. Finally, she opened her eyes only to see Jason lovingly staring at her. "How long have I been out?"

"About fifteen minutes," he replied.

She quickly brought her hand to her mouth, "Oh my gosh. I'm so sorry, Jason!"

He laughed and cupped her face, "Kelsey, you never have to apologize to me."

"But what about you, Jason? I felt your very large and impressive... you know..."

Jason placed his fingers over her lips. "Kelsey, I'm in no hurry. We have all night, unless you have somewhere to be?" he said with a smile.

She reached up and tucked a piece of hair behind his ear. "The only place that I was ever meant to be is right here in your arms." She leaned in and placed a kiss on his lips, then slowly let her tongue slide across his bottom lip. He let out a small groan and pressed his growing erection against her belly. With her mouth pressed to Jason's ear, Kelsey whispered, "I need to tell you something."

Jason pulled back to look at her face and, with a silent nod, encouraged her to speak. "I saw the doctor back in August and was placed on the pill." In complete shock, Jason asked, "When did you have time to do that without your mother finding out?" With a big smile, Kelsey responded, "Let's just say that it was a day that Courtney and I went to shop for our homecoming dresses. So we are safe as long as you don't have something you need to inform me about first?"

Jason dropped his head in disbelief. The fact that he wouldn't have to use a condom the first time with Kelsey was completely unexpected, and he nearly lost it when her breath carried across his ear. "Kelsey, I've been checked. You have nothing to worry about." With that, he removed the rest of his clothes and was on top of Kelsey, between her legs. Locking in on her gaze, Jason softly spoke, "Kelsey, you are so damned beautiful." Reaching a hand behind her back, he unhooked her bra. As he slid the straps down her shoulders, she moved her arms, one at a time, allowing him to remove the final item of clothing between them. Leaning over, he ran his thumb from her lips to her chin and down to her valley before he drew a figure eight path over her nipples. Kelsey gasped with the shock and desire it sent though her. "Kelsey, it may hurt and be a bit uncomfortable at first, but I promise to go slow. I just ask one thing." She looked at him with a hungry and puzzled look on her face. "Kelsey, please keep your eyes open and on me." Kelsey could only shake her head yes.

Resting on his arms on either side of her head, he gently pushed the tip of his hard cock into her, slowly rocking back out and slowly pushing a little deeper in the second time. By the fourth push, he went all the way. Kelsey let out a small yelp, but her eyes, now large and animated, stayed locked on Jason. "Breathe, baby. Just feel me inside of you. Oh my god you feel so good."

With that Kelsey wrapped her legs around Jason. They began to push and pull together and created a rhythm. Jason sat up and gradually drove deep inside her, then reached down and used his fingers to massage her center. "Keep your eyes on me Kelsey." As he continued to rub and push, Kelsey could feel another release coming from her toes and traveling up. She let out a massive moan as her muscles clamped down over him. They both went together, crying out in unison as their sweaty bodies paused to feel the splendid pulsing that had taken them to the edge and over. Jason collapsed back on his arms, resting his forehead to hers as she brought her arms around his neck and pulled him into her.

They spent the next several hours sleeping, completely sated and as one.

December 1994
Feed The Birds

With two days left until Christmas, Kelsey could hardly contain her excitement. She loved this time of year. She loved everything about it, and now with Jason in her life to share it with, life was even that much sweeter. The stories, the music, the lights. She wished that people would understand that joy and peace were something they could choose every day, but that was not reality.

The sounds of the season were upon them, and it made her truly giddy. She was especially excited to share the friends she'd made at the shelter. A few years ago she had an opportunity to volunteer at the local homeless shelter through her church. Kelsey's heart and eyes were open to a whole new world that day. She met people who were often ignored, mocked, and forgotten because they no longer had their own place to call home, weren't always clean, and would ask for money on the street corner. Many times she learned that people found themselves homeless for reasons that were beyond their control: even a fellow high schooler was living at the shelter as her family tried to get back on their feet again. Homelessness affected the young, the old, individuals, families, men, women, and even animals. Kelsey was grateful for the experience so young in her life, and while she may not be able to help everyone, she learned early on that these were people who, though down on their luck, deserved to be treated with dignity and respect. She made volunteering a regular part of her life, but this time of year the need for resources and volunteers always reached its peak.

One of the *regulars* at the shelter was Mary. She was a woman in her fifties and was mute. Kelsey had tried to learn more about Mary's past from several of the longtime volunteers, but they would simply say that it wasn't their story to tell. Mary spent most of her time each day in a local park, and once she felt the park animals were all tucked away into their natural habitats for the night, she'd make her way to the shelter. Mary had become the guardian of sorts to that sweet little park with the water fountains and swings. She had even adopted the birds and squirrels there. Always looking for spare coins and collecting cans and bottles that she could turn in for change, she'd take that money, walk to a local hardware store, and purchase cracked corn. She couldn't buy much, but it was her effort to feed those animals. She was like a female version of St. Frances of Assisi. Kelsey had met her the first day she volunteered, and Mary made it very clear that she had trust issues. It wasn't until six months into volunteering on a regular basis that Kelsey felt Mary warm up to her. Kelsey had to prove that she was there to help and not for any other selfish motive or ambition like volunteers too often do. Eventually, if Mary saw Kelsey arrive at the shelter, she would practically knock people over to give a warm hug.

As Kelsey and Jason pulled up to the shelter, Kelsey did the checklist in her head. "Jason did you grab the bag of wrapped gifts and the cracked corn?"

Jason laughed, "Sure did, it's in the trunk. I still have to say that two fifty pound bags of cracked corn have to be the most unusual Christmas gift anyone has ever bought."

"Just trust me on this. I think Mary is going to be thrilled. I know she's excited to meet you."

"I can't wait to meet her; the way you describe her; I know she's a special lady."

"I've learned so much from her about humility and true kindness. She has nothing, and yet she's still constantly doing what she can to provide for others. I have so much, and yet I'm never that selfless."

Jason thought about Kelsey's kindness and selflessness: her gentleness with her mother, even when Melody's love came across as strict rules; her willingness to stay sober at parties so she could take care of her friends; her desire to share her love of art by becoming a teacher; and her taking the time she could be having fun as a senior in high school to instead volunteer to help feed people in need. But because he so admired her humility, he decided not to point it out to her at that moment. Instead, he just smiled as she once again was about to put others' needs and desires ahead of her own.

As Jason put the car in park, he could see some of the homeless community starting to head in for the hot dinner that the shelter provided for them on chilly nights like tonight. He headed around the back of the car and opened the trunk and then proceeded to Kelsey's door, opening it for her. She and Jason grabbed the bags out of the trunk but left the cracked corn. She wanted to surprise Mary a little later with that. As she entered the main dining room, many of those who knew Kelsey, whether staff or homeless, jumped to their feet to hug her and wish her a Merry Christmas. Jason stood back and watched as Kelsey looked them all in the eye and listened to every word they all had to say. His heart was touched, but he was also a little mad at himself. Mad that he had never taken the time out of his own selfish life to volunteer his time to serving these people.

Kelsey didn't see homeless people. She saw individuals and treated them with love and dignity. It was a humbling moment for Jason, and he committed every detail of this night to memory so that he could be a small part of the solution in the future.

After greeting everyone, Kelsey motioned to Jason to head to the director's office with the bags, and then it would be time to roll up their sleeves in the kitchen. Once back there, Jason was put in charge of washing the dishes. Pots, pans, plates, utensils, cups, serving trays: it was a non-stop barrage that required Jason to scrape leftovers into the garbage, wash, and then rinse. He had a helper by the name of Lenny who was showing him the fastest and easiest way to clean and stack them as they went. At one point, Jason looked up and out the window to see if he could catch Kelsey's attention, but she was busy serving macaroni and sweet potatoes. A piece of her hair had slipped out of her ponytail, and Jason loved how adorable she looked.

"C'mon. Jason, we're getting behind in our dish duty," Lenny called out in his raspy voice. "On my way, buddy." Jason jumped right back in and easily fell back into the rhythm with his new friend, aware more than ever that the blessings he had in his life needed to be paid forward.

As the night wound down, Kelsey was finally able to introduce Jason to Mary. She had her pad and paper and quickly wrote down her greetings. *It's so nice to finally meet you, Jason. You're much more handsome than Kelsey described.* Kelsey burst into laughter, and Jason was blushing. Once Kelsey contained herself, it was finally time to surprise Mary with her gifts. Mary was so excited when she opened to find a new pair of warm but functional gloves and a scarf that she threw her arms around Kelsey to thank her.

"We have one more thing for you, Mary, but you have to come to our car," Kelsey explained.

Mary enthusiastically clapped and ran to put on her jacket, new scarf, and gloves. Once outside, they approached the trunk as Kelsey prepared her, "It might seem like a weird gift, but I sincerely hope you like it." With a raised eyebrow she looked at Kelsey and lifted her shoulders with a *whatever it is, I'm sure I'll love it* shrug. Jason opened the trunk. Realizing the perfectly-selected gift, Mary covered her mouth in utter shock. Tears immediately formed in her eyes as she began to make grunting noises of thanks and hug them both. Grabbing her pen and paper out of her pocket, she leaned against the car and wrote, *I will be able to feed the animals for weeks with this.*

As they continued to hug, Kelsey reassured her, "I'm so happy you're happy, and I already spoke with Artie, and he said you can store the bags in the back room of the shelter." Jason and Lenny unloaded the bags from the car and took them inside. Mary grabbed Kelsey's hand and squeezed it tightly as though she was still in disbelief. Turning to face Kelsey, she mouthed the words *Thank You.* It took everything within Kelsey not to burst into embarrassing, joyful weeping. "No, Mary, thank you."

December 2014
New Year's Eve

With two minutes left in 2014, Kelsey was spending them exactly as she wanted. Alone, in quiet reflection of the past six months. She stood on the front porch of her home, bundled up in Jason's coat, facing the western sky, talking to him as if he was standing right there. Kelsey hugged the coat closer to her body and caught a whiff of Jason's smell. Tears streaming down her face, she looked up to see the moon shining brightly and the intense sparkle of the stars in the cold night sky. She missed her husband, she missed her best friend, and she would have made a deal with the devil himself in that moment if it meant she could have him again.

Bringing her back from the brink was the sound of a FaceTime call coming in. She took the phone out of her pocket to see it was her sister. She turned the front porch light on and hit accept on the phone. "Happy New Year!" were the sounds coming from two of the three young voices that could make any dark night shine with brightness. Wiping the tears from her eyes and digging deep for her best cheery voice she answered back, "Happy New Year, my sweet angels! Where's your brother?"

"He was too tired to stay up," Sarah Jane beamed. "He tried really hard though," replied her younger sister Katie. "Have you been crying, Aunt Kelsey?" Sarah Jane asked in a low voice. "Just a little," Kelsey responded.

"Is it because you miss uncle Jason?" Before Kelsey could answer, Ellie was in on the call. "Say goodnight to your awesome aunt; she needs her beauty sleep." "Goodnight!" "Happy New Year, Aunt Kelsey!" Then she heard them pounding their feet down the hallway to their rooms. As Kelsey caught her breath, Ellie saw the sadness in her sister's eyes. "Well, you made it. I know you don't want to hear it, but you made it."

"I know," was all that Kelsey could say while looking out over the moonlit fields.

"You got through the holidays and New Year's Eve, and now the next big hurdle is the court date for jury selection and trial date, right?" Ellie asked.

"Yeah, my lawyer said that once that happens we can expect the trial to start mid-summer."

"A full year after the accident." Ellie shook her head. "I don't understand why the legal system takes so damn long when this case is so cut and dry. It also isn't helping matters that Jason had taken this guy under his wing only for this to happen." Ellie wasn't saying anything that Kelsey hadn't already thought about.

"I need to go," she interrupted her sister. "I need to get some sleep and feel rested before heading to the hospital tomorrow for the infusion. I'm thankful that the center is open, even if it is on a holiday. I'm hoping it will help keep my heart and mind distracted. I'm also going to stop by the shelter. I know Mary hasn't been in the best of health, and I need to check on her."

"Kels, before you go, I need you to know that I'm proud of you. The hardest part of this season in your life as your sister has been having to sit back and watch you walk this out, but you're doing it, and I'm proud of you, and I love you." Ellie's words brought more tears to Kelsey's eyes.

"Thank you, Ellie. I love you too." They ended the call, and Kelsey breathed in the cold air and let it burn in her lungs for a few seconds before exhaling, expelling the old and leaving it behind as she walked back into her home to find some rest before the dawn of 2015.

After a quick visit with Mary at the shelter that morning, Kelsey arrived at the hospital at ten o'clock on the nose. This was her second infusion since Jason's death, and she still felt as if she was walking into a foreign land even though she'd been in this room what felt like a hundred times. Without Jason by her side, and with a heavy heart from seeing Mary in declining health, she felt the sudden sadness that had become her new normal. The girls who worked in the infusion center were always professional and ready when Kelsey got there. They knew the situation, and as soon as she walked in the doors, they ushered her to the back of the room in a corner where she could pull the curtain and have some privacy.

Tracey, one of the nurses who had gotten to know Kelsey and Jason, was there to greet her and get her IV line in. She knew the old routine Kelsey and Jason had down to a science. When she heard Kelsey was coming back in, she wanted to be as much help as possible getting her settled and into a new routine as easily as she could. Once the line was in and the drip started, Tracey looked at Kelsey and said, "Okay, looks like you're just here for five hours today. Can I get you anything?" Kelsey shook her head no and put her headphones on and thanked Tracey for being so attentive and understanding. Tracey squeezed her other hand. "My pleasure, ma'am. I'll be back to check on you in a few."

Using her tablet, Kelsey caught up on some of her reading and eventually dozed off. As she slept, the Faurè piece played in her ear, and she dreamt that she was back on the beach with Jason, her back to his chest, looking out over the horizon. The temperature was perfect, complete serenity, complete peace. There was no need to talk; he was holding her, and that was what she had desperately missed for the past six months. She could smell him and feel him. "This has to be real," she thought. It felt like they were together for hours, but as the sun was beginning to set in her dream, Jason started to disappear. "No no no no, Jason. Please," she whispered. "Don't leave me. Please stay!" But before she could stop him, he was gone.

Tracey pulled the curtain back to see Kelsey's eyes flutter open as the big tears rolled down her cheeks. "Kelsey, what's wrong? What hurts? Is it your line?" Kelsey could barley talk and only shook her head no. "Did you have a dream?" Tracey asked. Kelsey nodded her head yes. "I'm so sorry, honey," she looked at the iron drip and looked at the time on the machine. "You're almost done; another forty-five minutes, and I'll get you out of here. Are you going to be okay to drive home?"

Kelsey was finally able to sit up and find her words. "Yes, I'll be fine." Handing her a tissue, Tracey carefully asked, "Do you want to tell me about the dream?" Kelsey stared at her for a moment and, as if replaying it like a movie in her head, retold the sequence and what happened. Tracey just sat and listened and grabbed Kelsey's hand when she was done. "I wish I knew why you had that dream, but until you understand, I hope it brings you some peace." Kelsey smiled and hugged her and thanked her for listening.

Once she arrived home and got settled, Kelsey headed out to the barn to clean Jedi's stall then groom and feed him. As she was finishing up she stopped and took a moment to look out over the fields in the west. She stood there and watched the sun slowly dip below the horizon. Though the ending was painful, Kelsey was thankful she'd been given the gift of that dream earlier in the day. It was the first time she'd seen Jason alive in her dreams since the incident. Watching the sunset that night, for the first time in a very long time, she let out a prayer of thanks to the God she was purposely ignoring.

JUNE 1995
TWO WEEKS AFTER GRADUATION

YORK, ENGLAND

"Gareth, meet Kelsey Chapman. She's our guest exchange student and will be staying with us for the summer while working with the Art Department at the University." Gareth Blythe was never speechless. He was the strapping, clever, youngest child, and only son of the Blythe family. Having two older sisters helped shape him into the charming gentleman he had become. Always having the right thing to say when they brought over their lovely girl friends prepared him later in life for how he could charm the ladies on campus. He'd just returned from the York University football complex when he was rendered speechless by the most piercing hazel eyes and electric smile that he'd ever come in contact with.

Kelsey stood, hand outstretched, and waited for him to respond but began to shrink back when she realized he was just going to stare at her as if she had something crawling out of her face. "Good Lord, Gareth, stop staring, and shake the poor girl's hand for pity's sake," his mother, Camilla, practically shrieked.

"Oh, of course, where are my manners?" he sheepishly replied while extending his hand, "It's wonderful to meet you!" When he touched her hand he nearly jumped out of his skin. He was quickly jolted back to reality with his mother's voice. "Gareth, would you mind fetching her luggage from my vehicle, please?" his mother asked half smiling as she watched the comedy of errors that unfolded before her.

"Yes, of course," Gareth replied. As he turned to head to the front door, Kelsey was right behind him, "Let me help you. Surely you shouldn't be saddled with all of it." It was no problem, he assured her, but when he opened the back of the Land Rover, he was shocked to see four large suitcases sitting there. His eyes widened, and he looked up at Kelsey then back down at the luggage. "Well, are you sure you didn't forget anything?" he asked with a hint of sarcasm and small smile. Kelsey shouldered him to the side, a bit embarrassed as the redness raced across her cheeks.

"I came prepared and brought some comforts of home. I can take it from here," she said with irritation in her voice. He hadn't meant to embarrass her, and as she reached in to take the first suitcase, he grabbed her hand and apologized. "Kelsey, forgive me. I promise I didn't mean to embarrass you. I just wasn't expecting you…I mean all of you…all of this!" he sputtered, and then before he could even think about his next words he practically vomited out, "You're quite beautiful, Kelsey." *Oh Holy Jesus did I just say that out loud?*

Kelsey abruptly pulled her hand back. "Gareth, while I appreciate your kind words, I'm sure you've seen your fair share of American girls in your life because of your mother's position at the University. Furthermore, this American is neither interested nor available. Do I make myself clear?" Kelsey abruptly snatched two of her suitcases from the back of the Rover and proceeded to the house.

Gareth leaned against the vehicle and heaved out a deep breath. "Nice job, you bloody idiot," he muttered under his breath as he grabbed the other two suitcases and headed back to the house. He managed to get them up the stairs where he found the door to Kelsey's room shut. He placed them in front of her door, lifted his hand, and reached out to knock but then hesitated and thought it best to just leave them there. He was embarrassed by the fact this eighteen-year-old American girl had reduced him to nothing more than a babbling oaf. Why in the world was she different? He honestly had no idea; he'd seen and been with plenty of beautiful women, but he felt something unexplainable and instant the moment he saw Kelsey.

He needed to shower off the football practice smell that had accompanied him home and get ready for the welcome dinner his mother always prepared for new students. His sisters and their husbands would be joining them. He had plenty of studying to do as well but was finding it hard to focus on much else except the hazel-eyed American that had crashed into his life just twenty minutes ago.

As he climbed in the shower, he found his thoughts everywhere. Attending the same University where his mother was the Vice Chancellor made life interesting at times, and Gareth definitely felt that his behavior was under a microscope. However, he was no slouch in the classroom or on the football pitch. He had plans to attend medical school in the fall, and when he wasn't at practice, playing in a match, or in the gym trying to stay in shape, he was studying. While he treated his classes and workouts like a Monday through Friday job, the weekends were for stress relief. Indulging in good alcohol and pretty women were completely justified and what any healthy university student did to survive.

While he had a small place of his own available to him on campus, since his father's passing a year ago, he liked staying in his boyhood bedroom, to be there for his mum who would otherwise be alone in a big, empty house. She and Gareth's father had been married for thirty-five years when he died suddenly from a massive heart attack. That was a day that could still steal the very breath from his body when he thought about it. His sister Becs had called him at his apartment as he had been studying for a big exam. She could barely speak above a whisper, and a wave of dread shot though Gareth. The only thing he was able to understand was "come to the hospital; it's dad." He ran out the front door only to get to the hospital to discover his father was gone.

Gareth pulled himself out of his thoughts, jumped out of the shower, dried off, and wrapped a towel around his waist. As he walked over to his dresser to grab clean clothes he heard a *thud* outside his door followed by a moan. Without thinking, he threw his door open and saw Kelsey on the ground, pushing herself up with her hands. Before her brain could process what had happened, Gareth was beside her, half-nude and franticly apologizing because, in his assessment, Kelsey must have tripped over the very luggage he left in front of her door. "Oh god, Kelsey, are you okay? I thought you would see your luggage, and after what happened outside I was trying to give you space. That's why..."

Before he could finish, he noticed tears streaming down her face and heard the sharp words, "Get your hands off of me, now!" Kelsey looked up and stared him straight in the eyes. Pushing her hair out of her face and behind her ears, she stared at him with such contempt that Gareth took three big steps back. While she was gritting her teeth, words seethed out, "How convenient that you should leave my luggage outside my door where you knew I would trip and then come to my rescue in only a towel?"

Gareth didn't dare speak. He saw the fire in her eyes, and while he was extremely turned on by it, he truly didn't mean for all this to happen. Kelsey turned around, grabbed both suitcases, took them back to her room, and proceeded to close her bedroom door, leaving Gareth to stand in the hallway holding the towel around his waist, wondering how in the world he would survive the next twelve weeks.

Kelsey sat on the end of the bed and was finally letting the tears flow, really flow. She was exhausted and also jet lagged and hungry, and this Gareth jerk was not helping matters. Yes, he was gorgeous and built, even a blind person could see that, but she wasn't interested in any of that. The one she gave her heart to was patiently waiting for her to come home in twelve weeks. She looked at the watch that he'd given her for graduation. It was five o'clock England time; she may be able to catch him at the office where he was putting in overtime on a Saturday. She grabbed her bag and pulled out her wallet with her international calling card. After carefully reading the instructions so that the Blythes wouldn't have a ginormous phone bill, she called from the phone in her room.

By the fifth ring she had all but given up hope, but just as she was about to hang up, a breathless Jason answered, "Please tell me this is my Kelsey on the other end of this call?" Kelsey's heart nearly burst, and the tears poured down her cheeks. "Yes" was all she could manage to get out before Jason realized that she wasn't speaking because she was crying.

"Kels, sweetheart, what's wrong?" She finally pulled herself together enough to tell him about her travels and how lovely and gracious Professor Blythe was but how awful her son was as she shared all the events of the afternoon. She could hear Jason gritting his teeth through the phone. "Kelsey, say the word! I'm on the next flight over, and I'll teach that son of a bitch a lesson in American diplomacy that he'll never forget!" Kelsey started to laugh, something five minutes ago she didn't think possible. "I'm not kidding, Kelsey. If you call me crying again because of this asshat, there will be nothing to stop me from coming. Do you hear me?"

Jason was her knight in shining armor, and the very sound of his voice threatening to come to her aid was exactly the injection she needed to know she would be okay. "I hear you loud and clear, Jason; I'm just a little overwhelmed and tired and missing you so much."

"I know you are, kiddo, but I miss you more, and I'm so proud of you. This is a really exciting time for you." She could hear the sincerity and love in his voice. "When is your first day in class?"

"Monday. So I'll finish unpacking tonight, try and get some sleep, and then Camilla, Professor Blythe, said that she would take me into town and on campus to show me around and also pick up the art supplies I'll need so that I'm not completely out of my element come Monday morning."

"Will you call me Monday to let me know how the first day of class went?"

"Absolutely! Who else am I going to share all my anxieties and excitement with?"

"Well, if that English fellow has his way..." and before Jason could even finish, "Jason, I gave my heart to you completely a few months ago; you have nothing to worry about."

"Kelsey, I don't doubt you or us for a second; I just don't trust Romeo over there."

She laughed, "I promise to tell him that you have a flight on standby in the event that you need to help improve diplomatic relations."

He let out a laugh. "I love you so much, Kels, and I miss you so much already. I knew that it was going to be hard to let you go, and I'm so excited for you, but I had no idea that my heart could hurt this much without you here." Kelsey could feel the giant lump in her throat forming, but she didn't want to get off the phone in tears, so she took deep breath. "Me too, Jason, me too."

"Shall we end the conversation like we do every night?" he asked.

"Of course," she replied.

"I love you, Kels. Dream of me."

"I love you too. Dream of me as well, Jason. Goodnight."

And with that she placed the phone back in the receiver on the table. Kelsey inhaled deeply and took a few minutes to refresh herself in the bathroom. As she looked in the mirror, after the conversation with Jason calmed her and brought home back into her heart, Kelsey thought of how irrational she'd been with Gareth. Being a rather self-aware individual, she tried to pinpoint why she'd become so incredibly enraged at his coming into the hall after she fell over her suitcases. For one, she'd been embarrassed. But it didn't make sense to believe her host's son was out to mortify her, neither with his remark about her suitcases nor with a diabolical plan to cause her to trip so he could come to her rescue, showing off his amazing body and perfect hair, still wet from the shower.

Kelsey was shocked at herself. There was the problem. She loved Jason with all her heart. She knew it. She was going to be with him forever. So why would she even think twice about a dashing Brit who would be sharing a home with her for the next several months? Kelsey knew she'd reacted as she did because she was tired and jet lagged and missing family and Jason—but also because she'd used the anger to push away a feeling she didn't want to admit. "You're going to see other attractive men in your life, Kelsey," she told her reflection. "It doesn't mean you have to push them away or worry just because you have eyes. Your heart is secure." Feeling affirmed, she headed downstairs ready and determined to enjoy the next twelve weeks knowing that the love of her life was back home waiting for her.

There were seven places set at the eight-person table. Coming down the stairs she noticed all the family photos in the hall. As she looked at all the pictures on the walls, she saw a one of a handsome man who looked just like Gareth and the *in memoriam* clipping from the local paper framed. She quickly put together that the professor's husband had passed away within the past year when she saw the name Duncan Blythe. She heard another set of footsteps coming down the stairs. As she turned, Gareth stopped midway. She could see he was contemplating running back up the steps, but she interrupted him mid thought.

"Gareth, are you joining us for dinner?" He let out a breath and cautiously answered with a "yes." Kelsey looked at the table to her right then back up at the stairs to Gareth when the front door opened. Rebecca and Phil walked in chatting away with Ana and Ollie. The girls were stunning in their own way. Rebecca was tall, with long brown hair and blue eyes while Ana was tall with long blonde hair and blue eyes. Both were perfect mix of both parents. Rebecca was the executive type while Ana was the earthy one. Ana looked to be six months pregnant. Kelsey could only hope to look that beautiful one day when she was carrying Jason's child. As they all greeted one another and came into the dining room, they made a beeline toward Kelsey.

"Hi there! You must be Kelsey! I'm Rebecca, Becs for short, and this is my husband Phil." Shaking both their hands, Kelsey was enjoying the energy both sisters brought into the room. "I'm Ana, and this is my husband Ollie."

"It's a pleasure to meet you all," Kelsey replied. "I'm sorry if I seem a little out of it. I'm exhausted."

"I can only imagine, you poor thing!" Becs exclaimed. Gareth stood back and watched their interactions not believing how much more smoothly it was going for them than it had for him. Camilla walked into the dining room with a gorgeous pot roast with all the perfect trimmings to go alongside it. Kelsey's stomach growled loud enough for everyone to hear. They all let out a good laugh. "Oh, you poor girl! You're starving!" Ana exclaimed.

As they sat down for dinner Camilla realized, "Oh, I forgot the wine! Gareth, would you mind heading to the cellar for a red wine?" Kelsey felt a knot in her stomach, but then Camilla proceeded, "Grab a glass of water for Kelsey as well, please." Camilla looked back at Kelsey, "I got the memo that you don't drink, and it isn't a problem."

"Well, I can't have wine either!" Ana exclaimed.

"Oh, yes, of course darling. Gareth, make that two glasses of water."

Kelsey let out a breath of relief as Gareth strode back in with a bottle of red wine and two glasses of water. He carefully walked over and placed water in front of his sister and then, taking even more time, walked over to Kelsey and carefully placed it down in front of her. She could sense his trepidation as he worked extra hard to make sure that he didn't spill it across her lap. All eyes were on him and found it comical as he placed it in front of her and stared at it as if in disbelief he'd done it without all the theatrics that seemed to plague them their first couple of meetings. Becs and Ana looked at each other then at Camilla who shrugged her shoulders.

"Thank you, Gareth." He let his gaze reach hers and see the slight smile that was on her lips. He took the two steps needed to reach his seat, and dinner commenced.

In a word, it was perfect. The conversation and food flowed. Kelsey loved listening to Camilla talk about life with her late husband, Duncan. They had met at the University their junior year, and she knew he was the one she was going to marry. Kelsey's heart warmed as she understood that exact feeling and was overcome almost to the point of tears. She managed to hold them back as to not interrupt Camilla as she talked about all the challenges of being a student, wife, mother, and eventually a professor. She regretted none of the challenges and wouldn't have changed any of the adventures she and Duncan got to share. Memories they created with each other and their three children were precious.

Kelsey was surprised to learn that Duncan was very involved as a volunteer with the local homeless shelter. Camilla went on to explain that they had contacted her to say they hoped to see her for the launch of the summer outreach program that was coming up as well as help with the delivery of the weekly meals that were shared with the elderly who were had no way to come to the shelter. Kelsey jumped into the conversation trying to not sound overly excited, but thrilled by the idea of serving in this capacity in another country to gain a perspective she wouldn't get in a classroom. "I volunteer at our local homeless shelter back home and would love to help."

Camilla perked up. "Really, Kelsey?"

With all eyes at the table on her, Kelsey enthusiastically responded, "Yes. The work back home has meant so much to me. If there is an opportunity at all to help here, I'd truly love to."

As Gareth listened to her, an unexpected wave washed over him. It wasn't the usual reminder from his manhood that there was an attractive college student that he wouldn't mind bedding. While she had his full attention down there, Kelsey hadn't even been in their home twelve hours, and he was experiencing a tug on his heart. It wasn't the painful pull that had been there since his father's passing. This tug was new. It was light, and he'd experienced it every moment he was near her, and the thought that crossed his mind at that very moment was *I'm going to marry this girl.*

Taking a sip of wine, Camilla placed her glass on the table and said, "Well I think we have a date then, don't we, Kelsey?" Kelsey nodded her head *yes*, and they all laughed before the conversation continued as the sisters began to share stories about their father's dedication to philanthropy.

Becs and Ana were just as funny and wonderful to listen to as their mother. Becs and her husband were both barristers. They worked for a firm and lived about thirty minutes away in Leeds. Ana was a math teacher for a private school, and her husband worked at the international offices of Vision World in York as well. This agency, among many things, provided education and medical vaccinations to third world countries, mainly in east and west Africa.

Kelsey felt so privileged to be sitting and sharing among them. She looked over at Gareth during the conversation. He sat and regarded his mother and sisters with the warmest smile as he listened to them retell stories that he had heard hundreds of times. Camilla looked at her watch, "Oh my goodness! Let me get the kettle on for some tea to go with our dessert. How does that sound?" Becs and Ana excused themselves to the restroom as Kelsey let out a yawn, "Oh my! That snuck up on me," she giggled.

The men at the table let out a snicker. "You don't have to have dessert and tea, Kelsey. My mum will understand," Gareth assured her. "Oh, but I'm enjoying this so much; I can hang in there a little longer." Ollie and Phil excused themselves to the library so they could grab a quick glass of brandy to go with their dessert. While they were the only two at the table, Kelsey decided to take advantage of the moment. "Gareth, I need to apologize for my reaction to the suitcases event earlier. My life has been so crazy for the past nine months, but especially the past two weeks. I graduated from high school, said goodbye to my two best friends and my fiancé, not to mention all the prep into getting here. I'm truly sorry that I had such a nasty response. I hope you can find it in your heart to forgive me so we can start over?"

Gareth stared at her for a long moment studying her face, processing what she said and, with a puzzled tone in his voice, asked, "You have a fiancé?"

MARCH 2015
THE TRUTH BOMB AND A REUNION

The phone rang, and Kelsey grinned ear to ear, something she rarely did these days. "Hello, stranger," Kelsey beamed.

"Hello right back! I'm calling to check in on you. I need to know how you are and get an update on everything."

Kelsey held the phone between her chin and her shoulder as she put her plate in the dishwasher and then headed over and plopped down on the couch. "I just got in from the barn, had a quick bite, and was settling in for the night. You know this is the hardest part of the day for me. When everything settles down. It's like pain and grief wait in the corner all day. Not that they ever go away, but sometimes a small window of my new *normal* opens up, and just when I think I'm getting the hang of it, they rush in and sack me. Your call at this very moment is helping me stay distracted a little longer."

Courtney just listened to her friend get it all out as she had always done. After all those years of being each other's sounding board, never in her wildest imagination did she ever expect that her friend would have to go through this. As Courtney listened, Kelsey continued,

"The lawyer called me on my way home from work to let me know that the jury has been selected."

"How did that call make you feel, Kels? I mean—you had to feel something?"

There was a long pause as Kelsey chose her words carefully, "I'm not sure how I'm suppose to feel. I don't feel relieved. I don't feel anxious. I still feel numb so much of the time. Yes, pieces of me are coming back a little at a time, but I'll never be the same, Court. No matter what happens to Michael James Dupree, I'm never getting my husband back. At the end of the day, that's all I come back to."

Courtney listened carefully and mulled over the truth in her friend's words. "When does the trial begin?"

"June fourth."

"Are you kidding me? Almost a year to the day of the incident?"

"Yeah, I know. Ironic, right? I'm choosing to trust the justice system. We have good lawyers who are representing us and the company as well. You know, Court, there are times when I think about coming face to face with Dupree just to ask him if it was worth it. After all Jason did for him, giving him multiple opportunities to start his life over again at twenty-one. A clean slate, no strings attached. All the support he needed to stay clean, and it all ends like this. That's the part I cannot reconcile."

"Look, Kelsey, you and I both know that you've come a long way in a year, but you still have a long way to go. I'm going to make two radical suggestions, and before you react, you have to hear me out."

There was a beat of silence. "Go on; I'm listening."

"What if you went and visited him in jail? Straight up asked the son of a bitch if it was worth it. Let him see the pain in your eyes and burden of sadness that you carry around. Not for his sake but for yours. You and I both know that, in the end, the only way you'll be able to ever move on and live in true freedom from this situation is through forgiveness. Maybe seeing him and asking him would begin that journey."

Kelsey let out a begrudging "ha."

"Just let me finish, Kels. I know it sounds crazy, but this harkens right back to our Sunday school days and nights at youth group and the really important lessons we learned about what it means to forgive."

Kelsey could feel her face growing hot and eyes filling with tears. "I cannot believe you're seriously having this conversation with me right now! Since when did you become the authority on all things Gospel?"

Courtney was able not to take the reaction personally as she knew her friend was still so broken, but, in true Freeman style, she soldiered on. "Kelsey, I may have my non-traditional views and am way more liberal for most people's liking, but twenty years later those lessons and my views on God have never been more important than they are today. I owe it to you as your best friend to remind you of that. If the roles were reversed right now, I know that you'd do the same for me."

Kelsey remained silent and let the tears slide down her face, using the back of her hand to wipe them away; she knew her friend was right, even if she didn't want to hear it. She took a deep breath. "Dare I even ask about your second suggestion?"

Courtney laughed, "Well, I think it's time you get your ass on a plane and come visit me." Kelsey let out a forced reply, "Ha, you do, do you?" "Yes I do, and I already spoke with Jasper, and he completely agrees and said the moment you say yes he's coming as well. Come on, Kels; we haven't seen you since the funeral except on FaceTime, and that doesn't count. You need to get out here; experience life outside of your sadness. It will give you some perspective and maybe some healing in this process."

Kelsey couldn't argue with Courtney, as she knew she was right—this really could be the perfect outlet to mentally and emotionally prepare herself before the trial started. "I'll sleep on it and text you both in a couple of days with an answer."

"The fact that you're thinking about it makes my heart happy!"

"Thank you, Courtney."

"For what?"

"For just being my best friend, for being real with me. If you were next to me right now, I'd hug you."

"Aww, I love you too, lady. Why don't you text me in a few days and let me know when you'll be delivering that hug in person?"

Kelsey laughed, "I can do that."

* * *

The Next Day

"Dr. Blythe, I presume?"

"Please, call me Gareth. I'm glad to finally meet you, Dr. Eaton."

Both men extended their hands in a friendly handshake as they greeted one another. "Please call me David." Dr. Eaton had stood when Gareth entered his office, and he motioned to a leather chair across from him. Both men sat as David continued, "How was the flight over; I trust you're getting settled?"

"I am, slowly but surely. Much of my stuff is being shipped and won't be here for at least a month, so in the interim I'll live with the basic necessities. It'll be a harkening back to my old undergraduate days."

Dr. Eaton laughed. "And I trust the staff here at EVMS has been welcoming as well those over at the hospital?"

"They've been amazing, truly a delight to work with."

"Good to hear. So no regrets taking the leap across the pond, so to speak?"

"Not in the least; it was time for a change, and I was ready for a new challenge. Don't get me wrong, York and the University are home, but this is where I need to be right now."

"Well, we're excited to have you come into the rotation, and you're filling some very large shoes." Gareth knew this to be the case and was completely aware that his new colleagues were going to be watching very closely. He knew he was going to have to earn their trust and respect, regardless of the resume he was bringing in with him. "Dr. Spaulding's retiring was not unexpected, but the man was a legend, not just here in the school but in the medical community.

But enough about Charles, you're here now, and we know you bring great things with you. You're a gifted cardiologist."

Gareth reflected for a moment, allowing the compliment to soak in. "After my father's death I had no idea that it would change the course of my life to the degree that it has. I'd planned on being a professional football player, but instead I've made it my life's mission to make a small contribution to this community, in particular to cardiology. I'm willing to do it one case at a time if it means that a family won't have to go though what I did."

Dr. Eaton nodded his head and replied, "That is the kind of passion and moxie that patients and students need to hear. Will you be attending the Congenital Heart Disease conference in Los Angeles with me and Dr. Cameron in a few weeks?"

"My assistant has already confirmed the dates on my calendar and booked my airline ticket and hotel."

"Excellent! Have her adjust your return ticket to stop in Jackson Hole, Wyoming. I have a hunting and fishing cabin, and I'd love to take you fishing out on the Snake River."

"That sounds amazing, but are you sure I won't be intruding?"

"Not in the least; it'll give you a chance to see a beautiful part of the country that will take your breath away."

"Well, I look forward to it."

"Monday is your first official day, correct?"

"Yes, Sir."

"Well, come back to my office at anytime; my door is always open."

Gareth stood and shook Dr. Eaton's hand. As he walked out of the office, he took a deep breath and headed for the car. He was tired and ready to fall asleep as his body had not adjusted to the time change. He pulled out his phone to look at his list of reminders and realized he needed to pick up a few things. He pressed the round home button of his smart phone and asked, "Where is the closest Istore?" Within a second he got a response, "The closest Istore is 2.1 miles away on Montgomery Avenue. Would you like me to get you the directions?" With that Gareth said "yes" and opened the door of his rented vehicle and was on his way.

The day had been a typical Friday in the store, just slightly busier as the weekend was kicking off. Kelsey was finishing up with a couple who'd just bought their first computer and was about to head off to dinner when another customer stopped her and asked about a charging cable. As Kelsey walked over and pointed them out, the customer asked a few more questions before asking to be rung out. Kelsey processed the transaction and wished the customer a great weekend. Just as she was about to turn around she heard a voice: "Kelsey, Kelsey Chapman?"

Kelsey froze and slowly lifted her head, turning on her heels to face the voice that had called to her. She immediately felt all the color drain from her face, and she looked up and felt all the air in her lungs being sucked out.

The only thing she could manage in response was "Gareth, Gareth Blythe?"

JULY 1995
GOLDEN HEARTS

The pace of the summer art program was intense, and while Kelsey was fine with that, she was having a difficult time connecting with classmates. Most of them would go to the local pubs and drink, as the legal drinking age in Great Britain was eighteen. Kelsey didn't drink, and she knew that her classmates would find that weird, so it was just as well that she returned to the Blythes' home after the long days, had a snack, and jumped right into her paintings and studies until bedtime. Besides, she looked forward to dinner with Camilla and Gareth.

Camilla was awesome about tuning in and making sure she felt less homesick, asking all the right questions and just being genuinely interested in how her day went and how she was doing. "I'm sure your classmates are out having drinks after class, and while I know that you don't drink, there are plenty of non-alcoholic beverages the pub would serve. Gareth could take you up the road a way to the Grey Horse. It's a great spot, and you need to experience at least one pub while you're staying with us. You don't mind do you, Gareth?"

Gareth sat wide-eyed, looking at his mother, then Kelsey, and just as he was about to finally say something, Kelsey quietly looked at him and said, "You can say no, Gareth. I understand if you don't want to."

"No, no, I'm fine with it. Are you sure you're fine with it?"

"Of course. I mean, I have homework tonight and then I'll be with Camilla and serving at the homeless shelter on Friday after classes, maybe we could go Saturday evening?"

What Gareth wanted to say to Kelsey was *I will gladly take you wherever and whenever, just say the word.* Instead he responded with a "Yes, that's fine, no problem. I'm actually planning to be at the shelter Friday as well."

"Oh?" Kelsey asked.

"Gareth's been so kind to volunteer a few times a month since his father died, even with his studies and football keeping him so busy. I think he's been over there more than I have," Camilla shared.

"It's important to keep involved in the work that meant so much to him," Gareth explained.

"Well that settles it then," Camilla said. "We'll all serve meals on Friday, and you two can enjoy an evening out on Saturday. Who's ready for a cup of tea?"

As they sat together, Camilla told stories of the local history, funny stories of her children growing up including the one of Gareth losing his first tooth and playing in his first football match. She also told stories of how his older sisters Becs and Ana would dress Gareth in makeup and their dresses. Family: Kelsey knew it well, and for as strict as she was raised, she knew the importance of how it grounded you and formed you into the adult you become.

As they finished tea and cleared the table, Kelsey volunteered to wash dishes. Gareth helped by drying them and eased easily into conversation with her about growing up as a Blythe. Gareth could see that Kelsey was genuinely interested and kept the stories coming. They bantered back and forth while putting away clean dishes and leftover food. Kelsey shared stories of her and her sister growing up in the country with animals like dogs, horses, goats, and the occasional raccoon or fox that took up residence. She went on about how much she loved horses and about her love of painting. Creating something out of nothing was therapeutic on many levels. Gareth leaned against the counter, and Kelsey leaned against the sink, wiping her hands with the towel when they heard the grandfather clock chime in the hall.

"Oh my goodness! Is it really ten o'clock? I still have work to finish!" She folded the towel and laid it next to the sink. "Gareth, are you sure you're okay taking me to the pub Saturday? I'd feel awful if you were only doing it out of obligation."

"Not at all. If I felt obligated I would tell you. I think you and I are at a place where we can speak freely with each other, don't you?" That brought a big smile to her face, which made his heart swell. "Well, you have me there. Goodnight, Gareth." When she was out of sight, Gareth tilted his head back and closed his eyes while he tried to figure out what this girl from America was doing to him.

* * *

That Friday

Class let out at three in the afternoon, and Camilla had Kelsey meet her at her office so that they could ride over to the shelter together. The ride over was filled with talk about what to expect from the shelter: they'd be prepping some of the meals to be served there and deliver some meals to the elderly residents who were living on very small pensions and were unable to physically come in for a hot meal.

Camilla explained that Duncan had discovered this specific need while at the local market one afternoon. He bumped into an older gentleman unable to reach some cans on the top shelf. Duncan went over to help out and then struck up a conversation with the gentleman. In that conversation he learned that once every two weeks he would stock up on canned beans, stewed tomatoes, lentils, and even lima beans to survive until his next pension check arrived. The older gentleman cared for his ailing wife, and while he did his best to prepare decent meals, most of it was thrown together with the cans of food he could purchase. Duncan was overwhelmed by the exchange and quickly learned that there were many other elderly in York in a similar situation. Camilla's sadness wore heavy around her eyes as she thought of all whom had been helped because of her late husband's goodness.

"You see, Kelsey, these dinners delivered three days a week may be the only hot meals many of these wonderful old souls will get. Some have no families to check in on them, and helping them became a mission for Duncan as it was his way of giving back. Continuing to help in this way keeps him close to my heart and makes it feel as if he's still by my side. I think it's meant the same to Gareth."

Kelsey could see that Camilla was carefully brushing away the tears that had snuck in as she talked. Reaching for her hand, Kelsey gave it a quick squeeze. "It's my honor to help in any way I can. Duncan sounds like a warm soul, and I bet we would've hit it off from the moment we met."

Camilla smiled, "Of this I have no doubt."

Gareth was already inside with the shelter director James helping bag the to-go dinners when Camilla and Kelsey came into the kitchen. Gareth made eye contact with Kelsey immediately and saw her smile that lit up the room and his heart. Once Camilla did the introductions, James explained that one of their drivers wouldn't be able to make the deliveries. In that moment Gareth spoke up, "I can do it. I'm sure I remember the route, and maybe Kelsey could assist me."

Looking a bit surprised but not hesitating for a moment Kelsey responded, "Anything I can do to help is just fine with me." James and Camilla nodded in agreement. James handed Gareth the address list as a reminder, and then he sent the two off. Gareth checked to make sure the rack that he set up in the back of the vehicle was secure. This would prevent the dinner trays from spilling over when they made turns. He also counted six paper bags that had a few packaged canned goods that helped the residents eek by until their next meal delivery or pension check, whatever happened first. Then Gareth hopped in on the driver's side and gave Kelsey the game plan, "We have six dinners to deliver along with the bags with food that each resident will get. Four of them are on the outskirts of town, so we will go there first and work our way back in."

"Six doesn't seem like a lot people; surely we could do more?" Kelsey responded.

Gareth loved that she wanted to serve more and smiled. "Oh it will be, trust me on that. You have to keep in mind many times these individuals are looking forward to not only the food, but also a visitor." As he put the vehicle in drive, he filled her in on all of the individuals she was about to meet. "I don't always do the deliveries when I work at the shelter, but I've done so many times. In the past year, I've come to know all of these people just like my father had. He would carry his toolbox with him to fix a leaky pipe or sticking window. There was always something that needed tending to." Kelsey listened on. "He volunteered with the Peace Corp for a year while in College before coming home and meeting my mum. He became very handy with a set of tools. Once he knew they were settled and enjoying their meals he would move about their house on a mission to fix odds and ends that could make or break their quality of life. He knew because of their limited income and most of them having no family to check on them, he could address these issues for them free of charge."

Before she could ask him if he had any favorites residents he liked to visit, Gareth blurted out, "I cannot wait for you to meet Hyacinth Collins. She'll be our last stop as she'll want us to stay around a little longer and visit. She loves to garden and is a painter, so I'm sure you'll both have much to talk about."

Kelsey smiled back. "I cannot wait to meet her as well." After listening to him, Kelsey knew that they were in for quite an evening. As they made their rounds, it struck her how at ease Gareth was with each of the elderly they visited. She didn't expect that from him. She was sure he was no different from the affluent families back home who only volunteered at the homeless shelter so that they could brag about it in their yearly nauseating newsletters they sent out. No, Gareth loved taking the time to connect with them, just like his father had. And, also just like his father, Gareth hated that so many had more or less been forgotten. He wanted them all to know that he truly cared for them. He wanted to show them the dignity they deserved, just as his father had faithfully displayed for all those years. She sensed that Duncan's death had so altered Gareth that he now felt it was his mission in life to carry on his father's kindness.

He introduced her to all the residents who welcomed her and of course offered her a cup of tea. Some of the residents watched football, some preferred cricket, and others rugby. He knew which teams to engage them in conversation about as he helped them settle into their favorite chair with the tray of food. For the ladies, it was a conversation usually involving their houseplants needing a bit of water and what their favorite characters on the soap *Coronation Street* were up to. He was always kind, never rushed through the visit, and looked them all in the eye with a kindness that Kelsey recognized. When they arrived to the home of their final delivery it was almost seven thirty in the evening. *The poor woman is probably starving at this point*, Kelsey thought to herself as they pulled up.

"All right then: let's introduce you to Hyacinth," Gareth said with a smile as he got out of the Defender. As they walked to her door and rang the bell, they stood there for what seemed several long moments as Kelsey noticed that the small front porch was covered with flowerpots of all shapes and sizes. Hyacinth even had a purple vine of what looked to be wisteria climbing a make-shift arbor around the large picture window that looked out over her tiny front yard. In the pots were purple and white flowers, many varieties that Kelsey had never seen before.

As they waited at the door, Kelsey asked in a soft voice, "If she's this good with the gardening I can't imagine what her paintings are like." He gave Kelsey a quick wink, but before she could even think about blushing, the door opened and revealed a woman in her mid seventies with long, silver hair. She wore a lengthy, floral, purple skirt, with a long white flowing top layered with a purple vest and finished with a long, glass-beaded necklace with matching earrings. She wasn't up to the latest fashion in her second-hand or perhaps vintage attire, but it was the perfect look for her down to her purple and white striped socks peaking out from her well-worn Birkenstocks that steadied her walk.

"Hello, Hyacinth."

"Oh, Gareth, it's so lovely to hear your voice! You haven't been on the delivery route in a while." Reaching out, she pulled him in for a hug. "Bring a guest, did you?" Since she was holding Hyacinth's dinner, Kelsey had to balance it in one arm so she could reach out her hand for a welcoming shake.

"Hello, I'm Kelsey Chapman." It was at that moment Kelsey realized that Hyacinth was blind. Smiling back, Hyacinth reached out her hand to make contact. She asked, "You're American?"

"Yes ma'am. I'm staying with the Blythes for the summer term as an exchange student for the art program."

"Oh, that is lovely. Well please come in, and we can talk over a cup of tea." Hyacinth slowly turned her upper body; reaching her arms out, she used the wall as her guide. "Please excuse the mess; I'd planned on cleaning up before you arrived, but I really wanted to finish this piece before the sun was completely gone." As they gradually walked down the small hallway, Hyacinth and Gareth chatted while Kelsey took in the beautiful pictures hanging on the walls. Kelsey interrupted their conversation. "When...how...did you do all of these?" Kelsey immediately heard how loud and rude she sounded and covered her mouth. "I am sorry. Where are my manners?" Gareth and Hyacinth both laughed while Kelsey turned many shades of red.

"Kelsey, come with me to my tiny studio, and I will show you my work while Gareth prepares my tea." She handed a smiling Gareth the tray and followed Hyacinth into what certainly was a tiny studio with the large glass window that looked out over the little front yard. There were medium canvases all around covered in multiple shades of purple and white depicting gardens that were lush and captivating. There would be the occasional red or orange for a splash of color, but most everything was purple and white. "I don't know what to say," Kelsey admitted quietly.

"Well if you don't like them, you don't have to say anything!" Hyacinth said with a laugh.

"Oh my, no! That's not it at all! I think I'm in just a state of shock."

"Would it be because you're trying to figure out how an old blind woman is able to put paint to canvas?" Kelsey got very still and quiet. Hyacinth raised her hand and placed it on Kelsey's arm. "My dear, it's okay to ask me that question." Kelsey paused and smiled and appreciated Hyacinth's effort to make her feel less awkward. "Let's go into the kitchen and have a seat, and we can get to know each other a little better." With a deep breath Kelsey gave an "okay" as they made their way in the tiny townhouse.

In the kitchen, they found Gareth putting away the produce, preparing the tea, and rewarming her tray of food since she had been the final delivery. As they got to the kitchen table, they each took a place as Hyacinth did not waste time with her questions. "Where are you from in the states my dear?" "The east coast, Virginia." "How long have you been painting?" "How did you know I painted?" Kelsey asked with raised eyebrow and shock in her voice. "Oh my dear, one always knows when she is in the presence of another artist."

Gareth started to laugh as he poured the hot water into the teapot. Kelsey looked over at him with the look of *really?* and quickly realized he needed to focus at the task at hand. "My mom enrolled us in a week-long summer camp when I was ten. It was a ranch where you rode horses, swam, and could take art classes. My main intent was to ride horses all week, but I decided to take an art class. The teacher made it so much fun and made painting come to life. I also happen to have a knack for it, and one thing lead to another. When I showed my parents my work they both agreed to enroll me in classes. As I grew and took additional classes, my art teacher had shared her stories of spending her summers here in York at the art school. She really encouraged me give the summer exchange program a go before stepping foot into a college art classroom back at home. She said I'd be much more prepared to take risks with my work and my teaching techniques. I really wanted to go to Italy or France to study, but it was all I could do to convince my parents to help me get here."

Hyacinth laughed. "York is small and is certainly not Italy, but the University does have a wonderful art department. Do you like to paint anything in particular?"

Kelsey thought about it for a few seconds. "I do find myself painting a lot of outdoor scenes. I think that's what caught my eye with your paintings. You're able to capture so much detail on the canvas without it looking overwhelming." Kelsey paused for a moment unsure how to phrase her next question. Hyacinth reached across the table for her hand. Kelsey obliged.

"I was diagnosed ten years ago with Macular Degeneration. I have, for the most part, lost my eyesight, but if it's a decent sunny day outside, I can see a small bit of detail and shadows. When I received my diagnosis, I knew that if I wanted to continue to paint I needed to start committing my techniques to memory. I would even blindfold myself and practice. I knew by doing so I was making deposits into my memory bank that I would need to withdraw from when my sight was completely gone. I also had to promise myself to not let my heart forget why it loved to paint." Hyacinth pulled Kelsey's hand across the table and placed it over her heart. "All your work and inspiration must always come from here, no matter what the circumstances are. Never forget that, young Kelsey. Do you understand?"

Kelsey could feel her eyes filling and nodded yes before remembering that she needed to verbally respond. "Yes, I understand."

"Good. Now, I'm starving. Gareth, where is my food?"

"Coming right up, Ms. Collins."

"May I ask you another question, Ms. Collins?"

"Yes, of course, and you can call me Hyacinth. Gareth, you know you can as well," she responded while releasing Kelsey's hand.

"Why do you only paint with purples and white and why do you use only medium canvases and why don't you sell them?"

"I believe that was three questions," Hyacinth laughed as she pulled her tea cup to her mouth.

"Oh, yes, I guess that was," Kelsey said with a sheepish grin.

Gareth placed Hyacinth's dinner in front of her. He was enjoying the interaction immensely and was equally interested in Hyacinth's answers.

"I'm on a fixed pension. I mean good Lord, I have to rely on the good people of York and their generosity to feed me three times a week. It all comes down to cost, and the only way I can justify spending the money on paint supplies is to save on colors and canvas sizes. Purple and white happen to be my favorite colors to use. As far as selling, I'd have to travel to different counties and find local galleries that would even consider having me. No one wants to lug a seventy-year-old blind woman around so she can peddle her artwork. I truly appreciate your kindness, Kelsey, but I'm okay living my quiet life, with my paintings and flowers to keep me company—and of course an occasional visit from Mr. Blythe." Kelsey loved watching Gareth blush across the table as Hyacinth was now cutting and eating her meal with a smile on her face.

After dinner and another cup of tea, they said their goodbyes and headed back to the Blythe residence. Kelsey was quiet for much of the trip home. Looking over he saw her looking out the window, biting her lower lip with her brow furrowed. She looked adorable and slightly perplexed which finally led Gareth to ask if she was okay.

"Yeah, just that Hyacinth's work and experience need to be shared. It seems like such waste of talent."

"Well, you heard her say that she was content."

"I know, but I can't help but think that if she got to experience the classroom for a day and was given an opportunity to show her work to the department and some of the students, then maybe it would change her mind. I mean, she's going blind and is still painting these beautiful works of art. If that's not inspirational, I don't know what is. Sometimes in life we think we're content until we experience something or someone that makes us realize that maybe we aren't."

Gareth was astounded at the gravity of the statement she'd just made. He found it hard to reply as he tried to reconcile why his heart had been so affected by her statement. Before he could reply, Kelsey spared him by talking again. "Thank you for letting me go with you today, Gareth. It was striking to me when these people shared their stories that they're so similar to so many of the homeless people I work with back home. Need and hunger know no age and have no borders." Gareth responded with a small smile as he felt that blasted tug on his heart.

"Right you are, Kelsey; right you are."

* * *

That Saturday

Gareth came in the front door a sweaty mess. As he walked into the kitchen looking in the fridge for some electrolytes, his mother came in. "Hello, love, just home from the football match?"

Filling his glass to the very top with orange juice he replied, "Yeah, I needed a quick drink before jumping in the shower. Have you seen Kelsey?"

"I believe she is upstairs working. I swear, Gareth, of all the exchange students we've had over the years, she has to be most intense when it comes to her studies. Are you going to take her out tonight to the Gray Horse?"

Gareth gulped down the last of the juice using his sleeved arm to wipe his mouth and giving a breathless "that was the plan."

"Great, you might want to knock on her door and let her know you're home so you can confirm a time."

Giving his mum a look he muttered, "I think I can handle this."

"I never said you couldn't; I'm just making a friendly suggestion." He leaned in and kissed the top of her head before he took off up the stairs. Stopping at his door, he decided that maybe his mother was right, that touching base with Kelsey to confirm a time was a good idea. He walked over to her door that was partially cracked and noticed she was lying across her bed with what had to be twenty books scattered around her along with her portable CD player. She'd fallen asleep. Gareth saw that she had her headphones on. He poked his head in the door and quietly called her name, "Kelsey." Nothing, not a budge. He took three steps; standing right next to her bed he loudly whispered, "KEL-SEY!"

She started to stir, and Gareth was immediately aware of her pouty lips and long brown hair as it swept across her pillow. The overwhelming ache came over him to press his lips down on hers. Just as he turned to step out of the room, a sleepy and slightly confused voice stopped him, "Gareth why…why are you in my room?"

He turned to see her pushing herself up on her bed with her elbows and taking the headphones off. "I wasn't trying to intrude, Kelsey. I swear. I was about to jump in the shower and get ready to take you to the pub. I thought I'd confirm we were still on and found that you were asleep. I was just trying to wake you."

She rubbed her eyes and yawned. "Okay, well, when do you want to leave?"

Relief flooded Gareth. "Can you give me thirty minutes?"

"Of course, take longer if you like," Kelsey said as she stretched from her nap.

Gareth walked to his bedroom and planned on taking a cold shower to remind him that she and her sleepy pouty lips were off limits. Thirty minutes later, Gareth, in a khaki pair of shorts and Ralph Lauren polo and zip up hoodie, found Kelsey sitting at the dining room table having a cup of tea with his mom. Kelsey had her dark brown hair pulled back and up in a pony tail and was wearing a simple and, in Gareth's opinion, sexy as hell form-fitting red dress with cap sleeves and thin black belt. She wore black sandals that matched her belt and simple silver hoop earrings. Gareth once again found himself looking for his next breath and wondered if he would even survive the night. Picking up her sweater Kelsey beamed, "Are we ready then?" "Yes, indeed," Gareth replied, and with that they headed out the front door to experience a bit of old fashioned British pub culture.

He loved listening to Kelsey talk on the way, but he could sense she was sad. The Gray Horse was hopping with people gathered around the bar watching the big match on television, summer students from the University, and local townspeople escaping reality for just a little while. Gareth found a small cozy table in the corner that allowed them both to sit facing out toward the bar to people watch and let Kelsey take in the sights and sounds. Kelsey loved every minute of it. She only wished that Jason, Courtney, and Jasper could be there to enjoy it with her. She couldn't wait to tell them about it.

Just as she was getting her bearings, a blonde waitress with Jennifer Aniston hair, dressed in a plaid skirt and white t-shirt that stopped midriff, approached their table. "Well hallo, Gareth. Where have you been about?" Kelsey watched their banter as Gareth struggled to look at ease when he was anything but. Gareth began the introductions, "Heidi, this is Kelsey. She's here from the states for the summer exchange program at the University."

"Oh, lovely, what part of the states are you from?"

"East Coast, Virginia."

"That's sounds nice. What can I get you to drink?"

"I will take a water, please," Kelsey said quietly.

Gareth jumped in, "Their legal age for drinking is twenty-one, so she's starting out easy. I'll have a pint of Theakston, and bring over two orders of fish and chips."

Bouncing the eraser tip off her lips she howled, "Oh, right, I forgot about the age restriction in the states. Let me know when you want something with a little more kick. Be right back with that ale, water, and fish and chips."

After she walked away Kelsey couldn't help herself. "Old girlfriend of yours, Gareth?" This was asked with a raised eyebrow.

Gareth looked down at the table with a bit of a smirk. "Why do you ask?"

"Oh I don't know, maybe it was the awkward conversation right before you introduced me?"

"I wouldn't say girlfriend," he struggled to find his words, his head rolling side to side.

Kelsey leaned in close to him. "A bedroom buddy?"

Gareth threw his head back and laughed. "Where on earth did you pick up that term?"

"I just created it, why?"

"It sounds almost…wholesome."

Just then the glass of water and pint of ale arrived. Heidi bent over, putting one arm over Gareth's shoulder and leaning her large chest into him, and whispered into his ear. Kelsey turned her head as to help shield herself from the awkwardness that was spilling out from his corner. As Heidi backed up, she winked at him and said, "I'll come back and check on you later, love."

Kelsey looked over at Gareth who was absolutely red. She grabbed her glass of water and raised it to her lips, "I think you may need this more than I do."

Trying to move on from that moment Kelsey asked another question, "Since you've never volunteered it, what are you studying in school?"

"Well, because you never asked," he said playfully. "I'm pre-med, with the hopes of one day being a cardiologist and contributing something important to that area."

"Really?" shot out of her voice with a shocked tone.

"Well, don't act so surprised," he said in a huff.

"Is it because of what happened to your dad?" Kelsey asked carefully. He looked right at her and nodded his head yes. "Were you going to play professional soccer, I mean football, before he passed?"

"That was the plan, but plans change."

"I understand that," Kelsey replied. They sat in content silence for a few minutes until

Gareth leaned over. "Can I ask you a question, Kelsey?"

"Sure."

"Why don't you drink alcohol?" Kelsey paused and took a deep breath. "You don't have to answer; I didn't mean to put you on the spot."

Brushing her hand in the air so that he would know she didn't mind answering the question Kelsey said, "I was raised in a very conservative home. Yes, before you ask, I attended parties in high school where the alcohol flowed, but if I'd ever come home with the scent of liquor on my breath…. Let's just say it wasn't worth it in the end for the price I would've paid."

"Your parents sound harsh."

Kelsey could feel herself getting a little defensive. "Yes, my parents were protective; you could even call it overprotective, especially my mom." Kelsey looked out over the bar with reflection in her voice, "However, we had a chain of events occur in the past several months that helped with that. It's not that she isn't strict anymore; she's just is a little more open-minded these days, but only a little." Kelsey pinched her fingers together to show what a little looked like.

"Would those chain of events have anything to do with how you have a fiancé?" Kelsey looked surprised that he even asked and this time nodded her head yes. "Care to share those chain of events?" Gareth asked as he threw back his glass. The sadness and timidness that Kelsey had entered the pub with seemed to lift as she looked over at Gareth and with a shoulder shrug said, "Sure, but you may want to order another ale."

As he sat there and listened to Kelsey, he realized how he was in serious danger. The more she talked, the happier she became, and he was falling in love with this girl he didn't even know. It made no sense, and he told himself so as she talked, but it didn't matter. Love at first sight was a popular theme in movies not just because it made a good romance story but because it really did happen, maybe rarely, but enough that people dreamt it would happen to them. Maybe it wasn't exactly love he felt that first day, but it was something instant and strong. And sharing the time volunteering together yesterday and now hearing about Kelsey's life made her more real to Gareth, and the more real she became, the more real his feelings became as well.

She told him all about how she grew up in a conservative home, talked about how important her faith was to her, though it left her questioning so much. How she loved her parents, regardless of how complicated their relationship had been. She talked about her younger sister Ellie, and how she wanted to be the best big sister and role model for her.

She shared about her adventures with Courtney and Jasper growing up and how precious their friendship was. She shared with him how much she missed her horse Triton, how she desperately missed the smell of the barn and quiet moments painting in the garden. She even remarked at how much she loved being in a pub called the Gray Horse as its name alone gave her, for some silly reason, some comforts of home.

Even when she talked about Jason, how they met and how from the first date she knew she would marry him, he didn't mind. Well, he minded a little, and in that moment wanted so desperately to be Jason. He watched as her eyes filled with tears that he so desperately wanted to wipe away while she told him about the accident and how Jason's heroics saved her. "Have I completely bored you into oblivion yet?" Kelsey asked with a half smile, jolting him from his inner dialogue.

"Not at all. I find this all fascinating. Truly and utterly fascinating." Kelsey eyed him as she couldn't tell at first if it was the alcohol talking, but she quickly realized he meant what he said when he leaned into her very close and said, "No, Kelsey Chapman from America, I am not in the least bit bored."

Just then Kelsey squeaked, "Oh my, Gareth," waving her hand in front of her face. "How many ales have you had sitting here for the past three hours?"

"I don't know, seven maybe eight?"

"Well, then I will need to drive home as I am not riding shotgun."

"Kelsey, I know how to hold my liquor."

"I'm not saying you don't, but if I refuse to die in a car accident in York, England, because it was under the influence of alcohol by the driver." He couldn't argue. As she helped him out of the booth he looked at her, glassy-eyed and with a bit of a slur, and asked, "Why do you call it *shotgun*?"

"I can explain that later; just give me your keys, and let's hope that I don't grind the hell out of your gears. Driving a stick is not a regular event back home."

He handed her the keys and settled the bill. She got them home, with all of the gears to the car still intact. She helped to make sure he made it to his room. "Gareth, stand by your bedroom door. I'll be right back." As she crossed to her own room, she was back in thirty seconds and handed him two aspirin and a bottle of water.

"I would start drinking this water immediately, and you'll want to take these in the morning as soon as you wake up. You're going to need them."

"Yes, Kelsey, I'm quite aware of what I need to do," he said with much sarcasm. He looked down into her shiny golden hazel eyes and felt his insides radiated by that red dress. Gareth sensed his breath stagger, and it wasn't from the alcohol. "Thank you, Gareth." He raised an eyebrow. "Why are you thanking me; you're the one who saw to getting me home in one piece."

"While that might be true, I'm really homesick for my family, for Jason, my friends, and my horse. Tonight, being able to get out and see more than four walls of a classroom or a bedroom and just having a friend to talk with, helped more than you'll ever know. You could've said no to taking me out and instead gone to your parties with all your friends, but you didn't, so thank you, and I hope you'll be able to get some sleep."

Kelsey turned on her heels and walked back into her room and closed the door. Gareth leaned against the doorframe, not sure what to do. Passing out from an alcohol-induced coma sounded perfect; then he wouldn't have to think. Think about her and how in two short weeks she had managed to turn his world upside down and on its head. Instead, Gareth lay in bed staring at the ceiling, replaying the conversation from the Gray Horse in his head and coming to terms that the American one room over was never meant to be his. That she indeed had a love story for the ages, and her real life awaited to begin when she arrived back home in ten weeks' time. Gareth had a decision to make. She may never truly be his, but why not make some serious memories with this girl? Why not make it as fun as possible so she would never forget him and the amazing summer they had together?

He got up, walked into the bathroom, splashed cold water on his face, dried it with a soft towel, looked in the mirror, and murmured, "For the first time in your life, Gareth Henry Blythe, you want to impress and befriend a girl with the full knowledge that there will be nothing in return but her friendship?" He continued to stare at himself in the mirror, almost expecting another voice to answer his question. "You're a bloody fool" was all he could muster, and he slapped the light off and crawled into bed, where he lay awake for several more hours.

MAY 2012
LUCKY NUMBER 13

Kelsey was sound asleep with the covers over her head when Jason leaned over, pulled them down, and very sweetly kissed her forehead, then her nose, then her mouth before he whispered, "Wake up, sleepy head." He continued to pick up her hand and kiss the top of it making trails back up her arm, then to her collarbone, then her neck. Kelsey moaned, "That feels amazing." She grabbed him and pulled him into bed with her. Jason started to laugh, "What do you think you're doing?"

"I am going to have outrageously great sex with my sexy as hell husband."

She climbed on top and straddled him, allowing the sheet to fall and expose her naked body. "Why are you showered and dressed while I was still in bed?" she asked, grabbing his hand and pressing it to her breast.

"Because we have an anniversary to celebrate."

"Oh we do, do we? Well what about my anniversary sex to celebrate thirteen married years with you?"

Jason let out a moan as she started to flex her hips and rock back and forth. He pulled her down to him so her breast brushed his chest and they were nose to nose. "Kelsey, I have a surprise for you, and I got up early to have it ready. Don't you want to see it?"

"Mmhmm, yes, but not until we're done here." Slowly she unbuckled his belt, methodically unbuttoned and unzipped him all while looking him in the eye and licking her lips. "Shit, Kelsey, you still know how to completely wreck me, don't you?" Jason said in shallow breaths. "I do my best, husband."

She slid her hand down, pulling his boxers out of the way until his large cock sprang forth. "There you are!" And before Jason could react, Kelsey took him in her mouth. The more he moaned, the more turned on Kelsey became. She sucked, she teased his tip with her tongue, and she used her hand on his shaft while she sucked to take him to the place that was theirs and theirs alone. His hands in her hair, grabbing and pulling, he spoke a tumultuous "oh fuck, Kelsey," and before he could utter another word, his head went back, and he found his release. Kelsey took every last drop of him and kept her lips and mouth on him as he came down and experienced his after shocks.

Once she released her mouth, she lay beside him with her arm and leg draped over him. "Happy anniversary, Jason." Ten minutes passed before Jason came back down safely to earth. He brushed Kelsey's hair back and finally spoke, "Best. Anniversary. Gift. Ever." Kelsey laughed. He pushed himself up on his elbows as she got up to get in the shower.

"With the surprise I have for you, I don't have time to even the orgasm score. Can you wait till tonight after dinner?" Kelsey sighed, "If I must," and then smiled as she walked into the glassed shower. "I won't be long."

As usual, Kelsey could be ready with makeup that always looked natural and flawless in twenty minutes. One of the many things Jason loved about her. When she came out with her hair in a hat and ponytail pulled through, white t-shirt and jeans that hugged all her curves, Jason sighed. "I love you in a good t-shirt and a pair of nice-fitting jeans."

"I thought you liked me naked best?"

Jason laughed, "And don't you ever forget it."

"Well if you would tell me where I was going I would know if I need to throw on a scarf to dress it up," Kelsey quipped.

"You won't need a scarf, but you will need your paddock boots."

Kelsey stopped in the middle of the kitchen. "Really? Wait! Did you buy me that new riding lawnmower I've been wanting?"

Jason stopped dead in his tracks and turned, "Do you think that for one second I would buy you that as an anniversary present?"

"Well, why not? You know I don't need fancy jewelry. I mean I don't mind it, but I don't use that kind of measuring stick for anniversary presents; you know this Jason."

"Well before you get your nose in a wrinkle, let me show you what you got before you make any more guesses."

"Okay, fine."

Jason reached in his back pocket and pulled out a bandana. Kelsey looked at him with a raised eyebrow. "I thought we were going to even the score tonight?"

"Ha, ha, ha, we are, but this is to blindfold you before we walk outside."

Kelsey immediately clapped her hands together and turned around. As Jason started to blindfold her he leaned over and whispered in her ear, "I truly hope you love your gift."

Chills shot down her neck. "If you don't show me right now, we may be evening the score here on the kitchen floor."

Jason laughed and guided her out the side door. Twenty-five paces later he walked her through the paddock gate and had her stand in the middle of the field. "Are you ready?!" Jason asked with the giddiness of an eight-year-old on

Christmas morning. "YES! Jason! Please let me see!" He removed the blindfold, and, standing across the field was her sister who was holding the most beautiful horse she'd ever laid eyes on. Ellie unhooked the lead, and the horse immediately trotted over to Kelsey and stopped right in front.

"Kelsey, this is Jedi; he's a sixteen hand tall, seven-year-old, Friesian gelding. Happy anniversary, sweetheart."

Kelsey stood there, speechless, tears filling her eyes then streaming down her face. She was completely in love. "Jedi? His name is Jedi?"

"I know, right! What were the odds I found the perfect Friesian with the most perfect name?"

Kelsey laughed and reached out, touched the long flowing black mane, and wrapped her arms around his neck. Jedi stood there completely square, head raised as if on the look out. So proud and so majestic. "Oh, Jason! He's perfect." Kelsey turned around and threw her arms around Jason. "Thank you thank you thank you. I love him, and oh my Lord do I love you." She kissed him hard, and she kissed him long.

"You guys may want to take that back inside," Ellie yelled from the gate.

"Thank you, Ellie!" Jason yelled while waving across the field.

"Happy anniversary, you guys." Ellie walked across the lane to go and visit her parents as their home sat across from the cottage that Jason and Kelsey had built two years after they married. "I need to run an errand in town; why don't you spend some time bonding with your new boyfriend. Can you be ready to leave for dinner at four?"

"Absolutely."

Jason put both of his hands on Kelsey's face and put his forehead to her forehead. "Thank you, Kels, I'm the luckiest bastard alive and was determined to make sure that thirteen was remembered as lucky number thirteen; you more than deserve it. You deserve more than I can ever give you." He kissed her hard and passionately one more time just as Jedi cut in. Jason laughed. "I think I made him jealous."

"There's plenty of room for both of you, so no need for favorites."

With that, Jason went on to run his errand as Kelsey introduced Jedi to his new home, the barn cats, as well as Rosie and Dodger, the dogs. After grooming him and even giving him a quick lunge to see how he moved, Kelsey fed him a big bale of hay, and made arrangements for her mom to come over around five to care for him while they were gone. Kelsey didn't know the evening's plans, but she couldn't even begin to think how this day could get any better, except maybe when it was time for Jason to even the orgasm score. That may just be the cherry on top.

Not only had he made secret reservations in Williamsburg at the Fat Cardinal, their favorite restaurant, he also managed to pack an overnight bag for them to have a two-night stay at the Williamsburg Inn. He packed her favorite red cocktail dress and black heels, loading them into the car without her seeing him do so. When he told her the news in the truck on the way, she was thrilled.

"Seriously Jas, you have really outdone yourself this time. How am I ever going to compete with this?"

"Kelsey, this is not a competition; you're my wife, and I, as your husband, get to do this for you, and nothing makes me happier."

"Well, in case you're wondering, I do have something for you that will come after dinner, and no it's not more sex, even though that is definitely happening again tonight."

Jason laughed, "Oh so sure of yourself are you?"

"Yes," she said with a big smile and total confidence.

They had caught some traffic in the tunnel but got to the Williamsburg Inn in time to check

Cobie Daniels

in and to allow them both ample time to change and get ready. It always struck Kelsey as funny how an hour drive could not only transport them in time but also give reprieve from life's realities. Once they finished their amazing dinner, they decided to take a short walk down the Duke of Gloucester Street to admire the beautiful colonial homes.

They walked and landed on their favorite bench in front of the Governor's Palace. Kelsey tucked into Jason's side, reminiscing of the past thirteen years. All the things they had done, the places they had seen, and the travel they had experienced. They laughed and reflected on how quick time seemed to be passing them by. It was hard not to stay focused on all the good things, but there was the cloud of uncertainty and the sharp pain that seemed to find itself in the middle of the tender moments like these, a pain and uncertainty that was brought on by a miscarriage six months prior to their anniversary. Jason pulled Kelsey close as they sat in a quiet solace, watching the other tourists walk by.

Looking down at the ground, kicking some pebbles, the words just flowed out of Kelsey, "I'm still so sad, Jason." Immediately looking at her and putting his finger under her chin, he lifted her gaze to him, lovingly kissing her

148

forehead, then her lips. Once again he knew how to make her feel so cherished.

"Kels, I wish I could make the pain and the disappointment stop. Just please know that I hurt right along with you."

"What if we never get pregnant again? It was six months ago. It's not like we haven't been trying?"

He traced his thumb softly over her lips. "It will happen when it's suppose to happen." Kelsey remained quiet as he continued, "If it ends up being just you and me walking this planet together, then so be it. As long as I'm with you, nothing else matters. Do you hear me?" Kelsey nodded her head yes while her eyes filled with tears. She threw her arms around him and held him close. "I don't know what I did to deserve you," she said quietly.

"Oh, quite the contrary, love. I thank God every day that he gave you to me. How he ever saw me fit to be your husband still astounds me thirteen years later."

"Let's start heading back and enjoy our room at the inn. How does that sound?" Kelsey leaned in, kissing him long and hard.

"Sounds perfect."

One of the evening ghost tours was beginning in front of the Bruton Parish Church. As they walked by, Kelsey couldn't help but stop and listen to the tour guide, in full colonial dress, as she spoke of the ghost that frequented the streets and buildings of Merchants' Square. "It's not uncommon on a quiet night like this to hear the cries of the infant daughter of Ann Burgess, as her mother sweetly sings her to sleep. For it was in childbirth that both daughter and mother lost their lives, and now their spirits roam the streets of the town trying to find their way back to their home in Isle of Wight, England."

In that instant, at the very sound of a location she had not been to in twenty years, her head jerked back in the direction of the tour guide's voice. "You alright, Kels?" Jason asked, as he felt her reaction.

"Yeah, it's just that story is so sad, and hearing her say the Isle of Wight, England, just brings back a flood of memories of the weekend I spent there."

"Ah, you mean that summer you spent in England and put me through the torture of waiting for your official *yes* that you would marry me?" he said with a clever smile on his face.

"You had not officially asked me or given me a ring, so I think the torture worked both ways," she shot back with her own clever smile.

They entered the inn with fingers entwined and approached the door of their suite. But before Jason opened the door, he pressed Kelsey against it and landed a passionate and demanding kiss, allowing his hands to travel up her sides, over her breasts, and then in her hair. Sucking all the air out of her lungs, Jason pulled back and rested his forehead on hers while they caught their breath. Kelsey opened her eyes and found Jason staring at her.

"What?" she asked breathlessly.

"Eighteen years later, even after thirteen years of marriage, you still do things to me, Kelsey. Kissing you like this reminds me how lucky I am."

Using both her hands, Kelsey held Jason's head, kissed his forehead, his nose and lips, then slowly let her hands slide down to his pants where she deliberately began to unbuckle his belt, unbutton his pants, and push the zipper down.

"Open the door, Jason," she said breathlessly into his ear.

He fumbled for the card, waved it across the magnetic strip, and they were in. Seconds later the "do not disturb" sign was slapped on the outside door handle. They landed hard on the four- poster, king-size bed, each taking a turn removing an article of clothing from one another. Kelsey pushed herself from the bed and slowly removed his shoes, then his socks; Jason, in turn, got up and began kissing the back of her neck, slowly taking off her necklace. Then removing her long dangling earrings, he kissed each earlobe and slowly unzipped the red dress that hugged her body so well. As he did, he allowed his forefinger to leisurely trace down to the base of her spine where he saw her black thong. He leaned into her ear and whispered, "You wore my favorite thong, I see."

"Well, you did pack my bags for me," she responded with a half smile on her lips. He placed himself in front of her where they looked in each other's eyes, and Kelsey began to unbutton his dress shirt. As she did, she replaced each button with a kiss on his chest. The farther down she traveled, Jason's breath hitched. "Jesus, Kelsey." As she pushed his shirt off his shoulders, she reached into his open slacks and stroked his very present erection with her hands. Jason hissed a breath and grabbed her hands. "Oh no you don't," Kelsey laughed as he spun her around and pushed her dress off her shoulders and let it drop at her feet. With her standing in a strapless black bustier, black thong, and black heels, it was all Jason could do to stay in control.

"Oh my god, Kels, you are a vision." Jason removed his pants and boxers, reached for the clip that was holding up her hair and unsnapped it, letting her caramel-colored tresses fall around her shoulders. Then reaching his splayed hand around to the front of Kelsey's belly he slowly pulled her to him, so that her back was to his front, and began to kiss her shoulder and neck as he removed the rest of her clothing. Kelsey was on fire in each spot he touched with his lips. His hands continued to explore her body as he asked, "Do you remember the first time we made love, Kelsey?" Barely able to answer, she managed a yes. He continued, "It was so tender and so sweet and so deep. I'll never forget the privilege of becoming the first to love you this way. The way you feel in my hands, in my mouth: I will never get enough of this with you."

Kelsey was a completely undone by him. The level of connection that one could feel with another human being, let alone her husband, was something many women simply dreamed about. Kelsey was living it. "Jason, I need you right now, please."

He let out a little laugh. "Patience, my love," he whispered into her ear before nibbling her earlobe. He carefully and slowly bent her over the bed. "Leave your heels on," he breathed into her ear. Jason moved behind her, slowly massaging the inside of her thighs, then moving his hand around to her front to find her center where he put in two fingers. "Oh, you're so wet and ready for me." He continued to slowly stroke his two fingers then added a third, hitting the spot. Taking his other hand, he used two fingers to roll her nipple. He was bringing her closer as she began to moan his name. "Jason?" "Yes, Kelsey, what do you need? "You know what I need," she huffed out as he pressed and rubbed more intensely.

He felt the spasms around his fingers as she bore down hard cried out. As she continued to come down, Jason entered her from behind replacing his hand with his hard cock. Kelsey gasped from the pleasure and the pressure as he began to move hard. His thrust became more desperate as he reached and took Kelsey's long hair in his grasp and pulled as he moved. Kelsey cried out from the satisfaction as they both climaxed together. They collapsed on the bed, sweaty and still coming down from the after shocks; Jason wrapped himself around Kelsey, tenderly kissing her breast and lips. "I think the orgasm score is now settled," he said with his eyes closed and a slight chuckle.

"Mmhmm, maybe," she said with her eyes closed as well and a teasing smile on her face. As they lay in quiet sated moments for a little longer, Kelsey finally cleared her throat.

"Jason?"

"Yes, Kelsey?"

"Can I take my heels off now?"

He laughed, "Allow me." He sat up, bent over her body and removed both heels and dropped them to the floor. As he came back up with the sheet, he kissed her hip then her shoulder then her lips and pulled her close as they both slipped off into a blissful sleep.

They both awoke at seven a.m. to the strips of sunlight filtering through the cracks in the curtains. Kelsey rubbed her eyes as they both stretched and yawned. She shot up as she remembered. "Oh my gosh! Jason, your gift!" She jumped out of bed and grabbed the plush hotel robe and ran over to her large purse that held everything needed to survive the apocalypse. Grabbing the package, she jumped on the bed like it was Christmas morning. Jason sat up against the pillows and the headboard.

"I truly hope you like it," Kelsey said, biting her thumbnail and intently watching Jason open the package, waiting for his reaction. Jason's eyes lit up as he slowly realized that he was holding the Tag Heuer Carrera watch that he'd walked by and admired so many times. "Kelsey! It's amazing! No, it's beyond amazing. I cannot believe you got me this!"

Kelsey let out a sign of relief. "You really like it? You're not just saying it, right?"

"Kels, this is so awesome." He reached for her, pulling her close. She placed her hands on her his chest as he leaned in for a kiss. "I haven't bushed my teeth yet," she pleaded.

"I don't care," was all he gave her as he took her, pushed her hair back and began to kiss her chastely all over her face. "I love that you bought me something that I would've only admired from afar but never would've spent the money on for myself. I love that you looked so nervous while I opened it and worried I wouldn't like it. I love you, Kels, and I truly hope you know that you could have bought me nothing, and I would have been absolutely okay with that."

She placed her hand on his face, cradling his right cheek. "There was no way I was going to show up with nothing! I'm just thrilled you're happy with it."

"I have the best life Kels, and you are all my reasons why."

They held each other, admiring the craftsmanship of such a gorgeous watch, and finally decided to get breakfast when both of their stomachs let out growls. They ordered room service with the plan of going nowhere. Jason spent the late morning returning some phone calls to his work site crews who diligently were working on the stadium being built for the new MLS team. The stadium was due to open in March of 2014. Jason had officially taken over their family construction company in 2005 when his father retired. While his father had created a highly successful commercial company, Jason was able to land the construction bid for the new stadium, making it the biggest contract in company history. He was completely confident in his crew and knew that they had the talent and work ethic to get the job done and done right.

After enjoying their breakfast together, Jason got Mac on the phone. "How are we looking on our deadline?"

"Everything's perfectly on time, Mr. B. You just enjoy some time away. You've earned it."

"Good! Keep me posted. I'm only an hour away if you need me, but only if it's an emergency, you got it?"

"Yes, sir."

With that Jason ended the call and looked over at Kelsey who was lying across the bed, wearing a white tank top and lace panties. She had her headphones on and was reading her book. He slid into bed with her. As he grabbed her hand and began by kissing her palm and working his way up, she placed the book down, removed her headphones, and sank into the pillows as the slow sensual kisses took over her entire body.

"Oh, did I disturb you?" Jason asked in between kisses.

Barely audible, Kelsey responded, "Not at all, why do you ask?"

"You just seem really into your book. While I was on the phone, I looked over and saw you all alone in bed; I couldn't resist coming over to check on you."

Jason slowly pulled her tank top down and freed her right breast from the constraints of her matching lace bra, taking the now-exposed nipple into his mouth. Kelsey threw her head back. "Jason, are we ever going to leave the room today?"

Jason laughed, "Not unless you have somewhere to be, cause I'm not going anywhere."

They stayed wrapped in the sheets and in each other until dusk, when they finally decided that room service and turning in early was the only way they would recover from such a beautiful anniversary weekend.

They checked out late Sunday morning from the hotel and made a quick stop by the office. There were a few employees working extra hours to keep the stadium on schedule. Jason never had a problem with paying his men overtime when it came to projects like this. He knew if he took care of them, they would let their work show for it. Kelsey ran in to use the bathroom while Jason grabbed some paperwork and spoke to the guys. When she came out, she saw Jason talking to Mac and someone she didn't recognize. As Kelsey approached, Mac let out a holler, "Well, well look at you, misses, looking as lovely as ever I see."

Kelsey could not help but blush, and Jason always got kick out of that. "Hello, Mac. As always, the pleasure is mine."

Jason put his arm around Kelsey. "Mac was just admiring my anniversary present, Kels."

"It's a gorgeous piece, Mrs. B. You did good!"

"Thank you, Mac."

Kelsey looked over at the young stranger who never said a word the whole time. "Oh, let me introduce you, Kelsey, to Michael James Dupree, our newest employee. Mac has been teaching him the ropes of what it means to be a safe and sane dump truck driver."

Both reaching out to shake hands at the same time, Kelsey noticed that Michael had a hard time making eye contact. "A true pleasure to meet you, Michael."

Mac began to brag on the young man. "He's doing a damn fine job learning the ropes.

He's patient, hard working, and may just be promoted to his own dump truck in the very near future." Kelsey was shocked that Michael showed no emotion to all the accolades except for a half smile that never seemed to consume his face.

"That's very exciting to hear, Michael. Congratulations!"

Jason beamed while giving him a soft slap on the shoulder. "Keep it up."

As they said their goodbyes, Kelsey tried to shake a raw feeling that came over her about Michael. Jason could feel her stiffen when they walked back to the truck. "What's wrong, babe? And don't say nothing because I know better."

"What is the story with Michael?"

Jason grabbed the handle of the door. "Hop in the truck, and I'll explain on the way home."

As they rode, Jason told her the story of their latest hire, Michael James Dupree. He was twenty-one and being given a second chance by the judge after modeling good behavior in federal prison for the past two years. His rap sheet was extensive and began way back when he was in middle school. When he came in and asked Jason for a job, what he was really asking for was a new beginning. He'd told Jason his story and promised he would do whatever he had to do, work however hard he had to work, to never go back to a federal prison. His days of moving drugs across state lines were over. Jason was struck by his candor and his sincerity. He hired him with conditions and put him in the passenger seat of the dump truck crew with Mac, the head driver. Mac didn't pull any punches and understood about second chances. Jason knew that he could be a good mentor for Michael.

Forty minutes later, they pulled into the driveway. Jedi immediately trotted over to the fence to welcome them home. Kelsey had stayed in silent reflection of Jason's story for most of the trip, and now she just sat and stared out the truck window as Jason held her hand. "Promise me you'll be careful with him, Jas. I know you've given other employees second chances, and it's worked out, but from what you're telling me, his history goes beyond recreational drug use. I mean—federal prison at the age of eighteen!"

Jason sighed, "Babe. I know, but you heard Mac; he's doing a great job. The kid just needed someone to take a chance on him."

Kelsey took a deep breath and looked over at him. "Jason, I love how big your heart is. I love that you can run a successful business and keep your employees' best interests at the center, but there was just something about this guy. If I were to describe it, it was sad, wild, and it made my insides ache. Just promise me you'll be careful?"

Pulling her hand up to his mouth and kissing it, he answered, "Kelsey, I promise I'll be careful. Now your new boyfriend is standing at the fence and waiting for you to come visit him."

Kelsey leaned over and kissed Jason lovingly. "I love you, Jason Holden Bauer."

And lovingly, Jason responded, "I love you, Kelsey Jane Bauer."

JULY 1995
THE PARTY

The workload for the summer experience abroad had not let up, but Kelsey was doing a better job keeping up and was beginning to enjoy herself. As week five of classes wrapped up around three on a Friday afternoon, she grabbed her large bag and made her way across campus, enjoying the bright sunlight. Getting used to the cloudiness and rain was another thing that Kelsey had to learn to do; so on afternoons like this, she found a welcome reprieve in slowing down her pace and allowing her head to roll back so she could enjoy the fullness of warm sun.

She was jolted back to earth when she heard her name being called. She squinted as she opened her eyes, looked in the direction of the voice, and saw Gareth walking towards her. Gareth had just finished a pick up game of football on the lawn and was heading to his car. "Can I give you a ride?"

"Oh, I appreciate it, but it's so beautiful out today that I hate not to walk home and enjoy it."

"Well, do you mind if I walk with you?"

With an earnest smile on her face, Kelsey encouraged, "I'd love the company, but what about your vehicle?"

"I parked by my apartment and plan on coming back to campus for a party tonight with some of my teammates."

"Oh, I see."

"*Oh I see* what?" Gareth asked with a confused expression.

"If you're leaving your Defender on campus for the purpose of returning for a party, that will no doubt be filled with thumping music and plenty of alcohol, you probably won't be returning home tonight, right? Should I come along and chaperone you like I used to for Jasper and Courtney?"

Gareth let out a deep laugh. "No, no need to chaperone, but you are invited to come along. It'll be loud and rowdy, and there will be lots of drinking and…other kinds of activities occurring, but if you stick close, I can look out for you."

"Don't flatter yourself, sir; I can handle myself. But I have plenty of work to do and…" before she could finish Gareth stepped right in front of her, causing them both to stop.

"Kelsey, do you realize that besides the evening dinners you've had with me and mum and the one visit to the Gray Horse Pub two weeks ago, you've not even thought about heading to a party, taking a weekend adventure to another part of the country, or just exploring this town? I mean, seriously, what gives?"

He could see Kelsey's brow furrow and shoulders stiffen. "I'm sorry that I'm not living up to your expectations, Gareth, but I'm not like the other girls here who can just freely get by with average grades for the sake of partying. That's not who I am."

"Kelsey, I would never dream of asking you to be someone you aren't. I just hate for you not to take one day during the week where you just relax and live a little."

As the awkwardness of the moment grew, Kelsey finally spoke, "Will you please move to the side so that I can continue to walk home? Jason is expecting my call." Gareth moved over and had to work to keep up with Kelsey's pace. As soon as they got to the front door, Kelsey breezed up the stairs and into her room, shutting the door. Gareth stood at the foot of the staircase leaning against the rail, completely confused. "Well, that escalated quickly," he muttered.

Just then, Camilla came into the dining room to set the table. "Hello, darling, is everything okay?"

"Yeah, everything is fine. I'm going to head up and shower."

"Okay. Dinner should be ready early as I need to step out. Would you mind letting Kelsey know?" He nodded his head yes and then dreaded the idea of knocking on her bedroom door when she'd just all but sprinted from him two minutes prior. As he got closer, he could hear Kelsey's voice, and it sounded like she was crying. *Jesus!* Was she crying because of him? He pressed his ear to the door and was finally able to hear her on the phone.

"Jason, I'm fine. I just had a long day, and I have a lot of work to deal with this weekend. Of course I miss you—how could you even ask that? I'm the one who should be asking you, considering I'm walking around thinking we're getting married, and I have no ring to show for it…I know that we agreed to wait for the 'formalities,' but I'm starting to regret that decision…NO! I didn't say I was regretting saying I want to marry you! Are you not listening to a word I'm saying?!!…Look, I have to go. I'll call you later…Yes, of course, I love you too." With that Kelsey all but slammed the phone to the receiver. Gareth felt awful for listening to her conversation, but his heart and mind were racing. If she wasn't "formally" engaged, then why should he not try and convince her *he* was the one that she was meant for?

As he turned back to head to his room, Kelsey came barreling out of hers and met him in the hallway. Red face and watery eyes greeted Gareth. "Oh, I didn't realize you were there," Kelsey sputtered.

Gareth quickly changed the subject; "Mother said that dinner would be early as she needs to step out." Kelsey stood there looking as if she was going to burst into tears or a ball of fire from being angry. It was all Gareth could do not to wrap his arms around her and hold her and let her know that everything was going to be okay. "Gareth?" Kelsey said with a catch in her breath from the crying. Her voice snapped him out of his dream. "Can I go with you to the party tonight?" A bit stunned but thrilled, Gareth walked over to her and rested his hand on her shoulder. "I think that is a fantastic idea." With sad eyes, Kelsey looked up in gratitude. "What time do we leave?"

* * *

Later that Evening

They walked back toward campus together in silence. The whole time Gareth was trying to figure out if he had just made a huge mistake taking Kelsey to what was sure to be one of the rowdiest parties of the summer. It's not that he didn't think that Kelsey could handle herself. She was a non-drinker, so he knew that alcohol wasn't going to be a problem. However, the college party scene was way different from a traditional American high school. Yes, there would be drinking, enormous amounts of that. There was going to be recreational drug use, and it was not uncommon for sex to be taking place in random rooms. It was definitely a mistake agreeing to bring her.

It was eleven p.m., and the party was just getting going. The students who stayed on campus for the summer term were flooding in. The music was thumping and could be heard half a block away. As they got closer, Gareth asked one more time, "Are you sure you're up for this? I know you had an argument with Jason tonight over the phone. You also didn't say a word on the walk here."

"How do you know I fought with Jason?" Kelsey asked with a raised eyebrow. There was an awkward silence, and just as Gareth went to explain himself, Kelsey held up her hand and stopped him. "Never mind, I don't even care that you know. I'm not here to think about him. Do you understand, Gareth?" Gareth stared back, nodding his head yes. They both walked down the sidewalk where they were greeted by scores of people. Several of Gareth's mates from the football team were there. One whistled through his teeth, "Who is that delicious dish you brought with you?"

"Don't worry about it, Harry; she's not available."

"Well, did you use your clever wit and devastating smile to captivate that sweet piece of ass?"

Before he could blink, Gareth was in Harry's face. "First of all she is more than a piece of ass, second she has a fiancé, and thirdly keep your hands off of her and bugger off."

"For someone who isn't available and not dating you, you seem awful protective of her." Harry asked with a raised eyebrow, "Wait, is she that American girl staying with you? The one that doesn't drink or go to parties?" Harry was almost giddy when he asked the question.

"I am not fucking around, Harry. You leave her alone."

"Oh, all right, captain—whatever you say, but I will at the very least make her acquaintance before the end of the night." Harry walked off, playfully slapping Gareth's cheek. "Stand down old man, and get yourself something stronger than the beer."

As Gareth calmed himself down, he realized he'd lost track of Kelsey. The music thumped louder and harder as he got closer to the room with the stereo. He could barely hear himself think. As he scanned the room, he found her: holding a beer in one hand and downing a vodka shot after licking salt off her wrist and then sucking a lemon. "What the hell is she doing?"

Getting across the room to Kelsey was no small feat. Using his body to push through, he kept his eyes on her the whole time as she guzzled her beer. Just as she pulled the empty cup from her lips, he snatched the beer out of her hand and grabbed her arm, yanking her from the room and into an oversized closet in the hallway. As he slammed the door behind them and turned on the light, Kelsey screamed and slurred, "What the HELL do you think you're doing Gareth?"

"What am *I* doing!? What the hell are *you* doing drinking alcohol at neck-breaking speed when you've never had a sip in your entire goddamned life. You're going to be so ill, Kelsey."

"Oh yeah, well fuck that and fuck you." Gareth couldn't believe her language or the amount of alcohol pouring from her breath. "Let me tell you something, Gareth." Kelsey used her arm to wipe her nose as tears welled up in her eyes. "I'm tired of being the nice girl. The one

who does exactly what everyone expects.
I HAVE HAD IT!" she screamed! "Tonight
Kelsey Chapman is going to live a little, and if
you or anyone else can't handle it, then get out
of my fucking way." Gareth stood there and
looked at her as she swayed back and forth.
"Kelsey, I want you to have a good time, but
you've been here for thirty minutes, and you're
already so drunk. There are people here who
will want to take advantage of that—that is
unless you don't die from alcohol poisoning
first."

Kelsey was now dealing with the hiccups
as she tried to respond. "Well, then I guess you'll
just have to keep an eye on me and make sure
nothing bad happens to me. Now it's fucking
hot in here, so get out of my way." She shoved
Gareth, struggled to open the door, and
stumbled back into the room with the thumping
music and alcohol.

For the next hour, he never let her leave his
sight. She hammered down more beers and at
least two more shots of vodka. She was dancing
with anyone and everyone in the middle of the
room. After more than an hour of her dancing
and drinking, he saw Harry approach her. "Son
of a bitch." Gareth clinched his teeth and
tightened his jaw. He watched as Harry, who
towered over Kelsey, jumped into the middle of

the room and begin to dance with her. He pushed a strand of loose ponytail hairs behind her ear. Harry leaned over and started to whisper in her ear. Gareth watched as Kelsey let out an over-the-top drunk laugh.

After ten minutes of watching them carry on, he saw Harry grab Kelsey's hand and push past the hoards of people into the hallway. Gareth immediately pushed through the crowd and tried to keep up. Like a salmon swimming up stream, Gareth shoved anyone and everyone out of his way, not caring whom he hurt—he had to get to them.

When he got to the hallway, they weren't there. He pushed through to the kitchen, not there. He pushed his way back down the other side of the hallway where he found two people making out in the bathroom. He then threw open the door to the closet they'd been in earlier, but it was empty. There were two doors left. He threw the next one open where he found Kelsey on her back passed out and Harry methodically unbuttoning her shirt.

"YOU SON OF A BITCH!" Gareth was on top of his teammate in no time, throwing him to the floor, punching him, and screaming obscenities. After the third blow, he realized he'd knocked Harry out cold and didn't care if he broke the asshole's nose or not. He dropped to his knees beside the bed and immediately started to re-button Kelsey's shirt. She began to stir, and as she did, she made the kind of halted gag that occurs before one vomits. "Gareth?" He leaned up over her, brushing her hair, which was now completely out of its ponytail, away from her face. "Gareth, I don't feel so good; can you get me home?"

She looked and sounded so pitiful that he scooped her up, praying that she could at least make it back to his on-campus apartment before the inevitable happened. Gareth realized in that moment, this would be the only time he'd get to care for her this way. He would make sure he did it with the utmost affection. It would be a memory; a very messy memory he could hold close to his heart when she went back to her real life in the states.

As he carried her, Kelsey remained quiet and kept her eyes closed, doing everything possible not to vomit all over him. Kelsey whispered into his neck, "How much farther?"

"I'm taking you to my apartment; we're very close, and my roommates are away for the summer. It'll be quiet, and you're going to need that while you recover."

Kelsey raised her hand to his face, "You're so kind, Gareth. You're going to make an amazing doctor one of these days." Gareth's heart constricted, but he didn't respond. They were steps from the apartment when Kelsey's head shot up in a panic, and she let out, "Gareth! Put me down right now!" Gareth did as she asked and stayed right next to her while Kelsey wobbled down the sidewalk into a set of bushes where she immediately projectile vomited. It splattered all over the bushes, her shirt, and black-sandaled feet. She fell to her knees and began to weep. Gareth was on his knees right by her side. "Ah, Kels, it'll be okay. Let me get you inside."

He coaxed her to her feet and then lifted her into his arms where she lay limp, cried, and apologized. "I'm so sorry, Gareth. I know I smell and…." She fought to put a sentence together when he stopped her; "Hey, just lay your head down. It'll be okay." Kelsey let the tears roll as they made their way into the apartment. Gareth opened the door and carefully put Kelsey on her feet. "Gareth? Where's your bathroom?!" Grabbing her hand, he quickly raced her down the small hallway where he lifted the toilet seat and Kelsey promptly heaved the contents of her stomach. She dropped to her knees and continued. Gareth sat on the edge of the tub and carefully held her hair and soothingly rubbed her back.

Once she was done, Gareth helped her lean against the now closed bathroom door while he took a facecloth, ran it under cold water, and brought it to her forehead. Tipping her head back just slightly so she wouldn't have to hold the cloth up, he used a second damp cloth to wipe her face. He then removed her sandals and placed them in the corner. "Kelsey, I need to get you in the shower. I know I'm asking a lot, but I'll start the water and leave to you to undress. Once you're done, hop in and close the curtain; I can come in and retrieve your clothes and get them in the wash."

Kelsey couldn't even open her eyes when she responded with a cry, "But I didn't bring any clothes with me."

Gareth stifled a laugh, reached over, and put his hand on her knee. "I know that, Kelsey. It's all right; I have a football jumper and sweats you can use to sleep in until your clothes are washed and dried." She sat there for another moment moaning. Gareth wasn't sure if she was about to vomit again, but in that moment she reached for his hand. "Can you please slowly help me up?" Gareth did, and once he knew she was stable enough, he started the water for the shower and, when the temperature was right, removed himself to just outside the door. Five long minutes later, Kelsey murmured, "Okay."

The steam coming from the hot water billowed out the door. As he stepped in he kept his eyes fixated on the floor and scooped up all her clothes. "Kelsey, I have all your garments; will you be okay if I go and get these on in the wash?"

"Gareth, I think I'm going to be sick again."

"Okay, well, it's okay if you do, better in there anyway."

Just as he said that, she reached her hand through the curtain for his and began to vomit again. Dropping the clothes to the ground, he held her hand, all while letting her know that she was okay. Once she was done and had rinsed off, Kelsey went to her knees in the shower and bawled louder and harder than the two previous times. Gareth dropped his head and, without looking at her, shut the water off reached for one of his nicest towels and draped it over her.

"Make sure you're covered, Kelsey. I need to pull the curtain back." As he waited for her to give the all clear, Gareth pushed the curtain back and dropped to his knees where he pulled her long hair out from behind the towel. "Did you get a chance to wash your hair?" he asked softly as he rubbed her back. She nodded yes, and Gareth grabbed his hairbrush and carefully combed it so it wouldn't dry tangled. "Kelsey, can you stay here long enough for me to go and put this on in the wash, and I'll be right back with some fresh clothes?" Kelsey nodded her head yes. "Right, be back in a moment!"

By the time Gareth started the load and came back with the fresh clothes, Kelsey had leaned against the tub wall and fallen asleep. He looked at the clothes in his hand then the towel she was wrapped in. The towel had flipped up on her side, and he saw an enormous scar. It wasn't a very old scar as the skin was still very pink and looked as if it were still healing. It dawned on him it must have been from the branch that had impaled her in the accident back home. Seeing that scar made him want her even more. To protect her and never let anything like that happen ever again. "Christ Almighty, why me?" he muttered under his breath.

He bent over from the hips and tried not to wake Kelsey as he carefully picked up her limp, damp body from the tub. She began to stir as they stood. "Wha...what are you doing?" Kelsey whispered. Gareth quietly responded, "Let me get you to a warm bed."

He took her to his room where thankfully he had washed and cleaned his sheets and comforter before the end of the semester. Pulling them back, he laid Kelsey down and covered her up. Kelsey was passed out cold by the time her head hit the pillow. Gareth put his clothes intended for her on the trunk that was at the end of the bed. He walked over to check on her one more time and decided to remove the damp towel from around her; he did so carefully without exposing or waking her, though she was so out of it she didn't notice the movement anyway. Gareth couldn't help but smile as he stared at her. Even in the midst of throwing up and now lying in his bed with a wet mop of hair, she was the prettiest girl he'd ever laid his eyes on. He leaned over her, and, using his fingers to tuck her hair behind her ears, he kissed her forehead. "Try and rest, darling."

As he turned to walk away, he stopped and leaned back against the door and just stared, wishing with every fiber in his being he could lay next to and comfort her, but she wasn't his to do that with. So he took a deep breath and closed the door. He looked at his watch, and it was three in the morning. He went into the bathroom where he cleaned and disinfected, grabbed a quick shower himself, then found a pillow and comforter from his roommate's room, and proceeded to the couch. There he could hear the timer go off when the wash was done and then move her clothes into the dryer. Gareth adjusted the pillow, laid his body down, and pulled the comforter up.

With one arm over his head, staring up at the ceiling, he knew officially for the first time in his twenty-two years on the planet he was beyond in love as he remembered the jealousy of seeing other men ogle her and Harry trying to have his way with her. Giving Harry the beat down of his life was completely worth it so that he would never treat Kelsey or hopefully any woman that way again. The only thing he wanted to do was to make all the bad stop for her. For once he wanted to be the knight in shining armor, to hold her and tell her it was going to be okay. That they were going to be okay, and that she should stay here in England and let him prove to her that he was the one she should be with.

"Bollocks. Fucking. Bollocks!" Why did his life have to be so complicated! This wasn't supposed to be happening. This was the stupid shit women read about in a romance novel. However, in this case it wasn't; this was his reality. She was only eighteen; he was twenty-bloody-two. "I have my whole life ahead of me, so much school left, and there will be plenty of other women who can fill this, whatever the hell THIS is!" Gareth continued to lay there awash in thoughts that eventually turned into a dream that took the two of them away from the reality they were living.

Kelsey stirred as the sunlight was breaking across her bed. Her head was pounding so hard she literally thought someone was beating drums in the room. Barely able to open her eyes, she began to feel around and figure out where she was and what had happened. She knew she was in an unfamiliar room; the pillow and sheets smelled like they had been freshly washed. Using her hands, she began to pat down her body. *Why am I naked?* she thought. When the magnitude of that discovery hit, Kelsey shot straight up so quickly, she had to grab her head to stop the room from spinning. Her breathing was in heaves as she tried to recall how the hell she wound up nude in a strange room and bed! *Think Kelsey! Think! Think! Think!*

With her hands still holding her head on her shoulders, her mouth shot open. "Gareth! GARETH! ARE YOU HERE?! GARETH! HELP ME PLEASE! WHERE ARE YOU?!" Hearing his name being screamed for from the back of the apartment, Gareth jumped over the couch so rapidly he forgot he was only in boxers. Flinging the bedroom door open he saw Kelsey holding her head and her eyes shut. Gareth leapt on the bed, grabbing her shoulders. "Kelsey, it's okay. You're okay! You're safe. Calm down! You're in my apartment. You're okay!" They sat there in silence while Gareth rubbed the sides of her shoulders reassuring her that everything was fine.

When Kelsey was finally able to slowly open her eyes, she could see that Gareth was only in his boxers. With an arched brow she looked at him, then looked down at herself, wrapped in his blanket and sheets, then looked back at him and in a low and tentative voice asked, "Gareth…did we?"

"Oh Jesus, Kelsey! Are you seriously asking me if we had sex last night? Do you not remember anything at all?" he asked in a harsh voice.

"If I remembered, Gareth, then why would I be in a panic asking you?!" she snapped right back.

"Well, let me see where do I begin? Ah yes, let's start with the phone call you made home to your beloved Jason, who apparently said or did something to piss you off."

"Were you eavesdropping into my conversation with Jason last night?"

Gareth sat silent and reluctantly responded but with a terse tone, "It was only because I could hear you crying. You were also visibly upset when you came out of your room and enthusiastically volunteered to go to the party. I had a bad feeling about it. However, I didn't stop you because you're an adult, and you were finally giving yourself permission to have a little fun." Kelsey went to interject, and Gareth raised his hand. "I'm not finished," he said through gritted teeth. "Once we got to the party, you were hell bent on being this 'new' person, and I was astounded when you went right for the alcohol! You never even tried to work your way up; you were doing shots in one hand and holding a beer in the other."

"Okay, I get it. I remember," Kelsey said, waving her hand in the air. Gareth was so annoyed at her flippancy that he grabbed Kelsey's face between his hands and in a controlled yet angry voice began his speech, "No, Kelsey, I don't think you do remember, because I found you in a room with Harry. That bastard had gotten you alone in one of the bedrooms, and I found you just in time to discover that he was unbuttoning your shirt while you were passed out on the bed. He had no intention of stopping until he'd gotten everything he wanted. I jumped on him, pulled him off of you, and gave him the beating of his life. Once he was out cold, I scooped you up, and halfway back to the apartment, you asked me to put you down."

"Put me down?" Kelsey asked as tears began to pool and stream down her face.

"Yes, Kelsey, I was carrying you, and I put you down so you could get sick, which you did, I might add, in spectacular fashion." He released her face and sat next to her. "You were so pitiful, and I just wanted to get you back somewhere safe and help you get cleaned up because I knew that's what you would have wanted. I knew that last night you were angry, and you were trying to live it up, but Kelsey, your actions almost… you could have been…last night was not the Kelsey I've come to lov…" He stopped before he could say it. "That was not the Kelsey I have come to care for, and I didn't want the one night where you made some bad choices to haunt you for the rest of your life."

They sat in silence for a good five minutes while the depth of his words anchored to her soul. Kelsey reached out and laid her hand on his arm. Gareth nearly jumped out of his body at the sensation of her touch. "I have no words right now, Gareth, to adequately fit the moment to show my gratitude. Would you allow me the opportunity to take another shower and pull myself together?"

"Of course. Your clothes are washed and are now in the dryer. I just need to run and fetch them. I'll leave them here on the bed for you."

With that Gareth got up and, five minutes later, brought the fresh clean clothes back to his room just as he said he would. He could hear the shower running, and while he desperately wanted to shower with her, feel every curve of her perfect body, wash her, and then worship her in his bed, he snapped out of it, put on a clean pair of jeans and a shirt decided to make some coffee and scrambled eggs to help Kelsey recover from her night. He'd have to take a mental cold shower instead.

Twenty minutes later Kelsey, showered, dressed, and with towel-dried hair, slowly came into the main room. The smell of coffee was bad enough, but the eggs almost made her sick again. She found Gareth in the little kitchenette with his back turned to her. He commanded rather decent skills in the kitchen, which she found amusing before she was quickly reminded of the awful headache that caused her eyes to water and stop her dead in her tracks. She reached for the chair that allowed her to sit up at the bar and slowly sat down. "Please tell me you have a glass of water and Advil nearby?" Before she could even finish the question, Gareth produced a bottled water and meds. An audible sigh of gratitude left her mouth.

"You're going to need to eat some of this. It'll help you recover quicker."

"I'm aware of this Gareth, thank you. Oh, of all days for the sun to be blazing a trail in

York," before she could even finish that thought out loud, Gareth produced a pair of sunglasses. Without a second thought, Kelsey placed them over her eyes. "Oh, Gareth, you are truly, truly, wonderful." There was a heaviness and happiness in his heart all at one time when he heard those words. He placed a single cup of coffee in front of her. "Cream or sugar?"

"I take mine straight black."

"Of course you do; you're American." he snickered. He then leaned over to hand her a small plate of scrambled eggs. Kelsey slowly sipped her coffee and struggled with the eggs, trying her best to get them in her system. As she sat in silence picking at the eggs with her fork, Gareth made himself two eggs over easy and two slices of toast. He grabbed his plate and nearly dropped it when he heard his name, "Gareth!" Kelsey exclaimed. He already knew what she was thinking, and so as he turned to face her, he gave her a look of reassurance. "Mum won't be worried. She knew that we were together and that I would watch out for you." Kelsey's shoulders immediately relaxed, but the questions were all over her face.

"Will she be disappointed?" Kelsey asked in a low voice. Gareth took the seat at the bar next to her and, with a perplexed tone, responded, "Why in the world would that even matter?" There was an awkward pause between them until Gareth spoke up. "For the record, no she would not be disappointed, but why does it matter what she thinks? You're a grown woman, you didn't bring any strange men back to her home, and you have more than proved that you are a trust-worthy guest and, more importantly, a friend. Disappointment is the last thing you are going to have to worry about."

Kelsey looked back down at her eggs as her fork continued to dance over them. Removing her sunglasses, she looked up at Gareth and reached over to touch his arm while he ate his breakfast. As he tried not to drop his fork, he turned to face her. "Gareth, I need to apologize to you." He sat there, listening intently, locked in her gaze and trying to convince himself that his arm was not on fire where she rested her hand. "Jason and I did have an argument last night, and while that does not excuse my behavior, I used the alcohol to escape the situation. And, honestly Gareth, I just wanted to not be me last night. I'm always the responsible one. Normally I don't mind that, but last night I needed to let go."

By the time she was done talking, Gareth could not help notice that her hand was still on his arm as she looked out the window. He knew that he was being given a moment here with her that he might not ever experience again, and he took it in completely. He let the sun bounce off her brown hair and turn it to a caramel and then caught the green flecks in her hazel eyes. Like a hot iron he allowed that memory to sear into his mind. It was a stolen moment that would now be his cherished memory.

"Kelsey, can I ask you a question?"

She came out of her trance and lifted her hand. "Of course," she said clearing her voice.

"How is it possible that you are eighteen?" A little unsure of how to take his question, she took a deep breath as if going to answer and then paused. "I'm not sure I understand the question."

"It's just that you're eighteen, and yet, you don't act like the average eighteen-year-old. Not to mention, what eighteen-year-old finds the love of her life so young these days? How do you know Jason is the one?"

With no hesitation in her response, Kelsey made direct eye contact with him. "Gareth, the day I met Jason my world went from being lived in black and white to full-blown color." Gareth sat in stunned silence. "Does that answer your question?" Gareth pushed himself up from his chair, picked up their plates, scraped the food off in the receptacle, and placed them in the sink. He could barely share his response because he did indeed understand the full gravity of her analogy. "Yes, Kelsey, you answered my question."

Looking out the window and across the lawn where he saw a late morning pickup game of football starting, he had half a mind to run out and join them. Taking a moment, he reminded himself that, as painful as letting her go was going to be, he needed to make memories with her. The kind of memories that would get him through the dark days when she was gone. He turned from the window to face her, and in a voice that was filled with hope he asked, "Kelsey, what are you doing tomorrow?"

MARCH 2015
THE REUNION CONTINUES

They both stood in stunned silence. Both taking each other in. It took Gareth right back to the first day he laid eyes on Kelsey. The day he met her at his parents' home in York, England. Her eyes were still the captivating hazel but had a shadow of sadness. Her hair was still a caramel brown sprinkled with a few grays, but her electric smile that would reach from ear to ear was diminished. Gareth immediately knew something had taken place in her life. Something had happened to his Kelsey. Forming her words took great effort, but in a low and confused voice she spoke, "Gareth, what are you doing here?"

"I live here now. You're looking at the new Division Chief of Cardiology at EVMS." His tone was light and hopeful as he tried to read her facial expression. Another moment of awkward silence slipped by when Jon, Kelsey's co-worker, walked up to her. "Everything okay, Kelsey?" he asked, snapping her out of the silence. She looked at Jon, then looked at Gareth, and before Gareth could react, Kelsey abruptly excused herself pushing herself through both men and running off the floor. "Kelsey, wait. Please!" Gareth almost felt panicked.

Jon quickly stepped in front of Gareth. "Are you a friend of hers?" he asked.

"Yes, but it's been a long time. I just need to talk to her!"

Jon put his hand up. "She's still recovering," he said calmly but firmly.

"Recovering from what?" Gareth asked in a curt tone.

"Her story to tell, not mine. If you're a friend, then you can ask her later, in the mean time, I would suggest that you give her some space." After a brief moment of eye contact, Jon walked off the floor to look for Kelsey. Gareth left the store confused as the American girl that he never got over in the summer of 1995 had suddenly reappeared into his life. She was broken and sad, and Gareth had to find out why.

"Kelsey? Are you in there?" Jon asked as he softly knocked on the door. He could hear sniffling on the other side of the door and finally heard a small "Yeah, I'm here. I'll be out in a minute." Jon waited by the door for his friend. When he heard the lock click, he stepped back. As Kelsey stepped out, she looked up with red eyes and nose and shrugged her shoulders. "Did not see that coming."

"Who was he?"

"Well assuming he did not turn into an asshole later on in life, he was a dear friend from my past, Gareth Blythe. No, wait, correction. Dr. Gareth Blythe, from York, England. I was a guest in his home as a foreign exchange student when I graduated high school."

Jon laughed, "You did *not* seem to be happy to see him; when I looked over and saw you, you were white as a sheet."

Kelsey blew out a deep breath. "I probably confused the shit out of him and maybe even hurt him, which he didn't deserve. I'm sure he has no idea what has happened to me in the past year."

Jon let out a snort, "Does he not watch the news?"

"If he just arrived to America, then he may have no clue."

Jon didn't pull any punches with his next question; he knew how to keep the conversations real as Kelsey had done the same for him when his fiancé called off their wedding the year before Kelsey's life had changed so drastically. "He said he was a friend—didn't you stay in touch?"

Kelsey let a half smile reach her lips and kept her eyes on the ground almost recalling the moment. "He was in love with me. He tried to convince me to stay in England, but I'd given my heart to Jason, and I had a life waiting to start when I returned home.

Jon looked at her with a raised eyebrow, "Ah, I see. So you figured time and space would remove that. What about eventually finding him on Facebook?"

"I wasn't about to look for a man who'd been in love with me, Jon. I wouldn't have wanted my husband to do that if the roles had been reversed. My marriage was sacred to me. Gareth and his mother had been beyond wonderful and kind to me while I was in York. I have many amazing memories with them both. Gareth was my friend, but he wanted more, and I was unable to give it to him. So the day I said goodbye, I got on the plane and never looked back."

Jon sat and waited a moment before he responded. "Well, he is back now, and I can tell he left with a lot more questions than answers."

"I know he'll be back, but maybe he'll give me some space. I cannot handle dealing with him and this upcoming trial. I will lose what I have left of my precious mind if he does."

Jon laughed as he leaned over and kissed the top of her head and gave her a reassuring hug. "You're stronger than you realize, Kelsey. Even if he turns back up sooner rather than later, you'll be fine." Jon released her and walked away, leaving Kelsey to blow another round of air out of her lungs while she murmured, "I'm glad you think so."

Gareth drove back to his apartment in a daze. Even after all these years, he never forgot about that summer with Kelsey. He knew that she lived in Virginia, and near a beach, but never bothered to ask her the exact city, mostly because he never wanted to be tempted to come find her. He loved her more than any girl who had ever walked into his life. Even with the bevy of women he'd been with after Kelsey was long gone, it was always nothing and continued to be nothing more than sex. He was just never interested in a committed relationship. Well there was one, Cora. He thought he loved her, and he knew she wanted more, but after two years, he knew he could give her the ring she wanted, but not the love he knew was possible. Cora deserved that love, and so he ended it.

He arrived at his new home in the Riverview building. Unlocking the door to this ultra chic, one-bedroom studio, he flipped on the lights and tossed his bags and keys on the tabletop bar. Grabbing a beer out of the fridge, he proceeded outside to the enormous deck with a gorgeous view of the Elizabeth River. Plopping down onto the deck chair, he took a long hard swig of the cold liquid and placed the bottle on the side table. Sitting up with his arms on his knees, Gareth ran his hands through his dark hair over and over trying to come to terms that he had indeed, twenty years later, come face to face with the only girl he ever truly loved. He desperately wanted to know what had happened to her resilient smile and why there was so much sadness in her eyes.

As he stared out, he watched the tug boats push the barges down the river and was immediately transported in time to the weekend when he took Kelsey to the picturesque town of Godshill, on the Isle of Wight. Looking out over the water took him back to the day they walked the beach of Shanklin. That day almost didn't happen as the night before the truth about his feelings had been realized. He remembered what she wore that day, her bright hazel eyes that dazzled against the ocean. It was a memory that got him through the dark days.

After spending twenty minutes letting the memories wash over him, he decided to get up and take a shower with the hopes of getting a decent night's rest. As he made his way back to his bedroom, he flipped on the television. He turned the volume up to listen to the local news. As he undressed and turned on the shower, he walked back into his bedroom when he heard the newscaster spout the name Jason Bauer, the murdered local businessman of Bauer

Commercial Construction and deceased husband of Kelsey Chapman Bauer. They played B-roll of Kelsey walking out of the Federal Courthouse in Virginia Beach with her lawyer who quickly ushered her to a waiting car. Gareth immediately sat on the edge of the bed, stunned but finally able to make sense of it all. The sadness, the tired weariness that he saw were indeed from an event that had happened in her life. He needed the details. He knew that Kelsey loved Jason more than anything. When did this happen? How did this happen? He knew he could Google it, but he wanted to hear it from Kelsey directly. Gareth knew that if she were in front of him right now, it would be all he could do not to pull her into him. Just to hold her and make all the pain go away, even if it was only for five minutes.

It didn't matter to him that it had been twenty years since they last spoke to each other. Gareth quickly realized that everything he had ever felt for this girl was still there. Resting his hands on his head, he knew he had to convince her to let him back into her life. He was prepared to wait and do whatever he had to do to earn her friendship again. Suddenly, the reasons for taking the job began to take on a whole new meaning. His mission would start tomorrow.

* * *

That Same Evening

After getting home and getting her animals and herself settled in for the night, Kelsey went to the very recesses of her walk in closet. Using a step stool, she withdrew a medium size photo box. She took it back to her bed where she sat on top of the duvet and leaned against the big pillows. Taking a deep breath, she pulled out about one hundred and fifty pictures that hadn't seen the light of day in twenty years. As she slowly started to look at each one, she felt a rush of memories wash over her. There were pictures of the beautiful landscapes, the beautiful flower gardens she had encountered on her walk to the university. Then she got to the pictures of her and Camilla sitting out on the veranda having tea and the picture of her on that blessed horse Higgins that she'd ridden the Sunday Gareth had surprised her with a visit to a local riding stable.

Then finally she came across two pictures of Gareth that she completely forgot she had. She found the selfie pic that he had taken of them the day they visited the riding academy. Both of their smiles were priceless. Then there was the one of them walking the beach of

Shanklin, on the Isle of Wight. A flood of memories began to shower over her. She stared at it for what had to be over ten minutes when a crash of thunder startled her and the dogs, who were asleep at the foot of the bed. "Holy shit! That was loud, wasn't it pups?" Just as she said that, she looked over at her nightstand to see a picture of Jason staring at her. Immediately, guilt washed over her. She quickly put the pictures back in the box and pushed them under her bed.

Grabbing a tissue from the box next to his picture, Kelsey tried to rationalize why she was feeling guilty when she was doing nothing wrong. Knowing that she had to be back to work at nine a.m., she decided to call it a night since Saturday always proved to be a day of non-stop interactions, and after the emotional day of being in front of Gareth Blythe again after twenty years, she felt drained. As she checked her alarm, she reached over and shut off the lamp. Breathing a deep sigh, she quietly asked Jason to please come visit her in her dreams like he had done a few weeks ago.

Kelsey found herself standing back on the beach with Jason by her side. He looked so young. He reached for her hand and began to walk with her across the sand. Never speaking, just granting her complete peace as they walked. After what felt like hours, Jason came to a stop.

Looking out, he pointed toward the other end of the beach. Jason carefully released her and continued to point. As Kelsey tried to grab his hand again, he began to slip away. "No, no, no, please, not yet," Kelsey cried. "I'm not ready yet." The next thing Kelsey saw as she carefully opened her eyes was her ceiling. Her alarm was sounding, so she reached over and hit *off*. She was too stunned by how real the dream was and lay there in silence for a good thirty minutes trying to recall all the details. Before long the dogs began to stir and forced her up to unwrap herself from the warmth and comfort of her bed and let them out.

The dreams about Jason had gone from being about the incident to being just the two of them on the beach. It was almost as if he wanted to visit the place they spent their first date. He was trying to help her remember this time in their lives. Why? She had no idea; as lovely as it was and as real as it seemed, these dreams were becoming extremely difficult to wake up from because they left her with nothing but questions.

As she finally climbed out of bed, she fell back into her routine; in no time she was out the door to see what interactions awaited her at work that day.

DECEMBER 2013
PIRATES AND PRINCESSES

"Oh dear god, this song is going to be in my head the rest of the day," Jason said under his breath into Kelsey's ear, so the kids would not hear them. Kelsey leaned into him and gave him a bit of an elbow. "Isn't this place just the best during the holidays!" Kelsey beamed. Sitting in the row in front of them were her nieces and nephew: Sarah Jane, Katie, and Will. They were pointing, singing, and having a ball. They had seen YouTube videos of some of the attractions, but now they were experiencing it in the flesh and loving it. As they rounded the corner of the finale, their boat bumped into the one in front of them as it slowly made its way back to the boat ramp.

Sarah Jane spun around, "Can we please go to Big Thunder now?!"

"Our fast passes aren't for another hour, so we need to do something in between. Do you want to meet a Princess?"

"SNACK!" Will screeched. "Dole Whip! NO! A Churro!"

"Will! You just ate thirty minutes ago!" she said, trying to hide her smile.

"I know, Aunt Kelsey, but I'm a growing boy." They all began to laugh at Will's honesty as they exited the ride. "Let Will go get a snack with me. I could use a turkey leg, and maybe we can find Captain Jack along the way. You can take the girls to see the princesses, and we can meet up at Big Thunder."

"Does that sound good, ladies?" Kelsey asked. In unison she got a resounding "YES!" An hour later, after chasing pirates and princesses, they met up at Big Thunder and had a blast hooting and hollering up and down and around the hills. Once they were done, they decided to head back to their resort to meet up with Kelsey's sister, brother-in-law, and parents to enjoy the pool and get a quick nap before coming back for the fireworks. On their way out they decided to stop and watch the stage show *Dreams Come True*. The kids ate it all up and began to recite the chant from their favorite characters who were in the process of defeating the villain in the show. "Dreams come true! Dreams come true." Suddenly there were fireworks on either side of the castle to indicate that the chant had worked, sending the young audience away believing they had indeed defeated the bad guy and that anything in life was possible.

As they all walked down Main Street, Kelsey looked over at Jason, who was talking to Will. Then she looked over at the girls who were splitting a bag of cotton candy. With a smile on her face, she realized that, even though she was not a mom herself, being the best aunt was a pretty awesome job, and if this is how it was always meant to be, she was truly okay with it. Yet, there was an uneasiness that she could not explain; she reached for Jason's hand, and the feeling immediately lifted. Kelsey took a deep breath as peace settled back upon her. She had kept the dreams she was having to herself. They were dreams laced in confusion and sadness and felt all too real. She felt ridiculous for having them, but as she repeated the chant in her mind, *dreams come true, dreams come true,* she could only think of how desperate she was that her recent nightmares never came true. Once they got back to the hotel and refreshed in the pool, the whole family went to their separate rooms to take naps and reset themselves for the evening that they would be spending in the park.

As Kelsey set her phone alarm for their nap, she felt Jason come up behind her and slowly release her pony tail, then run his hands down her shirtless arms. She immediately felt her knees go weak. "Can I at least jump in the shower before you continue?" There was a pause as Jason was laying a hot trail of kisses, "No. Absolutely not." His kisses grew more intense around her neck, and his hands traveled and began to push her bathing suit straps off her shoulder, reaching for her breast. "I have been waiting to have mouse sex with you all day," Jason whispered.

Kelsey let out a giggle, "Mouse sex? Really?"

"Come on, Kels, no one comes down here planning on having hot intense sex with his wife when the whole resort is full of families. It's not exactly like our honeymoon in Cabo."

"Ah, I see, well, can we pretend that we are in Cabo and go from there?"

"Absolutely, anything for you," Jason replied tenderly. And with those words, Kelsey let Jason have his way with her, and when they were done, they took a short but completely restful nap.

* * *

Later that Evening

The castle, draped in its shimmering lights, took all their breaths away. The *oohs* and *ahhhs* that came from the kids as they stared at the other end of Main Street were truly magical. The giant monstrosity that resembled a castle looked as if icing were dripping off of it, and all of the Christmas decorations transformed the park from magical to magical on steroids. Kelsey was in heaven. She leaned into Jason and whispered, "Thank you."

Looking over to her he whispered back, "Thank you for what, babe?"

"I know that taking the week off with the opening of the stadium just three months out was a big deal. You made a way, and I'm so grateful that we're all here."

He pulled Kelsey closer to him, "Kelsey, there is nowhere else I'd rather be." Jason had Sarah Jane on his shoulders, Coy had Katie, and her brother-in-law Jake had Will. They heard the talking cricket's voice project from the castle and start to tell the story about letting our conscience be our guide, wishes, and the blue fairy. Kelsey was overwhelmed by the innocence and love that surrounded her. For ten minutes, she was flooded with the gravity of just how blessed she was, but she could not figure out where this odd, sad feeling she couldn't shake was coming from.

She forced herself to be swept back into the moment, allowing her eyes to fill and her heart to swell. As the finale approached, the whole family stood with their mouths agape and tears of in their eyes. Kelsey looked over at Jason, and while the tears quietly streamed down his face, she knew that she would never forget this moment. It would be etched into her memory forever. The rest of the evening they ran from ride to ride, watched the evening parade, and made even more memories in the most magical place on earth.

* * *

One Week Later

Christmas Eve

The dreams were becoming more frequent and more frantic. They would start out serene. Jason would be there, and they always seemed to be on the beach. In certain dreams he would slowly disappear, and that would begin Kelsey's frantic search. She would find herself running down the beach, winded and calling his name. In some of the dreams he would reappear but not speak. He would only point. Kelsey would follow the direction of his finger and look out, only to beg him to tell her what she was looking at. Jason would never respond.

Feeling anxious, Kelsey rushed out of work to get home and wrap the last two gifts that needed to go to her sister and to get ready for the Christmas Eve service. Having not slept well since she arrived home from their trip to Florida, when the bad dreams she'd had infrequently before became far more frequent, Kelsey soldiered on and distracted herself with work and the busyness of the holiday season. She simply refused to allow her favorite time of year to be dominated with details of dreams that made absolutely no sense in her sleep and much less sense when she was awake. No, there were too many other things to be excited about.

Jason came into the kitchen where he saw Kelsey putting the finishing touches on the last two presents. "Are you about ready to go?" he asked as he came up behind her, wrapping his arms around her. Kelsey turned to face him, wrapped her arms around his neck, and took him in a deep kiss. "Well, if you continue to do that, then we won't make it to the service at all."

Kelsey laughed, "I just needed a passionate moment with my husband." Kissing the top of her forehead, he stepped back to look at her with a bit of a moan. "I want you so bad right now, but it'll have to wait until later." Understanding exactly what he was saying, Kelsey ran upstairs to freshen her makeup, as her second favorite church service of the year was to start in thirty short minutes.

Each member of the congregation, one by one, lit a candle. The candlelight shimmered off the stained glass. As the song finished and the service drew to a conclusion, the congregation turned to face the entrance of the church. At midnight, the ushers swung the doors open wide as the congregation sang "Joy to the World" and allowed the sounds of their voices to travel to the outside. It had become a tradition for the entire family to attend the Christmas Eve service, and each year it took on even more significance. On their way out the door, they greeted Pastor Murphy and thanked him again for another wonderful service.

"It's always great to see you both," he said warmly as he shook their hands. "I cannot thank you enough for all the donations for the homeless packages. We were able to supply one hundred blankets and toiletries to the homeless shelter to pass out tonight at strategic locations. Kelsey, once again you were instrumental pulling all of this together with the volunteers. What a blessing."

Jason looked on and smiled at his wife whose heart was so big when it came to caring for the homeless in the area. He'd known Kelsey's genuine compassion when he watched her volunteer countless hours at the age of eighteen. Over the years that passion and concern grew as she continued to volunteer when she could and found so much joy in pulling together the resources to donate to the church so that packets could be assembled. She worried about those living on the streets all year, but especially on cold nights and during the holidays. Kelsey remained quiet as she never like to receive attention for something she thought was both her privilege and duty such as serving these people. Jason spoke up. "It was our pleasure, Pastor; it's the least we can do to give back to the community." With that, they said goodnight and headed home.

As he drove, Jason grabbed Kelsey's hand and brought it to his lips. "What's on your mind?" Kelsey asked. He paused a moment before he spoke. "I was thinking how I'm so looking forward to this project being over with. While I'm honored that our company got to be a part of it, I'm ready for some consistency in routine and schedule again. It's been a long four years," Jason said as he let out a big breath.

"I couldn't agree more. I feel like, in some ways, we'll be getting our lives back." Jason nodded his head in agreement. As they pulled into the driveway, Jason looked over at Kelsey. Reaching into the glove box, he pulled out an envelope-sized package wrapped in a red velvet sash. Wide-eyed, Kelsey looked back over at him. "What is that?"

Jason laughed, "You have to open it to find out."

"I thought we weren't doing Christmas presents for each other this year? I distinctly recall saying that we would focus on my parents, your parents, and the kids?"

"It's not from me; it's from Santa," Jason quipped with that devastating smile that said all that Kelsey needed to know.

"Well then, let's go inside and open this in front of the Christmas tree."

With the tree lit and sparkling, they both sat down at the pre dawn of Christmas and opened the package. Inside Kelsey found two passports; a map of Florence, Rome, and the Amalfi coast; and two airline tickets with the departure date of June fifth and a return date of June twenty sixth. Kelsey sat in stunned silence and stared at Jason. After a few moments of awkward silence, Jason finally spoke up. "C'mon Kelsey. I thought you'd be excited? You've always wanted to go."

Jason could see that she was trying to rationalize everything in her head. Kelsey asked, "Are you sure you're okay taking that kind of time away from work?"

A bit stunned by her response, Jason replied, "I have all the right people in place. No need for you to worry about any of that." A few more moments of silence, which neither of them was used to, passed until Jason could not take it anymore, "Kelsey, baby, why aren't you excited? I expected you to be over the moon. What's wrong?"

Kelsey couldn't figure it out either. Well, she could, but she didn't want to tell him. "I don't know. I know I should be screaming with excitement, but something just seems off, and I wish I knew why."

Reaching over, he tucked a loose piece of hair behind her ear and spoke calmly, "We can go anywhere you want. If you don't want Italy, not a problem."

Kelsey waited a moment to respond. "No. I want to go; I guess...I guess that life has been at such a standstill with the stadium. We just took our first real vacation in four years to Florida and now this. I guess I just don't feel like, on some level, I deserve it." Kelsey didn't dare tell him about the dreams that were plaguing her and that added to the uneasiness of everything. She didn't understand the dreams, but the thought of traveling, of anything outside of their normal routine, made her anxious.

Jason pulled back and, with a puzzled look, he asked, "Why?"

Taking a deep breath, Kelsey started to talk, "I don't know...it's just that sometimes I feel like my life is too perfect. I know that sounds stupid, but it's how I feel." She drew closer to him and rested her head on his shoulder, taking in his smell as he brought her into his lap. Jason wrapped his arms around her and gave his gentle response, "Kelsey Jane, I have no idea why you feel guilty about your life, but please remember that we've had our fair share of trials and tribulations. If there's one thing I've learned in this short and crazy life, it's that we don't apologize for living, and we certainly don't need to feel guilty about it."

Kelsey smiled past the quiet tears that had formed and spoke quietly, "Now why is it, when you say it that way, it makes perfect sense?"

Leaning back to look at her, Jason smiled from ear to ear; then, kissing the top of her head, he spoke, "Because, sweetheart, it's the truth, and the truth always sets us free." He took the documents out of Kelsey's hand. "No more of this feeling guilty, you got it?" Before she could respond or get up, Jason gently picked her up and carried her up to the bedroom where they both crawled into bed and held each other close. As they drifted off into sleep, Jason leaned over, kissed her deeply, and whispered into her ear, "Merry Christmas, baby. Sweet dreams."

Kelsey did dream that night, and, once again, it was a desperate dream where she frantically searched for Jason: the louder she called for him, the more scared she became. At one point she was running down the beach calling for him, when off in the distance she saw what she thought was him running towards her. Just as it all came into view, Kelsey's eyes flew open, and she was awake.

* * *

Christmas Day

Christmas Day was a success. They started with a late breakfast with Jason's parents and then headed over to Kelsey's parents who were so surprised when they got their new computer. The kids went crazy when they each opened their new tablet minis that had their names engraved on the back. After a beautiful turkey and ham dinner, they sat in the family room on the couch while the girls played the games that Jason had helped them download. Will had curled up on the couch next to Kelsey and fallen asleep. Kelsey ran her hands through his brown hair and enjoyed the sweetness of the moment. She did spend parts of that day chasing away thoughts of her dreams from earlier. She was beginning to feel overwhelmed by them, but they just didn't make a bit of sense, and she knew that Jason wouldn't know what they meant either. Interrupting Kelsey from her thoughts, Jason brought her over a cup of hot chocolate and sat on the arm of the couch next to her as they enjoyed family time by the fireplace and Christmas lights. "Have you told your family where we're going this summer, Kelsey?" Caught off guard by his enthusiastic announcement, Kelsey replied, "I'd not yet mentioned it, but since you brought it up, why don't you tell them." Jason looked at Kelsey a little wary, but everyone's attention was now on them. With a huge smile on his face, he grabbed Kelsey's hand and brought it up to lips.

"Well! Spill it!" Ellie exclaimed.

Not to leave them hanging, Jason spoke up, "Santa is sending us to Italy for three weeks at the beginning of June. He thought we were long overdue for a real vacation."

"Ohhhh how romantic, you guys!" Ellie said. "Are you starting from the north then heading south?"

"That's the plan," Jason said while taking in another sip of his drink.

"I'm excited for you," Melody chimed in. "It's been an insane four years for you both with this new stadium and Kelsey working full-time and volunteering at the homeless shelter. You both have earned it—that's for sure."

"I appreciate that, Mom. We're definitely ready to get away for a bit."

"When is opening day of the stadium?" Coy asked.

Jason responded, "March 16th. We'll stay on board until the beginning of June to make sure that nothing structural needs to be addressed once they have a few home games. Our contract with the owners takes us up to June third, and we leave for Italy June fifth." Jason ran his hands through his hair and drew in a deep breath. "It's been a great experience, but it'll be a while before we bid on a project like that again." Kelsey laid her hand on his back and rubbed gently as he talked. She could feel the tension in his back and wondered where it came from. "I couldn't be more proud of my team and how well they all did."

"Well, they had a fearless leader who isn't afraid to make decisions," Coy chimed in as he threw back his cooled off cocoa.

"I appreciate that, but it took all of us to get it done." The clock in the hallway chimed that it was seven p.m. "Kelsey, how would you feel about heading home?" Hearing his abruptness, Kelsey responded with a shoulder shrug and quick "sure." She figured Jason was tired, and she had wanted to look at the map of Florence and start to plan in hopes it would help her struggle with all the uneasiness of it. After hugs and kisses were exchanged, they both bundled up to walk across the lane to their cottage to enjoy the remaining hours of Christmas 2013.

Once they got in, Kelsey let the dogs out for a quick break as Jason turned on the gas logs in the den and waited for Kelsey to come back in. He sat on the couch leaning on his knees and rubbing his stubbled jaw with his hand, lost in deep thought to Kelsey's lack of enthusiasm about the trip. Even after saying the right things to help calm her earlier that day, there was still distance. Then, there were the dreams she was having. She hadn't told him any details, but he knew when she was having them. She would thrash around in bed, waking him up. It would last for five to ten minutes. He would watch her, perplexed and concerned about what he was seeing and what he was hearing. It happened again last night: she kept calling for him, over and over. She even sounded as if she was crying in her sleep. Just as he was about to wake her up, she stopped. Had the stress and pace of the last four years taken its toll, and had he been so absorbed in building the new stadium that he had neglected her, neglected them?

As Jason's mind raced, Kelsey came downstairs after changing into her short purple satin gown and matching robe. Once she let the dogs back in and ordered them to their beds with their treats, she met Jason. She found him staring off into the heat of the fire. Leaning over the couch, she slipped her arms around him from behind. He kept his gaze on the fire as Kelsey leaned in and started to kiss him on the back of his neck. She could feel his resistance, and immediately pulled away. With little inflection in her voice she spoke, "Jason, what is it?" As if her words snapped him out of it, Jason turned and looked over at her, his brow furrowed with a look of hurt lurking behind his eyes. "I could ask you the same?" Not expecting the curt tone, leaving her hands on his shoulders, Kelsey responded carefully, "Apparently we need to talk?"

Jason stood up, brushing her hands off with a snarky "apparently." Kelsey came around the other side of the couch where he was. "Jason, we've had a lovely holiday, and this is how we're going to end it?" Jason stared back at his wife, trying so hard not to be mad and hurt, but he was, and there was no use in trying to hide it. "Jason, talk to me, please," Kelsey all but begged as she reached for his hand. "This isn't like you, isn't like us, not to be able to talk."

Jason stood there in silence; his gaze had gone back over to the fire when he finally spoke up. "I know about the dreams, Kels."

She brought her hand to her mouth but didn't say a word. He turned back toward the fireplace and kept talking, "Last night, while we were sleeping, you had a nightmare and started to talk in your sleep. You kept calling out for me like I wasn't there. You were getting louder and more worked up. Just as I was about to wake you, you stopped and settled back into sleep. This isn't the first time you've had these dreams, Kels. You started to have them a month before we went to Florida. Every time you have one; you wake me up with your thrashing and crying."

Kelsey's eyes filled with tears; she turned and ran up the stairs. Jason was right behind her, not knowing what to do as he wasn't prepared for her reaction. Kelsey reached their room and leaned against the post of the bed; the tears flowed from all the anxiety that had knotted into her gut over the past few weeks. Jason came up behind her and softly placed his hands on her shoulders. "Kelsey Jane, talk to me, please. What's going on?" Kelsey finally let the tears flow. She never wanted him to know about the dreams because they seemed so ominous and were so confusing. Maybe once she put it out there, maybe it would all stop. She pulled herself together and turned to look at Jason. "There are these dreams, and I've avoided telling you about because I don't understand them." Jason pulled her into him and rested his chin on her head. "Kels, please just talk to me. Tell me everything."

As she spoke, he rubbed her back, gently reminding her that they were both safe and she had his undivided attention. "I wish I knew why I was having these dreams, Jason. I want to know what's triggering them. I've sat at the table with pen and paper trying to figure out. Was it an event that prompted them? Was it something I ate? Anything to make sense." Letting her go long enough to pull the covers back on the bed, he guided her in, undressed himself, and climbed in behind her where he pulled Kelsey in close while allowing enough space for his hand to drift soothingly up and down her spine as she continued to talk.

When she was done, they lay there in silence together until Jason quietly spoke up. "I don't know what to tell you, Kelsey. I want to give you a why, but I just don't know. What I do know is that we've had to work really hard over the past four years on this new stadium, and while I know we didn't do it on purpose, we let the craziness of life sneak in and distract us. That's why I want this Italy trip more than anything for us. We both need it, and we've earned it; you've earned it putting up with me." Sitting up he leaned into her ear and kissed it tenderly and breathed a wanton breath. "Do you hear me?"

She lay there absorbing his words, warm breath, and kisses. "Has talking about this helped, Kels?"

"Mmhmm, it's helped so much. I truly feel a giant weight has been lifted." Now kissing her down her jaw line and allowing his hands to travel to change the heaviness of the conversation, he asked her, "And what happens when you have another dream?"

"I'll tell you immediately so we can work it out together."

Jason put Kelsey on her back in a fluid motion and was now on top kissing her with possessiveness that also begged for forgiveness for not being more in tune with her emotional needs. His hand moved down to release one of her breasts, making his kissing more urgent.

"Are we going to get through this, Kelsey?" She responded in a whimper. Jason couldn't help but smile and then asked, "Are we going to Italy, Kelsey?" A faint "yes" left her lips. Because he was enjoying making her want him, he then asked, "Is that a 'yes' we are going, or 'yes' keep doing that with your hand?" Kelsey moaned, "Yes to all of it." Jason kissed her forehead. "That's my girl." Freeing the other breast, he worshiped them with his fingers and tongue.

They let the intimate and meaningful love they expressed wash over both of them. For the first time in several weeks, Kelsey was able to truly let go and make love to Jason without the chains of the dreams and guilt weighing her down.

MARCH 2015
PLEASE LET ME IN

Kelsey called her mom's cell phone and got voicemail. Knowing her mother wouldn't be thrilled with the reminder, she decided to leave a detailed message. "Hey, Mom, just wanted to remind you I'm staying at my friend Zoe's place tonight. Yes, it's a girls' night out, and yes I will be careful, and yes even though I'm thirty-eight, I know whom I represent. See you tomorrow. Love you." Kelsey ended the call and hoofed it into what was most likely going to be a busy Saturday.

True to form, the morning had been bananas, and Kelsey was more than ready for lunch. She'd packed it and planned on walking down a couple of blocks to the sit under the tree by the Elizabeth River. It was turning out to be a gorgeous spring day and a much-needed respite from the cold winter they'd just endured. As she walked out of the store and turned the corner, Gareth was leaning against the railing. When their eyes met, he stood straight up. He was wearing a pair of khakis and a navy polo; Kelsey was struck that he was still as dashing as he was twenty years earlier, perhaps even more so. Contemplating turning and running in the opposite direction, she heard him call to her in a calm but deliberate tone, "Kelsey, please wait."

Kelsey froze in place, speechless as Gareth slowly approached her. "Gareth, why are you doing this? You don't want to talk to me right now. You really don't. My life is a mess. I am a mess."

He looked longingly at her and was desperate to grab her hand. "I know it's been a long time, and I know you're scared. I know you're tired, and I cannot imagine the thousands of other emotions you're having to process."

Kelsey looked at him with a quizzical eye. "Do you know everything?" she asked quietly.

"I know enough, and that's all that matters." Another moment of silence fell between them before Gareth spoke up, "I don't know anyone here, and to see a familiar face again helps so much. I may be being unfair, but I could use all the friends I can get." Kelsey closed her eyes. With tears threatening, she took a deep breath; when she opened them back up, Gareth was still there and staring at her, beginning to look a little desperate.

"I'm taking my lunch at the park; you can walk with me, but I make no other promises."

Relief shuddered though his body, as it had done so many times in the past with her. "That would be lovely, Kelsey. Thank you." The walk over was a moderate pace with no words exchanged. They walked past the Pagoda and then down to the USS Wisconsin Museum, then towards a bench that, later in the season, would be shaded by a tree that was just sprouting its new leaves. As Kelsey sat, Gareth waited for her to say something. Waving her hand at the empty spot, she gestured her invitation. "Please, Gareth, have a seat; just know I'm not the best company these days."

Gareth looked over at her and watched as the breeze blew pieces of her hair around her sad eyes. "Words aren't necessary, Kelsey. I'm okay just sitting here with you." Kelsey looked up with appreciation. They sat there for ten more minutes as she picked at her lunch, but too many questions began popping up into her mind. She finally spoke up, "When did you arrive?" Keeping his gaze out over the water he responded, "Wednesday." Another round of silence until Kelsey asked again, "How are Camilla and your sisters?"

That she asked about them made Gareth smile. "They're all doing splendidly. My mother recently retired from the University and has begun to do more traveling the world with my step-father George." Kelsey looked up at Gareth in surprise. "She remarried?" Gareth nodded his head yes and put his gaze back out over the water. "She did, about ten years ago. They really are a great match. We, my sisters and I, were all thrilled for them both. He's a lovely chap."

Another round of silence held them until Kelsey stood. "I have to start walking back."

"Yes. Of course." Gareth stood up with her. "Do you come here often for lunch?"

"Mmhmm," she said when stretching out all the anxiety bottled up in her body. Gareth desperately tried not to notice how beautiful her shape still was. "I try to escape out here in the spring as often as I can. When summer hits, it'll be too warm. It also gets me away from people long enough to reset for the other half of my shift. If you don't mind, Gareth, I really need walk back alone."

Gareth's heart sank, but he understood. One small step at a time was all he could ask. "Of course, it's not a problem at all. Do you work tomorrow?"

"No, I'm off. I'm actually allowing myself to go out with some girlfriends from work tonight." Even though Gareth would have given his right arm to know where she would be, he refrained from asking her. "Have a good time, and I hope to see you soon. Even it means we just sit on this bench and say nothing."

Kelsey gave a half smile. As she walked away, she found herself wanting to stop, turn around, and run into Gareth's arms so he would hold her. She knew it was selfish, and she hated herself for even going there. She knew there was safety and trust there, even after twenty years, but she was going to have to keep Gareth at arm's length. She may still be a young and have needs, but there was only room for one love in her life, and he was gone. Not all love stories get a happy ending, and she'd finally come to terms with that.

Gareth stood there and watched her until she turned the last corner and was out of sight. His heart was racing and aching at the same time. While it had gone better than he hoped, watching her leave was almost like watching her get on that plane and knowing she was never coming back. He longed to hold her and to try and make things a little better for her, but this encounter today reminded him that it was going to take a lot of time. He started his new job officially on Monday, and while work was going to be very busy and a nice distraction, Kelsey was not going to be very far from his thoughts.

JULY 1995
HACKING AWAY THE DAY

Gareth was on a mission. He had four more weeks with Kelsey, and he was going to make them amazing. After spending the morning recovering at his place, they decided to head back to his childhood home. Camilla was not in. Gareth immediately went to his room where he could have some privacy and contacted the York Riding Academy. When he hung up the phone, he could hardly contain his excitement. "Be cool, you bloody idiot," was all he could repeat to himself. He stepped out of his room and, as calmly as his hands would let him, knocked on Kelsey's door. She opened it with a yawn. "Oh, sorry, did I wake you?" he asked.

Waving her hand, "No, not yet, but sleep will come early tonight." At that Gareth smiled and said, "Well that might be a good thing as I have a surprise for you."

Kelsey looked over his shoulder and around his back. "Where?" she asked with a confused look on her face.

Gareth chuckled. "Not here, but somewhere. Can you be ready to go in the morning, say around nine a.m.?"

With a smile on her face, Kelsey asked, "Sure I can, but where are we going?"

"Nice try, but as I stated, it's a surprise, so if you want to know what it is, just be ready at nine."

"But what should I wear?"

Fair question, Gareth thought. "Wear jeans and t-shirt, and maybe bring a light jacket. We'll be outside mucking about, so maybe a pair of trainers?" Kelsey brightened, "I brought my paddock boots, would they work?" Gareth couldn't help but smile. "Perfect! Get plenty of rest as I think you're going to need it."

* * *

After breakfast, Kelsey excused herself from the table, as she wanted to change into her paddock boots and pull her hair up in a ponytail. As she slipped on her boots she thought of home, but the feeling didn't make her as homesick as it did earlier in her stay. She was grateful she had been able to get over her initial feelings about Gareth, that silly fear that shook her at the first experience meeting him. She felt firm and happy in their friendship, which had never been more real to her than with what she lived through with him Friday night. *I can't believe that I imagined either one of us would be so immature as to make this into something complicated,* she thought. *Gareth is a good guy and a good friend, and I'm so glad to have more going on during this trip than just schoolwork. I couldn't have asked for better.* With that, she walked into the bathroom to find a hair tie.

As Kelsey finished getting ready upstairs, Gareth and his mother sipped their morning cup of tea together. "What are you up to this morning, Gareth?" Camilla asked with a smile.

"Kelsey's been working so hard, and I thought a surprise visit to the York Riding Academy would be just what she needed."

"Ah," Camilla responded. "And how did the party go Friday night?"

Gareth's smiled immediately and began to blush. "It was okay. Kelsey nearly lost her liver to the alcohol fairy, but I was able to take care of her."

Camilla stared blankly at her son before she raised her hand to her mouth, never once tearing her eyes off of him. "Oh my Lord, how did I not see this until now?"

"See what?" Gareth responded in a defensive tone.

Another moment passed when Camilla leaned into the table and whispered, "Gareth, you're in love with her." Staring back at her, Gareth threw his napkin on his plate and pushed his chair from the table, taking his dishes into the kitchen. Camilla gave him a moment and then walked into the kitchen where she found him standing in front of the sink staring out the window.

Another beat of silence fell until Gareth finally spoke up. "I am. I am in love with her, Mum. From the day she arrived, I've had to work exceptionally hard not to make a total ass of myself, because I've fallen for a girl who is in love with someone else." She could hear his voice catch and saw his breathing hitch. "I decided that making memories with her was the best that I was going to get." Camilla walked up behind him and affectionately held his arm. Before she could speak, they heard Kelsey come bounding down the stairs.

"Okay, I'm ready!" Kelsey stopped hard when she walked in on Gareth and Camilla. "Oh, did I interrupt something?"

"Not a thing. Let's go," Gareth said, grabbing his car keys. Kelsey looked at Gareth and then his mother, who appeared as if she'd seen a ghost. As they walked to the car, Kelsey looked back at the house. Then, before sliding into the car, she looked at Gareth. "Are you sure everything is okay?" Holding the door open for her he responded, "Everything is fine. Now are you ready for your surprise?" Kelsey smiled as she nodded yes. "Alright then, off we go."

The fifty-minute drive through the English countryside took Kelsey's breath away. Even the giant billowy clouds made it more magnificent as the sun's rays pierced through them, sending gold fire across the fields, spilling over the stonewall fences that stretched the country side. "I cannot get over how beautiful it is here, Gareth. How old do you think some of those stone fences are?"

"Many of them date back centuries, as they were boundary dividers that the farmers used."

Kelsey sighed, "Who knew it would become such a work of art, thousands of years later."

Gareth smiled, "There you go again, sounding not eighteen."

"Oh yes, well I will get right on that, sir," she said with a laugh. Just as their banter ended, Gareth looked ahead and saw a large sign he'd been told to watch for. Kelsey, who was squinting, began to read the sign aloud. "York... Riding...York Riding Academy?!" she yelled, eyes large with delight and a smile so wide that Gareth didn't think it possible. Looking at him, she asked, "Gareth! Is this my surprise?"

Putting on his right blinker, he slowed the car and pulled onto the long driveway that bobbed and curved its way around the hill to the stable. "Yes, it is." They pulled up to a giant stone stable, the likes of which Kelsey had only ever seen and read about in magazines.

Kelsey took in the flurry of activity. There was a sand ring where youngsters on their ponies were enjoying a group class. In the other ring, there was what looked to be a private dressage lesson going on. Getting out of the car, Kelsey was gobsmacked and could barely speak as she never dreamed of experiencing her favorite hobby during this summer trip. She was here to study; riding a horse in the picturesque British countryside was never an option for her. She turned to Gareth who came up behind her and gently placed his hand on her shoulder and, in a concerned tone, asked, "Are you okay?"

After taking a moment to clear the knot in her throat, Kelsey was finally able to respond. "I'm more than okay, Gareth." Just as she finished speaking, a man with a sun-weathered face, in riding pants, English riding boots, and dark polo approached them. "You must be Gareth and Kelsey." Reaching out his hand, he introduced himself, "I'm Archer Livingston, head Riding Master. Kelsey, I understand that you ride back in the states and that you've been missing your weekly hacks through the fields?"

Kelsey could only smile and nod yes; she was so overwhelmed that she was trying desperately not to miss any of the details of all that was happening. Archer laughed, "I believe you're the first American girl I've met who's had so little to say!" They all laughed, and Kelsey finally breathed what felt like was her first breath in ten minutes. "I do miss my weekly hacks, Mr. Livingston, very much so."

"Well, your friend Gareth here has arranged an afternoon of hacks and picnics if that is alright with you?" Astounded, Kelsey looked back and forth between both men. "I cannot think of anything that sounds more lovely."

"Wonderful! Let me introduce you to your horse."

As they walked towards the stable, Kelsey turned to look for Gareth. "You're coming along as well, right?"

Gareth couldn't help but smile when he responded, "And miss this adventure? Not for all the tea in China!" Standing at the cross ties, Gareth watched Kelsey groom Higgins, who would be her horse for the afternoon. He watched as she talked to him as if he were another person. Then she wrapped his legs and added bell boots and then the saddle pad and saddle and then the girth. Just before adding the final piece of the bridal, she gathered her hair into a net that Archer had provided and put on her helmet. Gareth had to grin. She looked so happy. If he'd known that this was going to make her this thrilled, he would've arranged the event weeks ago.

As she removed the cross ties and the halter, Kelsey glanced at Gareth with a puzzled look on her face. Leaning with his shoulder against the stable door, he asked her quietly, "What? What is it?" As she continued to put the bit in the horse's mouth, she looked over at him and asked, "Do you even know how to ride?"

Gareth chuckled, "As a matter of fact I do, and you can thank my sisters for that."

"Really?" she replied.

"Yes, really. When I was twelve, as a part of my Saturday morning sporting activities, riding was a requirement. My sisters trained to ride when they went through their horse phase. Thankfully I never fell off and broke any bones, and my parents finally let me focus on football the following year. But, my sisters' horse obsession prepared me for a day like today, so that, to me, is the bonus."

Kelsey smiled, "Well we shall see how good your seat really is and if those lessons paid off won't we?" Archer came around the corner to see how Kelsey was coming along and was pleased at what he saw. "Fine job there, Kelsey. Gareth, your horse, Digby, is outside with the stable hand. We can follow you out and all make our way to the mounting block. We'll ride for three miles through Grangers Field and then stop by the river where we can picnic and make our way back."

After rechecking girths one last time, Kelsey, who was hardly able to contain her excitement, was the first to mount. Once Gareth was on Digby and Archer on his horse, they both came along beside Kelsey and Higgins. "The kitchen crew will meet us by the river with the Land Rover and have lunch prepared in a couple of hours. Are you ready to see the English countryside on horseback, Kelsey?"

With a smile that stole Gareth's heart, Kelsey confidently responded, "Absolutely."

The clouds hung low and created an ethereal fog up the side of the mountain where they found themselves on the trail. Going up the side of the hill and finding it steep at times, they followed the banks of the river. While it was a warm day, the cloud cover and breeze kept everyone cool. Archer told them stories of the rich history of the county, how he had worked as a young man in the Queen's stable where he helped in overseeing the care of her Majesty's race horses, including the famous mare Burmese. He told tales of his adventures there and at other stables he'd trained under in England. Kelsey loved hearing the stories as they dotted the hillside.

Once they reached the end of the trail, they arrived at a cottage next to the river. It had a restroom inside that Kelsey was delighted to see. As the stable hands tended the horses, Kelsey used the facilities and stretched her legs.

Taking in the view of the country side from the top of the vast hills they'd spent the morning winding through, and now listening to the sounds of the river as it flowed over the rocks and down into the valley, Kelsey stood there and absorbed every detail knowing that she'd want to be able to recall it one day. As she stood there, she was unaware that Gareth was behind her, taking her in along with the setting. After several quiet moments, Gareth cleared his voice to let her know of his presence. Kelsey turned her head halfway, catching him in her peripheral. "Come join me, Gareth. This view is too beautiful not to share with someone."

Gareth obliged and came along side of her. His hands in his pockets, he struggled to find the words to speak, but before he could, Kelsey spoke up, keeping her gaze out over the view, "This weekend started out wrong on so many levels, Gareth, and had you not been there, I could've found myself in major trouble." She paused and took a deep breath before continuing, "Then you surprise me with this. I was lost for words yesterday when I needed to thank you for taking care of me, but now...now you've completely swept my vocabulary clean." Gareth let out a full laugh while facing Kelsey. She turned to meet his gaze, "Thank you, Gareth. Thank you for everything this weekend."

Desperately wanting to touch her, he kept his hands in his pockets and, in a deep, gentle tone, responded, "You're most welcome, Kelsey."

"Oh, wait! I have my camera. Didn't you bring yours, Gareth?"

Archer had carried them in his messenger bag on the ride. As Gareth came back from retrieving them, the two began to shoot photos of each other: ones of them making funny faces, serious faces, fashion model faces, pouty faces, and, as best as they could, normal faces. At one point, they began laughing so hard at each other, they both had tears in their eyes. Finally, Gareth said, "Okay, let's take one with the river and country side behind us. My arms are longer; just squeeze in next to and smile. Or you American's like to say 'cheese,' right?"

Kelsey smiled and pressed her body next to his. When she did, Gareth could smell her, the soft vanilla bean scent that he wanted to drink in forever. "Okay, on my count say 'cheese.' One. Two. Three." And in unison and with giant grins they both exclaimed, *"CHEESE!"* and laughed again. "I cannot wait to have these developed," Kelsey laughed. "You and me both," Gareth sighed back.

As they began to come down from their laugh together, they turned their gazes back out over to the countryside, standing in a quiet contentment for another five minutes until Archer came to retrieve them. "Lunch is served, my friends. Meet me at the tables down by the alcove and river." Offering his arm, Gareth looked at Kelsey. "Shall we?" With a wide and grateful smile, Kelsey reached out to receive his offering. "Let's."

Lunch was a delicious traditional British picnic that consisted of homemade Scotch eggs, pork pie, and toasted pine nuts mixed into goat's cheese and spread over Parma ham and smoked salmon. The ham and fish were rolled in spears and then cut into mouth-size pieces. Dessert was succulent sliced strawberries with meringue and Chantilly cream served with a raspberry champagne cocktail that caused Kelsey's face to turn green when she saw it. Gareth, who was paying close attention to Kelsey, intervened before the staff approached her and made sure that a bottled water was offered instead.

Relieved, Kelsey looked over at Gareth and mouthed, "Thank you."

After spending an hour eating and letting their food settle, it was time to mount back up and take in the view as they returned in the direction of the stables. Archer was satisfied with how well Kelsey rode, so much so that, as they found themselves back at the bottom of the hill, he posed a question to Kelsey, "Would you like to gallop and take a few of the steeple jumps on our cross country field?" Kelsey could hardly contain her excitement as she squeaked out a "YES!"

With a sheepish smile Gareth cleared his voice, "Well, Digby and I shall make our way over here and watch you if that's okay. I never learned to jump."

Kelsey laughed, "Of course, Gareth, I need you in one piece for the drive home."

Pleased, Gareth and Digby trotted off away from the fences and came to a stop far enough out where he could watch Kelsey and Archer. Alone with his horse and his thoughts, Gareth watched Kelsey, his Kelsey, gallop through the field and move effortlessly over jumps that seemed obscenely high. She and her horse became one entity, moving and flowing together. She smiled the whole time and even let out a "whoop." That made Gareth laugh.

Closing his eyes and breathing a deep breath, he committed this moment, another gift, to memory. Soon after, Kelsey brought him back to reality as she came trotting up beside him. Rosie cheeks, big smile, and breathless, she eagerly asked Gareth, "Well! How did I do?"

With a giant smile to meet hers, he boasted, "It was like watching a scene from *National Velvet*."

Kelsey's eyes widened as she asked, "You actually know that movie?"

Rolling his eyes, he responded, "I have sisters, remember?"

Archer came up a moment later and told them, "The last mile back to stables will be good way to cool your horse down, so if you're ready, I'll let you lead the way, Ms. Chapman."

"I'm sure that I can handle that," Kelsey beamed.

They reached the stables, and Kelsey helped to finish cooling down her horse, untack him, and groom him. Then she asked if she could offer him a few of the sugar cubes she took away from the picnic. Archer smiled and said, "Of course. I'll meet you in the parking lot." As she gave Higgins his treat, she whispered in his ear. Standing off to the side, Gareth could see the tears filling her eyes but didn't say a word; he just listened. "Thank you for a lovely afternoon,

Higgins. I'll never forget you." She kissed his forelock, gave him the cubes and one last pat, and, before facing Gareth, wiped the escaping tears from her eyes. Turning, she tried to disguise her sadness in her best fake cheery voice, "Are we ready to go then?"

Ignoring her red eyes and puffy nose, he came up beside her, put an arm around her, and responded, "Yes." Archer met them in the parking lot. Hugs and handshakes were exchanged along with thank yous. "It was my pleasure, Kelsey. You're a lovely rider and talented horsewomen. Don't ever stop riding." Kelsey could feel the tears returning; she hugged Archer again and kissed him on the cheek, then quickly walked to the car. Gareth was right behind her. Again exchanging no words, he opened the car door and allowed Kelsey to slide in.

Ten minutes into the ride, Gareth noticed that Kelsey, who had her eyes out the passenger window and her head against the headrest, was fighting to keep her eyes open. Feeling bad for her, Gareth spoke up, "Kelsey, we have an hour drive home. It's okay if you want to sleep." Rolling her head to the side to face him in mid yawn, she asked, "Are you sure?" as her eyes grew heavier and heavier. "Yes, I'm sure." Before he could finish his sentence, Kelsey was out.

Gareth smiled. Carefully keeping his eyes on the road, he brought his hand up to her face to push back some of the hair that had fallen out of her ponytail and over her eyelids and nose. Taking in a deep breath, he allowed the smell of a beautiful day of adventure, countryside, and Kelsey seep deep into his car as they made their way home. Once they arrived and Gareth pulled into the driveway, he turned the car off and took a moment to watch her sleep. He realized in that moment how emotionally exhausted he was. He was going to have to tell her; he was going to tell her because she needed to know that he loved her and that he was an option for her—that he was the better option.

She was so peaceful to watch. As he stared, he thought about all the things that made her this lovely creature who'd come in and stolen his heart. She was funny, kind, so damn smart, and driven. Yes, she was young, but god she was so beautiful. He knew they could make this thing, whatever this thing was that was so special between them both, work. She just needed to give him a chance to prove it. Yes. He was going to tell her. He needed to come up with a plan. He sat there a moment longer thinking, but Kelsey began to stir and blink her eyes open.

Letting out another yawn and a stretch, she looked over at Gareth. "Are we home?"

"Yes, just. Let me come get your door." It was half past six in the evening when they walked in the front door. Camilla greeted them, "How was your day, Kelsey?"

"Oh, Camilla, it was lovely, just beyond words, lovely."

"I'm so glad to hear this. Would you like some dinner?"

"Oh, we had such a huge lunch, I'm not hungry myself but would love some tea."

Smiling back and touching her arm Camilla responded back, "Of course, dear."

"Would it be okay if I got in a quick shower?" Camilla nodded a yes with a smile as Kelsey took the stairs two at a time. Gareth walked through the door, taking off his jacket. Camilla took his jacket from him and folded it over her arm. She continued to stare, waiting for him to say something. As he walked into the kitchen, he looked back over his shoulder at his mother. "Are you going to follow me or not?"

"Oh Gareth, don't use that tone with me."

"And what tone would that be, Mum?"

"We need to finish our conversation from this morning." Gareth turned and walked into the kitchen, grabbing the tea kettle, filling it with water, dropping it on the burner, and snapping and twisting the dial in the on position. Camilla leaned against the doorframe and watched her son. Placing both his hands on the counter, he kept his eyes down. "I'm going to tell her, Mum. I have to let her know."

Camilla waited before speaking, "Gareth, darling, I just don't know if that's a good idea."

Gareth jerked his head up in disbelief, "Why?"

Cognizant that Kelsey would be back down, Camilla walked over to her son. "Have you made some memories with her? Memories that will live here and here," she asked pointing to his mind and heart. Gareth could only answer with a head nod of yes. "Then let them stay there. You have four more weeks, create more, and let them be what gets you through until..." Camilla stopped mid-sentence.

"Until when, Mum? Until I find someone else?"

"I'm just trying to help you. Your sisters and I will be the ones here to pick up the pieces and help you get through this once she's gone."

Gareth cut her off, "Dammit, Mum. I don't want to get through anything. I want her to know that I love her and I can make her happy too—no, I can make her happier than that Jason chap."

Another round of silence stood between them until Camilla spoke up, "Oh Gareth, how did I not see this from the beginning?" Camilla sighed.

"You act as if my loving her is such an awful thing?" he replied defensively.

Just then they heard Kelsey coming back down the stairs. The kettle started to whistle, and Gareth announced. "Perfect timing."

Camilla hung Gareth's jacket on the hook by the back door and spoke up as if nothing was amiss, "So, Kelsey, tell me all about your adventure."

Kelsey went on non-stop. She talked about how surprised she was when she saw the sign, her horse Higgins, the amazing views, the spread of picnic lunch, and the jumping lesson on the way back to the stable. She smiled so big the whole time she spoke that Gareth seriously thought his heart was going to burst. He'd made Kelsey so happy with what in his mind was a simple visit to a farm but had turned out to be so much more. By the time Kelsey was done, she'd had two cups of tea and let out a huge yawn just as the clock in the hallway chimed that it was nine p.m.

"Oh gosh, you guys. It's late, and we all need sleep." Kelsey got up and took her cup to the sink; rinsing it out, she placed it in the dish drainer to dry. As she crossed the floor to the doorway leading to the stairs, she said to them both, almost as if humming a song, "I shall sleep and dream so well tonight. Goodnight, Camilla, Goodnight…" and before she could finish, she stopped and turned on her heels to look at Gareth and, without so much as a second thought, took three big steps and threw her arms around him. No words exchanged, no rush to pull away, they hugged each other. When Kelsey finally pulled back, her eyes were full of tears and gratitude. She turned and walked upstairs and closed her bedroom door.

Gareth looked at his mother, who was staring back with tears in her own eyes. He walked over. Placing a hand on either side of her arms, he kissed the top of her forehead and quietly said, "You're right. I won't tell her." Putting his dish in the sink, he made his way upstairs and went to bed. That night, while he should have been angry at the universe and himself, he found himself at peace for the first time since Kelsey's arrival and slept soundly through the night.

March 2015
Girls' Night Out

At seven o'clock, Kelsey punched out and was off the clock; Zoe was right behind her. "Are you ready for a thrilling and fun girls' night out, Kelsey?"

"Oh, you have no idea! I trust that you have a plan for the evening?"

"Who are you talking to lady? You know how I roll." They both let out a laugh. With long, dark black hair, deep green eyes, a heart-shaped face, porcelain skin that was embellished perfectly with a nose piercing and a beautiful sleeve tattoo on her right arm, Zoe was the quintessential bad girl who would drop anything and everything to help a friend in need. In her early thirties, she was amazing with people and knew how to fix any computer she was given.

She quickly laid out the plan for the night. "Let's walk across the street to my apartment and get ready. We can head over to the Pub House for drinks and food and catch that handsome Irish Pub singer they have, then meet Mariah, Shannon, and Lori later over at Hells Kitchen. They have a live band starting at ten o'clock, so we can talk and see where the night takes us. Lori will be our designated driver if we need it, but since I live close, getting home shouldn't be a problem."

"Well, it sounds like you have it all figured out. I won't drink at all, so if Lori wants to, she can go for it."

"Nice try, Kelsey, but this night is exclusively for you to let loose a little and have some fun."

"I appreciate that...but just being out is a big step in general."

Once they got to Zoe's place, Kelsey grabbed a quick shower and was in the process of drying off when Zoe came into her room to find herself something to wear for the night. Kelsey marveled at how gorgeous Zoe was: tats, piercings, and toned muscle that were evidence of hours spent in the gym. She even found herself a tad bit envious. "Zoe, did getting all that artwork and getting your nose piercing hurt?"

Zoe was used to those questions and didn't mind answering. "Well, it doesn't tickle, but you just deal with it because you know how it's going to look and how it'll make you feel."

With a coy smile on her face, she looked at Kelsey. Kelsey had a puzzled look and asked, "What do you mean *how it will make you feel*?"

Zoe let out a little snort. "Well...I guess if your mind is in the right place, then what would be painful could actually be pleasurable."

Kelsey's mouth dropped open. "Oh, my Lord! Are you for real?"

Becoming very serious in tone, Zoe responded, "Kelsey, I never joke about that. I take pain and pleasure very seriously."

Kelsey sat on Zoe's bed, a bit dumbfounded but also intrigued. "What else do you have pierced, Zoe?"

"Just my nose and a couple other places." There was a beat of silence, and Kelsey's eyes widened. "Oh, for Pete's sake, Kelsey, my nipples are pierced."

"WHAT? No way! That had to hurt like hell?"

"Oh, it hurt like a bitch, but after a few treatments of soaking my nipples in sea salt, I was fine. Plus, they make sex so much better... well when you have a man who knows what to do with them." Kelsey just sat in stunned silence as Zoe threw her head back and laughed at her expression on her face. "Are you going to be okay, Kelsey, with that extra special glimpse into my life?"

Clearing her throat, Kelsey responded, "Um, sure, yeah...I'm fine." Kelsey decided to excuse herself. "I'm going to slip into the bathroom and finish getting ready." Kelsey closed the bathroom door and leaned against it, taking a big breath as she looked in the full-length mirror. There were days she wished she could be more like Zoe. She let the towel she was wrapped in drop around her feet. Assessing herself, she was thankful her breasts were still full and round; gravity had just started to creep in, but was doing nothing that would send her running to a plastic surgeon's office. She had never considered getting an additional piercing outside of her earlobes, and since her tolerance for pain was pretty weak, she knew that a tattoo or a piercing was pretty much out of the question.

Or was it? A tattoo was just too permanent; a piercing, however, now that was a consideration. If she didn't like it, she could take it out. Kelsey thought about it for a half a beat more when she rolled her eyes at herself. Who was she kidding? The days of living dangerously and carefree were far behind her—not that she ever really lived it up in her youth.

She quickly got ready, applying her makeup and then dressing in a black, form-fitting skirt, red tank, denim jacket, and black heels. She put on simple, silver earrings and a black scarf to bring out the silver earrings and her hazel eyes. She wasn't out to impress anyone anyway, but it did feel good to dress up and not deal with her reality. Even if it was just for the night.

As she applied her lip-gloss, a thought quickly passed through her mind. *What if she saw Gareth tonight?* Looking at herself in the mirror she began to talk out loud, "Oh no no no, DO NOT go there, Kelsey. You pull it together. That is the absolute LAST thing you need to think right now." There was a knock at the bathroom door. "Everything okay, Kelsey?" Kelsey flung the door open. "Yes, absolutely. Just having a moment. Shall we go?" Ten minutes later, both ladies hopped into Zoe's car to make their way to their first stop at Pub House.

* * *

Later that Evening

Gareth's Office

Gareth had decided to go and organize what he could in his new office. If he went back to his apartment, he knew that he'd only be able to think about Kelsey, so it just seemed logical to head to the office where he wouldn't be interrupted. Some of his personal effects would not arrive for a few weeks, yet he was able to line his new bookshelves with his medical journals and other important resources that he packed in a separate suitcase when he came over. He rearranged his furniture to make it more inviting when he needed to consult with patients, students, and colleagues. He hated how sterile some offices were and wanted people to feel immediately welcomed in his. Just as he positioned the leather couch by the window-less wall there was an unexpected knock on the door. As Gareth opened it, he was greeted by Dr. Dylan Cameron. "Sorry to disturb you, but I wanted to take a moment and introduce myself. Dr. Blythe, I presume?" he asked, reaching out his hand. "I'm the attending pediatric cardiology doctor over at the children's hospital and am also teaching my first course this semester."

"Ah, yes, great to meet you. What are you doing here on a Saturday?"

"Grading papers, which takes up way more of my time than I ever imagined. Sometimes it's just easier to do those things on the weekend when it's quieter around here. I also had a patient to check on after a procedure yesterday. I heard a bunch of movement in here and saw a light on and thought I'd take a chance." Meeting another colleague was exactly the distraction that Gareth needed. He offered Dylan a seat. "How are you getting settled in, not too much culture shock I hope?"

Gareth laughed as he sat across from Dylan. "Not too much, mainly just trying to understand and obey the traffic laws."

"Do you have a family that'll be joining you over here?"

"No, I've been so focused on my career, that I never made time for anyone in my personal life. I do have a wonderful mum, stepdad, sisters, and nieces back in York, but nothing beyond that." Gareth knew he was speaking in half-truths, but it was just easier that way.

"I know exactly how you feel. I grew up in California in a close-knit family as well. I broke my mother's heart when I told her I was moving across the country. Not only have I not given her any grandchildren, I practically moved to another planet." They both got a good laugh when Dylan asked, "I know it's kind of late, but do you want to grab a beer? I know a place with great beer and wings."

Gareth laughed, "Well that sounds positively American and perfect. Let me grab my keys."

* * *

Pub House

After spending a couple hours at Pub House, Zoe was slowly nursing her third margarita and a couple of appetizers. Kelsey stuck to the appetizers and water so she could drive to the second stop of the night. They took in the sounds coming from the Irish troubadour on the small stage in the corner. He was covering Irish pub classics from the motherland like "Whiskey in a Jar" but also played Dave Matthews and Jack Johnson for the young med students and faculty who frequented Pub House. Zoe glanced around and laughed. "Look at all these poor kids, they look like they're barely hanging on. That one looks like he combed his hair with a brick today."

"Yeah, I was just noticing that table over there; they look as if they just rolled out of bed. But you know, that hair style could be all the rage—maybe we're just old farts, Zoe."

"Speak for yourself. Thirty-three is the new twenty-three, and I have plenty left to offer."

Kelsey laughed, "Do you think you'll ever settle down, maybe get married?"

"I was married once." Zoe's eyes darted to her drink as she lifted it to her lips. Kelsey looked at her, unsure if she was allowed to pursue the conversation. She leaned into the table. "Really?" Knowing she needed to explain the situation a little more fully, Zoe continued, "I was twenty. We met in college. I loved him, and I thought he was it. Two years later, he left me for someone else."

Kelsey's heart sank. "How did you handle it?"

"I've had to work for everything I have in this life, and I wasn't about to lose it because he decided to walk out. From that moment I swore that 'love' was not what all the romance books set us up for, and I signed the divorce papers as fast as I legally could to get on with my life."

"That was so long ago; don't you want to try again—I mean fall in love. Being older and wiser, you could ease into it a little slower this time."

"Yeah, maybe, I don't know. I'm having too much fun, and, honestly, giving my heart away like that just isn't in my cards. Sex, on the other hand, that is always on the table." Kelsey stuck her fingers in her ears, "La la la la la la, I'm not hearing this." Zoe laughed, and as she took another sip of her drink, she looked wide-eyed over Kelsey's shoulder as she saw a tall male wearing a navy blue oxford button down shirt and khakis walk in. His blond hair was wavy, his eyes a startling deep blue, and he flashed a rakish smile. "Hold.the.phone." Taking the look on her face in with concern Kelsey spoke up, "Zoe, what is it?" Zoe used her head to point in the direction she was looking. Kelsey turned to see what Zoe saw. Not only did she notice the handsome man Zoe had lost her words over, she also saw Gareth entering right behind him. Panic took over.

"Oh my gosh!" Kelsey exclaimed bringing her hand to her mouth.

"What Kelsey? Do you know him?"

"No, not the first guy, but I do know the second one. Which one are you checking out?"

"Well this night just got real interesting. I'd take either, but I was eyeing the first," Zoe said with a raised eyebrow.

"No. We need to leave and now. Where is our waitress?"

"Wait, slow down. You said you didn't know him, so I'm not stepping on your toes here, right? Why don't you get your hot friend to introduce me to his hot friend, Kelsey?" Jumping up to expedite their exit, Kelsey caught her heal on the corner of the booth. The next thing Kelsey saw as she slowly blinked her eyes open were three faces peering over her. She had an instant headache, and her hand immediately reached for the bump on her head and her lip that felt abnormally lumpy.

Then she heard a voice, his voice, and she turned her head in the direction it was coming from. "Kelsey, can you hear me?" She could only nod her head yes. "Okay, good. That's a start. I want to sit you up. Are you hurting anywhere?"

Searching for her words, she finally choked out, "Head and wip."

"Yeah, I imagine that you'll have a nasty bruise on your head, and it looks like you bit your lip when you smacked your head."

"We need to take her to the ER to rule out a concussion" came from a male voice she didn't know.

"No, no, just sit me up swoly. Zwoe, can we just get back to your apartment?"

"Yes, sure—but, Kelsey, I just finished my third margarita, so I shouldn't be driving, and you certainly can't drive."

Kelsey started to feel nauseated and snapped, "Fine, it's a ten minute dwive. I'll just dwive."

"Oh no you won't," Gareth snapped back when he grabbed her. With his hands on her shoulders as he squared up to her, his voice was all too familiar. She could have sworn she was having Deja vu. "Kelsey, look at me. I'm concerned you have a concussion. I'm going to take you to the ER. Dylan is going to stay with your friend whose name escapes me at the moment...."

"ZOE! I am Zoe," she exclaimed as she extended her hand to Dylan. He extended his hand back with a big, devastating smile. "Pleasure to meet you; unfortunate it is under these circumstances." Zoe turned bright red and began to fan herself. "My, is it warm in here?" she mumbled.

Gareth, smirking at what he'd just witnessed, turned his attention back to Kelsey, "I'm going to help you up now, but I want to take off your heels first." Kelsey nodded her head yes. Once he removed her shoes, he looked at her again. "When you stand I want you to put all your weight on me. Are you ready?" In a low voice, she answered, "Yes."

"Okay then, here we go." As Gareth gathered her in his arms and stood her up slowly, Kelsey's world immediately started to spin, and she held on to him even tighter. "Whoa, you okay?" Gareth asked as he tried to steady her. Kelsey nodded her head yes but failed to mention that she was incredibly nauseated. Half the restaurant was still watching the scenario that played out. As they finally reached the exit, Kelsey leaned over to Gareth, "I'm going to be sick."

"Okay, don't panic. I've got you." He saw a row of bushes and was able to get her to them just in time. As she hurled the contents of her appetizer, Gareth rubbed her back and talked her through it. When she was done, he was completely convinced that she had a concussion. "Like old times, yeah?" Kelsey started to cry. "Oh, Kelsey, I'm so sorry. Let's get you to the ER."

Kelsey didn't even bother to fight him, and his comment about old times wasn't lost on her. Between the vomiting, her head throbbing, and her puffy lip, she murmured out, "I must be a swight to bwehold?" Gareth laughed, and before he could stop himself, he let his words spill out, "You've never looked more beautiful to me, Kelsey." Kelsey didn't dare look at him and didn't respond. She just wanted the pain in her head and lip to stop, and she wanted to fall asleep. He opened the passenger door and buckled her up. They drove in silence the short distance to the hospital.

When they arrived at the ER, Gareth pulled into the ambulance drop off, jumped out of his car, and grabbed a wheelchair. Wheeling her in past registration, he was met by the head nurse who stomped behind him, demanding he identify himself. The bright hospital lights and the sound of the nurse yelling were all too much for Kelsey who was keeping her eyes closed and praying that she would avoid getting sick again as a wave of nausea rippled over her. He stopped rolling the wheelchair long enough to identify himself so the nurse barking at him would calm down. He flashed his credentials and explained why they were here. She continued to stare a hole though his head when Gareth finally decided he'd had enough. Crossing his arms then widening his stance he spoke with confidence, "I'm sorry—I didn't catch your name."

Taking a moment to absorb *his* name and job title, but not taking the sting out of her tone, she replied, "My name is Janie. We can register her bedside."

"Thank you. The patient and I truly appreciate it."

Pointing to the right she barked, "Roll her into that room." She walked away in a huff and made no eye contact.

"You swure know how to make a first imprewssion. That won't count against you your fiwrst week?" Kelsey asked.

"You let me worry about that. We need to get you out of these clothes and into a gown so we can get a CT scan."

"Gareth, I'm swure if I go back to Zwoe's apartment and sweep this off I will be fwine."

Gareth was loving the lisp because of her swollen bottom lip. "Nice try, Mrs. Bauer, but when you sustain a head trauma, someone needs to wake you regularly to make sure your symptoms haven't worsened. I'm sure the CT scan will come back negative, but it doesn't mean you don't have soft tissue damage or swelling." Reaching into the cabinet like he had worked there for years, he tossed the green hospital gown on her lap. "I'll stand on the other side of the door while you change. I'll be right out there if you need me." Gareth looked at her and waited for a response.

"Okay. Fwine."

After slowly helping her to stand and lean on the bed, he turned to walk out. With a smile on his lips, Gareth saw the hardheaded Kelsey was still there all these years later. A few minutes passed when he heard her call his name. Poking his head back in the door, he saw her perched on the bed, head back, a bump on her forehead, a swollen lip, and eyes closed. She looked pitiful but just still as lovely as the first day he'd laid eyes on her. Gareth's heart felt a familiar twinge that he hadn't felt in years. He cut the main florescent light off, leaving the smaller, less intrusive light on.

"Thwank you," Kelsey whispered.

Just as he reeled in his thoughts, Nurse Janie came in right behind him, pushing a wheeled cart with a computer attached to it along with a stand holding a blood pressure cuff and thermometer. Gareth stood on one side of the bed while the nurse stood on the opposite and began to ask her the basic questions that one would ask at registration. "Can you state your first and last name?" "Kelsey Bauer." Nurse Janie continued, "D.O.B.?" "August 19th, 1976." Pointing to Gareth, Janie asked, "Am I safe to assume this is your husband?"

Gareth felt the oxygen get sucked out of the room. Kelsey whipped her head up and almost vomited on the bed from moving too quickly. "No!" she said is a forceful voice that she immediately regretted. Bringing her voice low and keeping her eyes on her wedding band she answered, "My husband is deceased."

Nurse Janie didn't bat an eye and moved onto the next question. "Do you have your insurance information and driver's license?" Sounding defeated she responded, "I …I don't know where my pwurse is at, and it has awll that information."

Gareth rested a hand on her arm. "Your purse is in my car. Give her your address information. I'll take care of the billing." Kelsey raised her eyebrow on the side that didn't have the bump and looked down at his hand. Clearing her throat, Nurse Janie looked at Gareth for direction. Lifting his hand off of Kelsey he responded, "I'll take care of the billing. Now when can we get her up for that CT scan, and how about some ice for this bump on her head and lip?"

Glancing indignantly at Gareth, Nurse Janie looked back over at Kelsey. "Do you have any allergies?" "No." "Blood disorders?" Kelsey was hesitant to respond but knew she had to. "I am anemic and require iron infusions every quarter. I come to the infusion center here." Gareth was astounded at that answer and tried not to stare at her.

Done with her questions, Nurse Janie filed out of the room. "I'll have radiology down shortly to get you for the scan and will be right back with the ice." Kelsey turned her head away from Gareth, as the emotion of the past hour and a half was starting to hit her and spill over her cheeks. How had this evening gone from being about an awesome girls' night out to being in the ER with Gareth? As if knowing what she was thinking, he quietly spoke up, "Kelsey, what can I do? Do you want me to leave? Call your parents? Call Zoe? Just tell me, and I'll do it."

Kelsey could barely think and was pretty much numb even without drugs, but she did know she wasn't ready for Gareth to leave. "No, don't weave," was all she could manage to say. Relieved to hear her words, Gareth took a deep breath. The nurse came back in with the ice as promised, but Kelsey was too tired to hold it to her lip. "I just need to cwose my eyes, Gaweth; I don't care about the ice."

Wishing he could do more, he grabbed the ice from her hand. "Lay your head back, Kelsey, and close your eyes." She did exactly what he said, and as she did, he gently held the ice to her swollen lip. Kelsey drifted off. Gareth stood there dutifully holding the ice, staring at the face that, even after twenty years, still caused his heart to twist and turn like no other woman had. Seeing pieces of her hair fall across her face, he carefully and lovingly swept them away. "Lady Kelsey, my girl, why is the universe doing this to us?"

Twenty minutes passed, and there was a knock on the door. Radiology was there to wheel her down for the scan. Carefully waking her, Gareth could see the exhaustion as she opened her eyes and he looked at her. In his best reassuring tone, he leaned in and whispered, "I'll be right here when you get back." She let a half smile fall on her face, "Thwank you." He watched as they took her down and decided to run out to his car to retrieve her phone and her purse. The plan was to call her friend Zoe to give her an update on how Kelsey was doing and try to survive the rest of the night.

August 1995
Two Weeks before Kelsey's Departure

York, England

Kelsey allowed the tip of her paintbrush to bounce off her lips as she studied her progress. She had two final projects due for her classes, and she'd already thrown herself into working away on them both. One had to be an oil painting of a picture taken over the past ten weeks. She'd be graded on interpretation of her subject, capturing natural light, color saturation, and realism. The second project could be her pick, and she decided to challenge herself by creating a stained glass window. Her plan was to use those projects as thank you gifts to Gareth and Camilla. She wanted to acknowledge them with something special to always remind them of the summer she spent there.

Two weeks ago, after the trip to the York Riding Academy and after receiving the details of both assignments, Kelsey looked through some of the pictures she'd developed at the local camera shop. They included the pictures from her walks about town, some shots of Camilla's garden, photos from the visit to the farm, and then images of Gareth that she had snapped while he was playing a soccer match on campus. She'd been walking across campus and saw him and thought it would be fun to capture him when he least expected it. She found a picture that showed his side profile with his foot on the ball, his hair weighed down with sweat, and the muscles in his calves and arms glistening with sweat in the sun. Then there was the tightness in his jaw and the intense competitive look in his eye. She'd quickly determined that this would be the perfect one to use, as long as she was able to do it justice. And, so far, the painting was coming along perfectly. She'd also decided that Camilla would receive a stained glass window of the family coat of arms. With just one more week to finish, she knew that it would be tough to pull this off, but she was up for the challenge.

It was early afternoon on what was shaping up to be an overcast and unseasonably cool Saturday. Needing a break from staring at the canvas, Kelsey grabbed her hoodie and made her way downstairs to see if anyone was home to share a cup of hot tea. When she saw she was alone, she filled the kettle and placed it on the now warming burner with a twinge of disappointment. She decided to step out on the patio to wait for the whistle and take in the cool breeze and Camilla's garden. As she walked through the middle of the garden, she admired each of the plants that Camilla took so much pride in planting and tending to: the hollyhocks, Sweet Williams, marigolds, lilies, peonies, tulips, crocus, daisies, foxglove, and lavender. She felt like Lizzie Bennett taking a turn in the garden.

An unexpected sadness settled upon her as she realized she would be leaving all this soon. She'd become such good friends with both Gareth and Camilla, no longer having them in her life was going to take some adjusting. She'd write them regularly, of course, and even invite them to the wedding, but it would be different.

The sound of the sliding door opening brought her back to reality. Spinning around, she saw Gareth. "I was wondering where you and your mom were." As Gareth came closer, she could sense he was tired and not himself. In reality he'd been that way off and on for about two weeks. At dinnertime he seemed just okay, but he hadn't been his usual talkative self when they cleaned the kitchen. She chalked it up to him reading all the pre-med books he'd acquired on a recent trip to the school bookstore.

"The kettle was just starting to whistle when I walked in. I cut the burner off, but the water should be nice and ready for a cup if you're ready. Do you mind if I join you?"

"No, not at all," she said, and she followed Gareth back into the house where he pulled out the tea bags, milk, and sugar. "I think we have a few fresh biscuits are you interested?"

"Yes, I was in need of a little something before lunch. After breakfast this morning I lost track of time working on one of my final projects."

"You've been so secretive about them all week. What kind of projects are they?"

"Oh, I have to create an oil painting and a stained glass window."

"Oh, that's it, aye?" Gareth said with a snicker.

"Ha ha. I have it under control; don't you worry. My progress is actually ahead of schedule, thank you very much." Kelsey sat at the table as Gareth brought over their cups and the pot of steeping tea. "I was reflecting in the garden on how sad I'm going to be once I'm gone and don't get to see you and your mom on a daily basis." Gareth's heart constricted and must have also shown on his face because Kelsey immediately noticed. "Are you okay, Gareth?" she asked in worried tone.

"I'm fine, just haven't been feeling that great, probably because of the lack of sleep."

"What's bothering you? Do you want to talk about it?"

Of course the voice inside his brain was screaming at him: *just tell her you bloody fool!* The color began draining from his face, and he needed to change the subject and fast. "No, it's nothing. So is there anything else you wish you'd done while here in England?" Bringing over the biscuits to the table, he sat down to gather himself and pour each of them a cup of tea.

Not understanding the non sequitur of his question, she indulged him in an answer, "After our riding adventure, I wish I'd planned a road trip of some kind for a weekend. To where, I have no idea, but to be able to take a long drive through England and explore something other than a traditional city would've been nice. I find it funny that back in Virginia many of our cities and counties are names from here. Obviously we know from history why, but to know that there is a New Kent County, Loudon County, Prince George County, Norfolk, and Isle of Wight is pretty fun."

As she continued to talk, Gareth had another brainstorm. His mother's closest friend ran a bed and breakfast on the Isle of Wight. That was an island six hours south of York. If he could convince Kelsey to skip class on that Friday, they could head there for a long weekend. Gareth would do his research, but he needed to see if Kelsey was game. "How far along did you say you are you with your projects, Kelsey?"

Kelsey added milk and sugar, stirred her tea, and took a quick sip, "I plan on using every spare moment this week to work on them. The professor is giving us off this Thursday and Friday from class so we can focus, but I plan to have the majority of both of them done by then. I should have the oil painting done by Tuesday so it has more time to dry." *Brilliant!* swept through his mind. He set his biscuit down, took a deep breath, and looked across the table. "Would you like to take a road trip Thursday, just for a couple of nights?"

Kelsey looked up with wide eyes. "Where?"

"Well, as you were talking, I thought of how my mum's close friend Pam and her husband run a bed and breakfast on the Isle of Wight. It's an island, so we'd take a ferry to get there. It would be about a six-hour drive from here, so you'd get to see plenty of countryside. She lives in Shanklin, a small quaint village, but popular place, that sits near the beach. I totally understand if you don't want to go, but it could be a great way to end your summer here if you're up for it." Gareth was trying hard not to look desperate as he saw Kelsey mulling it over.

"I don't know if I have the extra money for it," she said quietly.

"I invited you, and that would make you my guest, so no need to worry about that."

Looking at him intently and not mincing her words, she came right out and asked him, "Why are you being so nice to me?"

Gareth could feel the panic rising, but before he let it get out of control, he shrugged his shoulders. "You've become a good friend, Kelsey, and I just want to make sure that, before we send you home, you have nothing but fond memories of us here."

Kelsey smiled, "Please be reassured, Gareth, if I were to leave tomorrow, you need to know that I hold you and Camilla so dear to me, and I will never forget this amazing summer. My final two projects are huge, and they'll heavily weigh into my final grades for each class. Can you give me a day to think about it?"

He sighed on the inside but gave a small smile on the outside. "Of course. I'll need to see if Pam has any 'room in the inn,' so to speak."

"Well then, let me finish my tea and head back upstairs, before I can even consider this, I need to jump back into my work and really process how much is left."

As Kelsey went upstairs and closed the door, she couldn't shake the feeling in the pit of her stomach. She chalked it up to realizing how much work she had ahead of her, especially now with this invitation on the table. She stared momentarily at the canvas, smiling at how well she felt she was already capturing Gareth, and immediately got back to work.

Gareth remained downstairs finishing his tea and gazing out the window. He contemplated the negatives of confessing to Kelsey. She'd probably lock herself in her room the rest of the time she was there and only come out for classes and dinner. She'd no doubt tell Jason, who'd be on the first plane here to defend her honor and kick his ass to a pulp. As he let that scene play out in his head he then contemplated the other scenario. Maybe she would just listen, hear him out, and give him a chance. There was always hope, wasn't there?

He heard the front door open from the jangling of keys. Camilla came into the kitchen with an arm full of groceries. "There are a few more bags in the car. Do you mind helping?"

Springing up from his chair, he headed outside with her. Knowing what kind of reaction, it could elicit, he asked her a question, "Thinking about taking a road trip to Isle of Wight next weekend. Can you contact Pam and see if she has any availability?"

As they reached the Rover, Camilla stopped and looked at her son with a raised eyebrow. "Would you be going by yourself?"

Reaching for two bags, he looked directly at her. "No, I've asked Kelsey to join me, and so I'll need two rooms." Camilla stood there staring. He knew she wanted to say something, but instead she responded while grabbing the last two bags. "I'll call her once I get lunch started." Not expecting that response, he walked back into the house behind her. Giving her just a minute as he placed the bags on the counter he finally spoke, "I know you want to say something, so why don't you just get it out of your system."

Unpacking the groceries, she stopped mid kitchen and paused before continuing. "Gareth, ever since you were a little boy, the minute you got an idea into your head, there was no changing your mind. I'll never forget the day, it was a Sunday—you couldn't have been five maybe six-years old—you wanted to go to the park down the way and play football with the adults. While your father and I loved that you thought you were ready for that, we both said absolutely not, that you were too young for their grown up game. I left you in the back yard long enough to turn off the kettle and make you a sandwich while your father continued to fuss in the garden. I came back, and you were gone. At first I figured you were sitting in a corner of the yard pouting, but two minutes later I realized you were gone. I ran out to the street, looking in both directions, yelling for you, and there was no response. I ran to all the neighbors' doors to see if you'd gone there. Nothing. Halfway down the street and ten minutes later and after knocking on every one of your friends' doors, it dawned on me that you'd gone to the park. You and your tiny little body carried the ball all the way to the park. I went from scared to furious to scared out of my mind in a record time. I grabbed my keys and yelled for your father, and we both jumped into the Rover and franticly made our way to you. When we pulled up we leapt out of the vehicle to see all of the adult men cheering you on as you were one on one with the goalie. We both realized they were letting you have your moment. Apparently, when you arrived breathless, you pleaded that they let you play before your old mum showed up to steal you away home."

Gareth couldn't help but smile and was about to ask her why she told him the story when she picked back up. "I learned two very important things that day. First, never underestimate a fiery five-year-old, but especially my Gareth Henry. The second thing I learned that day is that you were my decision maker; once you had made your mind up to do something, there would be no talking you out of it. You had absolutely no fear. Even if that decision meant that you could be making a mistake, we knew that, as long as your life wasn't in danger, we had to let you decide on your own; you'd learn and be a better young man later for it."

"Did I learn anything that day?" he asked with a snarky grin.

Smiling right back, she answered, "Oh, yes, after we got you home you received three swats of your father's hand on your backside for scaring the shit out of us. There was no point in taking away the telly as you never watched it anyway, so we took your football away for a week. You would've thought we ruined your life from the amount of tears you shed, but you seemed to have learned your lesson that day as we never had to take it away from you ever again."

They both had a good laugh when Camilla finished saying what was on her heart, "Just know, Gareth, that it's been very hard watching you hurt and mourn the past year over your father's passing, and the idea of seeing you hurt again for love, makes every bone in my body ache. I know better than to stop you, and I hope you also know that I'm here no matter what."

Gareth took two big steps over to his mum and held her. Being six-two to her five-seven allowed him to fully embrace her, kiss the top of her head, and quietly speak, "Thank you, Mum. Love you."

And with the most tender of responses only his mother could reply with, she leveled him, "Oh, my dear boy, I adore and love you."

Kelsey spent the rest of the weekend working diligently on her final projects, in her room toiling away on the painting so that Gareth would not see. Then, when she needed a break and change of pace, she took all her tools for the stained glass outside into the garden and began to work on that. She'd found a plaque hanging in the formal living room with the family crest and sketched it out as her guide. She just had to keep Camilla away from the outdoor workspace so she wouldn't spoil the surprise.

Sunday afternoon, Gareth stepped out on the patio. "How's it coming?"

Covering her work so he wouldn't see either, she looked up at him and smiled, "Wouldn't you like to know?"

Grabbing his heart in a mocking manner, he said, "Well, I'm only asking as Pam has rung to let us know that she has two rooms for us for arrival on Thursday if we want them." Kelsey just stared at him while processing his words, thirty seconds later she heard her name. "Kelsey?"

"Oh, sorry! I have some touch up that I need to do with painting, and then this needs to set. Then I'll need to add a few more pieces, but I feel comfortable that I could have all that done by Wednesday."

"You're sure? I don't want you to feel pressured into saying *yes*; your grades are way more important."

"Oh, no! I'm game. What I'll have to present to the professors will be great." Liking the confidence in her voice, he gave her two thumbs up.

"I'll call Pam to confirm. We can talk details over dinner."

"Okay, sounds great." Kelsey went back to working on the glass, excited about another adventure. Gareth went inside relieved and yet almost sick as he knew it would be the last chance that he'd get to tell Kelsey how he really felt.

APRIL 2014
ONE MONTH AFTER THE OPENING OF THE STADIUM

Spring was in the air, and the weather had cooperated for every home game since the opening day March 16th. The new Major League Soccer Club Virginia United was now officially open. Enjoying the Bauer Construction luxury suite that came as a part of their contract, Kelsey sat next to Jason just as they had every home game to date and watched him beam with delight. His crew had met every deadline for this place after four long years. Each home game he invited his staff to come and enjoy the fruits of their labor. It was a great way to build on the strong relationships he already had with his crew.

Kelsey got up, "I'm grabbing a soda. Do you want a beer?" Thinking for a moment, Jason answered, "Yeah, grab me a Yuengling, babe." Inside there was a fully stocked bar and a fresh spread of food: one of the perks of the luxury suite. She came in on some of the employees cutting up and enjoying those well-deserved perks. Mac, the head driver, stood around with the others, swapping war stories from the past four years. Kelsey noticed that Michael wasn't present, and, as she pulled out the drinks from the fridge, she asked aloud to the group where he was. It grew very quiet, and no one made eye contact.

Mac finally spoke up, "You may want to ask Mr. B about that."

All of the sudden, the sinking knot that had resided in her gut many weeks ago returned. "Did something happen?" she asked in a low, tentative voice.

"Yeah, you could say that, Mrs. B, but it's not our place to tell."

"Of course, Mac. You're absolutely right." Not wanting to make the moment any more uncomfortable, she changed the subject, "I hope you're all enjoying yourselves; you have a boss out there who thinks the world of all of you and couldn't be more proud." They all tipped their drinks to her as Mac said, "We couldn't work for a better boss." With that, Kelsey smiled at them, but Jason had some explaining to do, and it would begin the moment they got in the truck to head home.

When the match ended, Virginia United was still undefeated. As they walked to the parking lot, as always Jason could tell something was on Kelsey's mind. With a smile and treading lightly, he asked, "Care to talk about what you're thinking, or do I need to drag it out of you?"

Smiling back yet with a more serious tone, she grabbed his hand and said, "Oh you think you know me so well, do you?"

"I think after almost twenty years of being together, I may have you figured out just a little."

She loved how, after so many years together, the ease of caring and the love between them was still there. Sure they had endured their rough patches, but what they'd both discovered in all that time together was that working out those rough patches required a higher level of communication, trust, forgiveness, and sex. Lots of sex. It sounded simple, but it was anything but. In the end, *both* people in the marriage had to decide that they wanted to make it work.

As they got to the truck, before letting her hand go, Jason pressed her against the door and, taking his other hand, tucked her hair behind her ears. Kelsey's breath hitched as she playfully asked, "What are you doing?"

"Since I've been asking you for the past five minutes what's on your brain with no response, I figured if I pinned you here, you might tell me." Kelsey laughed as he sweetly asked, "What is it, Kelsey Jane?"

After taking a minute to swallow, she looked up. "I don't know that I want to know, but I noticed that Michael wasn't here tonight, and when I asked Mac and the guys sitting inside the suite, they wouldn't look at me. Mac spoke up a bit confused and said that it wasn't his story to tell."

Jason's gaze was locked on her; then he leaned forward to kiss her forehead. "Hop in the truck; we can talk about it on the way home."

Kelsey listened to Jason's explanation in stunned disbelief. "What did you say to him next?"

"I told him that I was beyond disappointed." As they pulled into the driveway and parked, Jason looked over at Kelsey for a long moment. "I should've told you last week when it happened; I need you to forgive me for not telling you. I just didn't want you to worry."

Wringing her hands, she put her head back against the headrest and looked out the window. "Did he tell you why he took the money?"

"Apparently he'd gotten himself into a hole in a game of poker. He knew where the safe was and eventually found the code on Bonnie's computer."

"What happens next?" Kelsey asked with a strained tone.

"He's going to work it off, and I've agreed not to report it to his parole officer. If I did, he'd be thrown right back in prison. I think what I find beyond sad is that he's one of the hardest workers we've ever had. It's like he doesn't seem to believe that he deserves any of the good in his life, especially when he's earned it. He allowed himself to get involved with the wrong crowd again."

Kelsey looked over at him. "Is he a danger to anyone? Or the people he's associating with, are they dangerous?"

Jason took deep breath. "Only to himself."

"Are you going to let him stay with the company once he works off his debt?"

After a long pause, he looked back over at her. "Yes. He whole-heartedly regrets his actions and has assured me that it was just a momentary lapse in judgment."

Desperately trying not to lose her temper, she unbuckled her seatbelt. "Jason, the only one having a momentary lapse in judgment is you." After a pause, she regained some level of calm and continued, "How'd you catch him?"

"Bonnie noticed on a few occasions that items on her desk had magically found new homes, but the big one was when she took the deposits to the bank, and they came up short. We went back and watched the video from the hidden camera. We showed him the footage, and he burst into tears." Grabbing her hand before she could jump out of the truck, Jason continued, "He just had six-month drug test that came back clean. He's done amazing keeping clean for the past four years. He made one very bad decision because he was desperate, and I don't think that warrants erasing four years of hard work with us."

Now her anger level was at a boiling point. "You cannot keep giving this guy chances that he's going to throw away. Think about this, Jason, what if you hadn't caught him, and then what if drugs came back into the picture? Can you imagine that hitting local news just as we were nearing the completion of the park after four long years!"

Jason could see that rage. "I know you're angry, but let me get him through this, and if he messes up again, then it's game over. I just know in my heart it's the right thing to do." Kelsey sat there, a perfectly good night ruined by information that she should've been told about a week ago, and it was all related to Michael James Dupree, an employee of her husband's who never sat right with her from the first day they met.

Before getting out of the truck, she put her gaze back on Jason. In her most deliberate tone, a tone that Jason hated but respected because he knew that she was trying to drive home the seriousness of her point, she told him, "I'm holding you to one more chance, Jason, one more. That is, it. If he screws up again, I'm counting on you to follow through with your word to me because you value me, our marriage, and your other employees more than this one employee who only truly cares for himself. I love you, and I love your heart, but there are some people who, in the end, just don't want to be helped."

Kissing her hand, Jason said, "I've heard every word you said. I know you're holding me accountable, and I love you." Kelsey opened the truck door and slid out. Jedi was at the fence to meet her. "I'm going to head out to the barn for a bit," she said. With that, she shut the door and walked away.

Jason sat in the truck and watched her leave. The barn is where she spent alone time. Sometimes to decompress from a long day at work or, in this case, get away from her husband with whom she was royally pissed. Rubbing his stubbled jaw with one hand while the other one rested on the steering wheel, he realized sometimes he let his heart do too much of the thinking, an overused skill that now made his wife believe that she, her opinion, his safety, all the other employees' safety, and business were less important than this one employee. When he saw Michael in his office crying and pleading how sorry he was, it just made his heart ache, but now he had to repair a breach of trust with Kelsey. He needed to make sure she knew that everything was going to be okay. His words to her tonight were a promise to fix the first crack in the foundation of their trust. It was now his duty to make good on them. Kelsey deserved nothing less.

AUGUST 1995
ROAD TRIP

Thursday had arrived. Kelsey stood back in her room and gazed at the oil painting and the stained glass window. She'd worked tirelessly for nearly two weeks. She hadn't been super sociable at dinner, usually skipping dessert and tea as she needed to get back upstairs to finish. But she was very happy with the final outcome of her projects. Carefully wrapping them, she looked at her overnight bag lying on her bed.

She went into the bathroom, grabbing the last few items, and then back into her room where she picked up her color palette and an eight-by-eleven canvas just in case she could do a quick painting, maybe even offering it to their hostess as a *thank you* since she was not charging them for the weekend. As she confirmed with one more glance that all she needed was packed away in her bag, she zipped it up. Hearing a knock at her door, she opened it to see Gareth standing there. Seeming a bit jittery, he asked, "Are you ready to go?"

"Yes, do you think you could help get my projects to the car so we can drop them off on campus on our way out?"

"Yes, of course. You wrapped them already? Why have you been so secretive about these? I was looking forward to admiring all your hard work."

"I want all the flash of a big reveal," she replied with that smile that made Gareth's heart skip a beat. As he walked in to get the painting, Kelsey all but tackled him. "I'll get that one! You get this one." Startled, Gareth put the painting down. "I didn't mean to scold you," Kelsey explained, "I just needed you to carry this one." Kelsey pointed to the wrapped stained glass and immediately felt bad for her overreaction. "It must be something special," he said back with a nod. "Yes, it is…well both pieces are, but I'm little more protective over this one." Kelsey quipped as she held secret the painting of him to her tightly, squeezing by him and heading down to the car.

Camilla met her at the bottom of the steps. "Oh, is that one of your projects?"

"Yes, I'm taking them to the school to leave with the professors for grading before we head out on our trip." Camilla smiled and looked up to see Gareth coming down the steps carrying the other project. With a wink aimed at his mother, he decided to tease Kelsey, "Well I'm glad the school is just three kilometers from home; apparently this is precious cargo." Kelsey whipped around and threw a smile at Gareth, "Yep, they are precious cargo. Glad to know we're on the same page."

Camilla interrupted their banter, "Okay you two, is there anything I can do to help?"

"Actually, Mum, you take this and follow Kelsey out to the car and help her load them. I'll go get her overnight bag to save another trip into the house." As Gareth carefully handed her the wrapped project, which he knew from the weight was the stained glass, he took the stairs two at a time. Upon reaching her bedroom, he grabbed the rather large bag off her bed when he stopped dead in his tracks and saw the picture of himself sitting on the easel. He walked over to it and stared in total shock. How had he not seen it five minutes ago when he was up there? He studied it and could recall the day with clarity but didn't recall seeing Kelsey take his picture. *What in the world would she want with this?* he thought to himself.

"Gareth, are you coming, slow poke?"

He quickly bounced out of her room. "Yep, just trying to make sure I didn't forget anything, and I grabbed your bag."

"Okay, perfect. I think I'm all ready then."

As they headed out to the Defender, Camilla hugged Kelsey. "Have a marvelous time, my dear. See you in a couple of days."

Kelsey returned the hug warmly and got in the passenger side. As Camilla turned to hug her son, she pulled back and looked long and hard into his eyes. "You know I love you and want you to have a good time. Just mind your heart, Gareth." Bending down, he kissed her forehead. "Promise." Gareth got in on the driver's side, and they made their way out of the driveway and onto the main road. Gareth caught Camilla in the rear view mirror, her face full of concern as she faintly waived.

Twenty minutes later, Kelsey hopped back into the vehicle after dropping off her artwork. "Okay, the professor said that he'll evaluate and have them graded by Monday, but we have to leave one of the projects there until the reception next Thursday." Gareth was reviewing the map one more time and then pulled out the brochure that confirmed the ferry times, making sure they'd be able to catch the last five o'clock ferry. "I bet you feel relieved," he said. "You have no idea. Now I can just enjoy our trip!" As Kelsey put her seatbelt on, Gareth reached for a book that he'd obtained and stored in the console between them. As he handed it to her, she looked at him with a raised eyebrow. "What do we have here?"

Smiling, Gareth replied, "We have a book that I got from Dr. Jeffries, Professor of British

War History. You see, where we're going is the home to the famous warhorse Warrior. Many historians believe he's responsible for saving the British military from the Germans. He was known as *the horse that the Germans couldn't kill*." Kelsey studied the book as Gareth drove and made their way to the A42. Thinking he must have made a mistake in assuming she would like it, he spoke up, "I thought since we had five hours in the car, you could read, and it would give you something to look forward to on the island."

Kelsey looked over with her big smile and bright eyes and gave him her most overdone southern accent, "Why thank you, Mr. Blythe." Gareth laughed out loud and shook his head and sarcastically let out "typical American girl." Kelsey snorted, "Okay! Whatever that means!" She settled in and immediately delved into the book as they made their way. Gareth drove and desperately tried to reconcile in his mind if he would actually be able to speak his heart. Would the truth set him free or make him full of regret?

After a stop to refill the Defender with diesel and grab a snack, they arrived at the ferry docks at four-thirty. As they queued up on the bridge behind the other cars and waited to load, he looked over at Kelsey and could see some tears had formed in her eyes as she was more than halfway through the book. He didn't look at her when he asked, as he didn't want to embarrass her, "Are you learning anything?"

She let out a sniffle and used the back of her hand to wipe away two tears that had escaped. "You could say that," she said quietly as she looked up and gave her best smile. "Yes, it's a wonderful story. I had no idea." She sat quietly and stared out at the passenger window a few more moments before she spoke again. "I'm looking forward to walking the trail." Just then the horn from the ferry sounded, and they prepared the cars to board. "Once they secure our spot on the boat, we can get out and stretch our legs. The drive to the inn will take twenty minutes once we reach the other side. So I think we should arrive for a dinner at half six."

"I've worked up an appetite for sure. Somehow road trips do that to me. Do you have any idea what you'd like to do tomorrow?" Kelsey asked.

"Well, honestly, I thought we could take it easy in the morning and see how we feel. There's really no agenda. Maybe just take in the village and the shops, or if you wanted to paint?" Kelsey's head whipped around, "How did you know I packed my pallet?" He waited a beat before he answered. "Lucky guess?" Kelsey shook her head and smiled. "Typical British know-it-all." Gareth laughed aloud and put the Defender into drive as the boat crew directed them to the spot they'd be in for the forty-minute ferry ride.

They arrived at Fox and Hounds Bed and Breakfast at six fifteen and were greeted by the innkeeper and Camilla's close friend Pam Davies. She was a tall, thin, striking beauty who was complemented with perfect makeup on milky white skin and dark brown hair. Her sparkling blue eyes danced as she came to the parking lot, giving Gareth a big, welcoming hug. "Oh my, dear boy, could you get any more handsome if you tried?" Kelsey stifled her laugh as she watched Gareth turn at least four shades of red.

"As always you are too good to me, Pam. Let me introduce you to my friend Kelsey."

Kelsey stepped around the car, extending her hand. "It's a pleasure to meet you, Mrs. Davies."

"Please, Kelsey, call me Pam. It's my pleasure to have you both here. Roger's inside and has dinner just about ready. Let's get you and your bags in and have supper." Gareth grabbed both bags from the vehicle as Pam walked arm and arm with Kelsey. The inn was a large ten-room cottage with beautifully manicured gardens. Kelsey couldn't wait to investigate them when the sun was brightly shining as dusky shadows were now covering. When they walked in they were greeted by the aroma of dinner and by Roger Davies, Pam's husband. Immediately shaking Gareth's hand with a warm welcome, he then turned his attention to Kelsey.

"Welcome, Ms. Kelsey, it's a pleasure to meet you. Camilla rang and told us how lovely of a student you've been this summer and that she values your dear friendship that grew so naturally."

Kelsey could feel her cheeks warming up as she took in the compliment coming from the good-looking gentleman in front of her. He was tall himself, with a ruggedly handsome face and the fiercest blue eyes Kelsey had ever seen. "Thank you, Roger. Do you have a restroom I could use to freshen up in?"

"Yes, of course! Pam will show you your rooms. I need to go check on dinner and make sure I'm not burning the place down."

As they followed Pam to the stairs, Kelsey caught Gareth gazing at her from the corner of her eye. Trying to get a read on his thoughts, she leaned into him and whispered, "What?"

With a bemused look on his face Gareth leaned into her, "Roger looks as if he has you all hot and bothered."

Kelsey's eyes grew wide with embarrassment as she struggled with a retort, "Gareth, I...oh never mind." Bright red, Kelsey turned and made her way up the stairs while mumbling under her breath. Gareth decided to have fun with that again later, but he knew that she was tired, and he really wasn't trying to embarrass her; he just wished she blushed like that for him.

"Okay, Kelsey, here's your key to the Warrior Room, and Gareth, here's your key to the Hound Room across the way. Dinner will be ready and on the table in ten minutes." Kelsey opened her door to a beautiful mahogany four-poster bed and red gingham canopy. Over the headboard was a painting of Warrior the warhorse. Next to it was a nightstand with a French horn lamp and a statue of a fox in riding gear blowing his horn. There were pictures of hunt scenes and beautiful castles throughout the United Kingdom. There was a writing desk that sat by the large bay window that overlooked the back gardens. Then she saw the quaint bathroom with a claw foot tub that begged to be soaked in for hours. "Do you like it, Kelsey?" Pam asked with a curious look.

"Oh my, yes! It's truly lovely. Thank you."

"Excellent, I'll see you downstairs then."

As Pam left, Kelsey closed the door behind her and quickly freshened up. When she finished, she met Gareth, who'd been standing in the hallway. "Were you waiting on me?" she asked. "Of course. I wasn't going to go down without you; we're here together." Kelsey smiled and tucked her arm under his, "Okay then, Sir Gareth. Lead the way." Gareth's heart soared, and he allowed himself to steal another moment that he knew wasn't his.

Dinner and conversation was with just the four of them. The other guests had dinner at a local establishment, which freed up Pam and Roger to spend their evening with Gareth and Kelsey. Kelsey enjoyed hearing about how they became the owners of the beautiful inn. They'd been best friends with Gareth's mom and dad for years and still weren't over the shock of Duncan's untimely death. Kelsey could hear the emotion in Roger's voice as he quickly changed the subject. "So, Kelsey, we hear you're an artist and that you paint very well. Any truth to this rumor?"

Kelsey could feel her cheeks warming and couldn't form a sentence when Gareth grabbed her hand under the table and squeezed it and then started to speak for her. "*Talented* doesn't even begin to describe how good she is. She's been painting all summer in our garden as a part of her classwork, and I've been astounded at how wonderful she is."

Gareth released her hand while never looking at her as Pam chimed in, "Did you bring your brushes with you? It would be lovely to see you do something in our garden."

"I did bring my watercolors and one canvas. I might be able to give it a go."

"That would be grand, Kelsey." Pam exclaimed. The grandfather clock chimed in the hallway, which was Roger's cue to ask who wanted a spot of tea. They all agreed to one cup, which was served with coconut macaroons. After another wonderful hour passed, Kelsey tried to hide her yawn when the clock struck nine. Instead, she stood and thanked her hosts for the warm welcome.

"I'm afraid that I'm about to turn into a pumpkin. I'll see you all in the morning unless I am allowed to help with the dishes?"

Pam and Roger shook their heads no. "That is not necessary. Please go get some rest, and we can talk more tomorrow." Gareth stood and thanked them as well and followed Kelsey. They both climbed the stairs together in silence. When they reached the landing, Kelsey stopped at her door and Gareth at his. Both facing each other, neither exchanged a word for a long moment. It wasn't uncomfortable, just a rare moment that neither had shared before. Gareth broke the silence. "Why don't we plan on being down for breakfast at eight a.m.? Then take a stroll through town before lunch?" Kelsey nodded her head yes. Gareth looked at her with a raised eyebrow. "I'm not used to you having nothing to say. Are you all right?"

"Yes, it's just been hitting me how, in about a week, when I go back to America, this life I've grown accustomed to and grown to care for will be gone." Gareth's mind raced, trying to interpret what he was hearing. Was she saying that she'd come to care for him more than a friend? Should he tell her how he really felt right then? Gareth felt like he was in the water and swimming against the current.

He finally spoke up, "Kelsey, you must know how fond my mother and I have become of you. Getting back to our lives as usual will be very difficult as well. We've grown so use to having you around, especially me." Kelsey looked up and met his gaze. They stood there a little longer in the quiet. Gareth was desperately trying not to run to her, gently take hold of either side of her face, and beg her to stay.

Kelsey took a deep breath and turned to open her door. Before stepping through he heard her say his name. "Gareth, I'd be lying if I said I hadn't grown attached to you and your mother.

It's not going to be easy for me to say goodbye." With that she stepped into her room and quietly closed the door. Wasting no time, Gareth did the same. Inside his room, he saw the writing desk and stationery on it. Taking a moment to collect his thoughts, he knew he wouldn't be able to sleep. As he plopped down onto the chair, he decided to write a letter to Kelsey pouring his heart into words on paper. It seemed completely cliché, but at the moment it was all he could come up with.

At promptly eight a.m. Kelsey opened the door to her guest room and peaked her head out. She'd barely slept. Gareth wasn't yet out, and she decided to wait a couple of minutes so they could go down together. Sitting on the top step, she relived their moments on the landing from last night. Was Gareth saying that he cared for her more than the genuine friendship that had developed between them? Why would he even allow himself to fall in love with her when he knew her heart was Jason's? Sure, maybe in another life they could've had something, but this wasn't another life. She loved and adored Jason, and her life in America was waiting for her.

Her heart ached as well at the thought of not having Gareth in her life any longer. He hadn't once tried to overstep and force himself.

He'd been the perfect gentleman and friend. He was so easy to talk to, they laughed about so much, he could tease her, she could tease him, and at the end of the day they could be sitting in the same room—her painting, him studying—and it all be as content as if she were with Jason. Letting her head fall back with eyes closed she whispered, "Dammit, Kelsey, pull your shit together."

As she did Gareth's door opened, and she shot straight to her feet. Catching the quick motion out of the corner of his eye and seeing how flush she was, he quickly asked, "Are you feeling okay?" In a high-pitched squeak she responded, "YES!" Not believing her, in two strides he was in front of her with the back of his hand on her forehead. "Kelsey, are you sure? You don't look like yourself." Dropping his hand and stepping back, he made eye contact with her until she finally responded, "I'm fine. I just didn't sleep well last night and was hoping to feel more refreshed than this." Eyeing her and biting his lip, Gareth responded, "Well, let's have a light breakfast, and then we can take the walk into town and get some fresh air. We're so close to the ocean, the nice salty air will be good for us."

She smiled and answered with a quiet "okay."

Breakfast was the four of them again. Kelsey could feel her cheeks warm when Roger asked if he could take her for a turn in the gardens when they returned from town. Taking a quick sip of her tea in hopes it would hide her cheek color she finally responded, "Yes, of course."

Gareth cleared his throat, "Well, Kelsey, let's go ahead into town to see the shops open and the village come to life." As he pulled out her chair, she ran upstairs to grab her camera and sunglasses. Pam approached Gareth as they waited for her at the bottom of the steps. "She is a lovely lovely girl Gareth." Looking up the stairs and not hearing himself say it aloud, he let out a sigh: "the best kind of girl." Pam looked at him and put her hand on his shoulder, giving it a squeeze before walking away.

As Kelsey came down, Gareth couldn't help but notice that, with her pony tail, light denim jeans, a white t-shirt, and her paddock boots, she was the picture of innocence and sexiness in one amazing package, and if he caught any other man looking at her today, there was going to be a fight. "Ready then, Sir Gareth?" With a bow and a dramatic sweep of his arm, he answered, "At your service, Lady Kelsey."

Kelsey was speechless as she walked the quaint town of Shanklin. Fresh flower carts stood in the square; The Thatched Tea Room sat on the corner with the fresh aroma of tea and pastries wafting through the door. After exploring the many shops, they saw one that sold local artists' work, which immediately caught her attention. "Can we go in there?"

Gareth smiled, "Why are you asking? Of course you can go in."

As they did, Kelsey was drawn directly to the wall that showcased watercolor and oil paintings. She was instantly moved by one of the pictures. It was of the beachfront cliffs in Shanklin. The morning rays of light streaming across the bluffs and the waves that crested the shoreline were beautifully interpreted. There was one right next to it that was an oil picture of the main road and square in town. It focused on all the colorful doorways into each shop and captured all the activity of the small village. They were each eight by ten and two hundred and fifty pounds.

"It's kind of hard to choose, isn't it?" Gareth asked.

"Mmhmm, yes, but I think I'm leaning towards the town square. I love how the artist communicated the light in both—it's truly stunning, but I'm captivated by how he captured all the activity here."

Gareth looked at the work and wrinkled his nose. "Hmm, they're okay, I guess."

Shocked, she looked up. "How can you say that? These are gorgeous!"

Leaning in for a closer look he responded, "Your work is just as good if not better."

Stunned, Kelsey muttered, "Oh, well that is certainly a matter of opinion."

Straightening back up and looking directly at her, he asked with complete sincerity, "Does my opinion not matter?" Again stunned and left speechless, Kelsey just stared at him. With their gazes locked, he reached and pushed a stray piece of hair that had come out of her ponytail behind her ear. Kelsey blinked, and before she could utter a word, Gareth's voice filled in the space where her voice failed her. "If we go back now, we can have lunch, and you can take a turn in the garden with Roger." Gareth winked at her as he saw the blush in her cheeks come to life.

Pam and Roger prepared to have lunch for the four of them out in the garden when they returned. As Pam put the finishing touches on the sandwiches, Roger walked Kelsey through the garden as he'd promised. There was a light breeze that kept the sun from being too warm. Kelsey was astounded and marveled at what she hadn't been able to see the night of their arrival. She'd been so impressed with Camilla's green thumb, but Roger's garden was a sight to behold. "How many hours do you spend out here?" Kelsey asked, trying to not sound trite.

Beaming back his response through a smile, he answered, "A lot! You're seeing this garden at its peak. The butterflies are in abundance, as are the dragonflies, damselflies, and bumble bees." Holding her hand up over her eyes to shade them from the sun, she could see the beautiful waterfall and the insects bouncing from bloom to bloom in a rhythmic and graceful tumble. "If you're still okay with it, I'd love to bring my brushes out after lunch and do some painting." Smiling again he responded, "I would love nothing more."

As they came back to the table, Kelsey noticed Gareth had a small smile on his face. When he locked his gaze with hers she immediately was mentally and emotionally transported back to the shop where he tucked her hair back behind her ear. She'd felt nothing but calm and peace when he did it. The only other person to ever do that to her was Jason. Thinking of Jason allowed her to break her gaze with Gareth. *What is going on with you, Kelsey? Snap out of it.* She jumped back into the conversation Roger had been having with her as he pulled out her chair.

As Pam brought the final dish to the table to begin lunch, Kelsey took a deep breath to relax and was looking forward to some time in the garden later where she could clear her mind and paint. Thankfully the conversation at lunch was very easy and full of laughter as Roger and Pam saw it their duty to tell every embarrassing story they knew about Gareth growing up. Gareth shook his head the whole time. "My mother must have phoned ahead with some of these, as I recall not one of these instances ever occurring."

"Oh, I promise, dear boy, these stories are all true! Especially the one when your family visited when you were eight, and you used all your boyish charm to dazzle some of the older ladies from the British Romance Writers Society staying for a long weekend. If I recall correctly," Roger chimed in, "you had them so smitten. You brought them tea to their table and fluffed their pillows in the drawing room so when they sat they'd be more comfortable. Then when they were all ready to check out, you offered to bring their luggage down. When they tried to pay you, you refused!" Kelsey swung her head to see the look on Gareth's face.

He shrugged, "It was nothing."

Roger let out a howl. "Nothing! Kelsey, don't let him fool you. He made ten quid that day! Those ladies refused to leave without him taking money, so much so, they came and got his parents, gave *them* the money, and thanked them for raising such a fine young man."

Kelsey was laughing when she asked, "What did you ever do with that ten quid, Gareth?"

When Gareth caught her gaze, she immediately started to feel her cheeks grow hot. Leaning in and putting his arms on the table and not taking his eyes off of her, he answered, "I did what any responsible English boy would do, and I bought a new football."

With that everyone laughed except Kelsey; she shot up from the table. "Excuse me...I need to go...I mean I need to gather my things...my brushes."

Looking on in concern Pam asked, "My dear girl are you okay? You look peaked."

Feeling her cheek with her hand, she noticed how warm it was. Why had Gareth made her feel so flushed? "No, I'm fine. Thank you for another lovely meal. I'm going to go get set up in the garden to paint." Standing up with her and feeling concerned Gareth asked, "Can I come watch?" Kelsey desperately needed some space but dare not mention it. "I...I guess, yes, sure." Smiling he answered back, "You're sure?" Kelsey nodded her head yes and quickly disappeared back into the inn.

In the past twenty-four hours something had changed between them. She couldn't put her finger on it. She desperately cared for Gareth; they'd had an amazing summer becoming friends. Kelsey felt tears starting to flood her eyes. Taking deep breaths, she calmed herself down and reminded herself that she was a grown woman and that she was going to have other male friends in her life that she cared for, but it didn't mean that they were in love with her or that she was in love with them. She was a week away from being back in Jason's arms, and the thought of that made the very core of what made her a woman ache. She simply adored and loved Jason.

Then, as had become the norm, a wave of sadness washed over her at the thought of never seeing Gareth ever again. Kelsey closed her eyes as they'd filled with tears that she brushed away with the back of her hand. *Why did he tuck my hair behind my ear this morning? It was so tender and sweet, and it didn't scare me or make want to run. Should I have been upset?* Going into the bathroom she turned on the cool water in the sink and used a face towel to press against her eyes to help with the redness. Giving herself a few more minutes, she looked back in the mirror. Refreshing her light makeup, she made a deal with herself. *Just trust the friend that Gareth has become. How lucky are you that he's respected your boundaries and your relationship with Jason? Don't mess this up because you feel like there is something more. Pull your shit together now, Kelsey.*

Standing back from the mirror, she blew out a breath and gathered her painting tools and headed back downstairs. Roger saw her and stopped, "Ahh, I was going to let you know that if you need a bit of a break from your masterpiece, I'll have a fresh tea and scones on at three."

Not quite back to her normal voice after her crying session upstairs, she cleared her throat, "Thank you, Roger. That sounds perfect."

"Oh, and Gareth is out on the other side of the garden near the fountain. He said that you might prefer the natural light over there."

Smiling back her second thank you, she made her way over to Gareth. "There you are; I was getting worried." Kelsey couldn't help but brighten when she saw him.

"Oh...I needed to make sure that I had everything." She hated not being honest with him, but what good would it have done to tell him that she'd spent the last thirty minutes in confused tears? "I only have one shot to get this right as I want to surprise Pam and Roger with what will hopefully be a decent one-of-a-kind painting of their garden."

"That's a lovely idea, Kelsey." She noticed the text he had in his hand. "A little light reading?" she asked.

"Yeah. I didn't want to be a distraction, so I brought one of my medical journals. I started to read these last year and use them to keep me up with all that's going on with the latest in cardiology advancements. Dr. Frei, who was good friends with my father, lends them to me. I figured I could read this and quietly keep you company." She smiled and relaxed as she realized that this is just who Gareth was. A kind and gentle soul. Her friend. All the stories she'd heard about him had a consistency. While he was certainly a charmer, and a bit of a rake with the ladies, he always had others' best interest at heart. With so few days left together, she was going to honor what they had between them, a friendship she'd treasure for the rest of her life.

At some point during their time in the garden together, Gareth had stretched out across the bench and fallen asleep. Kelsey continued to focus on the details she wanted to capture in the garden when Pam approached with a tray of tea and scones. "I'm so sorry to interrupt, but I thought you might enjoy a little siesta." Looking over at Gareth she chuckled, "It looks as if someone took serious advantage of his time in the relaxing garden."

Upon hearing them both laugh, Gareth startled awake and had four eyes staring at him as he tried to remember where he was. Finally realizing, he rubbed his eyes. "Having a good laugh, are you?" He stood up and gave a large and impressive stretch with his six foot two, muscular frame. Walking over to meet Kelsey at the tea tray, he endured her teasing, "Enjoy your nap, Sir Gareth?" Popping a scone into his mouth as if it were a piece of candy, he looked at her, still half awake. "Yes, I did. Thank you for asking."

Pam had zeroed in on the painting and was spellbound. "You did all of this in the past two hours? All this detail?"

Kelsey nodded her head yes. "I'm not finished yet. I need another hour to get it just right."

"My dear girl, if you were to stop right now, I'd be elated; this is astonishing. Roger is going to absolutely love it and want to buy it from you!"

"Buy what from her?" As Roger approached, his eyes grew wide. "You did all of this in two hours?" Kelsey nodded her head yes for what felt like the hundredth time. Gareth, now fully awake and admiring her beautiful work, came up behind Kelsey and placed his hands on her shoulders.

"We are absolutely buying this from you, Kelsey. How much do you want for it?" Roger asked.

Kelsey was both humbled and elated that they loved it. "My intention was to give this to you in appreciation for hosting us this weekend." Pam brought her hand to her mouth.

"Oh, Kelsey, it'll feel like highway robbery if we don't pay you. Don't you agree, Roger?"

"Absolutely, Kelsey, we insist."

"But it was my plan the whole time to make this for you and leave it with you… assuming it turned out okay. Please accept this as my thank you. If you want to repay me, just find a nice place to hang it so that people can see it and hopefully admire it." Studying the painting in greater detail, Roger backed away, shaking his head in disbelief and excitement that someone had captured such a unique impression of his garden. "We graciously accept that offer," he said. With a sigh of relief, she hugged them both.

"Let me finish up the last details of the painting, and then I'll bring it inside. We should place it in a room to dry for a few days."

"That will not be a problem!" they both said beaming. Pam and Roger went back inside to prepare for guests who would be arriving. After releasing her shoulders, Gareth sat back on the bench and watched Kelsey add the final embellishments. He was struck at how graceful and precise her strokes were. God, he was going to miss this so damn much. Just them together, no words having to be exchanged to enjoy each other's presence. The late afternoon sun had fallen across her hair, turning it the sweet caramel he loved seeing on her, and was catching the green flecks of hazel in her eyes. It was taking every amount of control not to go and cradle her head between his hands and make her listen as he poured out his heart to her.

He stood to change the direction of his mind. Kelsey got up and took two steps back to look at the painting once more. As she did, she backed right into Gareth. Almost falling, she spun around, but he caught her. "Whoa there, miss. Where are *you* going?" he asked, laughing as he steadied her. Kelsey started to laugh as well. "I didn't know you were behind me; I'm so sorry." "I'm not," was his response. Kelsey's laugh immediately halted as Gareth looked down at her. He gently grabbed her brushes from her hand, bringing heat to her fingers at the touch, and placed them on the easel. Her eyes followed his hands. He calmly said her name, "Kelsey." She looked back up at him as he started to talk. "I thought tomorrow we could go walk the trail and spend some time at the beach. Would you be okay with that?" Taking in the tender moment, she finally responded, "Yes, I'd like that."

Smiling down at her, he replied, "That sounds grand. By the way, you know you really blew Pam and Roger away with your painting today, don't you?"

"I really didn't think they'd be so happy."

"You have such a marvelous talent. I know you made me proud."

Kelsey felt full from his words and smiled. "That means the world to me, Gareth. Thank you." She interrupted the weight of the moment with a change in subject. "I need to get this all cleaned up."

"Can I help you carry anything inside?"

"If you don't mind grabbing my color palette and easel, I'll carry the painting." With that, they made their way back inside. As they got to the door, Gareth said, "Pam recommended a pub in town for dinner. Thought you might be interested in trying it. They have bangers and mash. Have you ever had that?"

Cringing, she responded, "I haven't; what exactly is it?"

"Oh, I think we just added an element of surprise to the night. Can you be ready in an hour?"

"Have you learned nothing of me in the past eleven weeks, Gareth?" she asked sarcastically and immediately regretted it as she saw his smile chased away from his face. This time Gareth changed the subject, "Do you mind walking? It would be a lovely night for a stroll; just bring a jacket."

"A walk sounds nice," she responded, keeping it light as they headed up to their rooms. "See you in an hour." Gareth smiled and acknowledged, "An hour." In his room getting ready, Gareth decided that he needed to tell her everything. To finally be honest with her and himself. He was prepared for her reaction and that it might mean they leave first thing in the morning, but after dinner he'd see if they could take a walk through town so he could share his heart and then the letter he wrote her.

The August evening in town was busy, even for a summer weekday. Turner's Tavern was the hub of that activity. They made their way in and found a table that would seat the four of them. Gareth had been very quiet on their walk over. Kelsey could tell something was wrong and asked if he wanted to talk about it, but he shrugged it off. "Nothing that you can help with; I'll manage." Kelsey noticed his tone was flat and a little indifferent. He again used the tact of changing the subject, "Pam and Roger said that they'll be up here in an hour to meet us for drinks but to go ahead and have dinner."

A handsome young waiter came bounding over and spoke directly to Kelsey, never even looking at Gareth. "What can I get you tonight?" Smiling back at him she responded, "Well, I'm not sure yet; do you have a menu?" Looking a bit sheepish, he reached into his back pocket and handed her a menu. "Oh, yes of course; here we are." She reached for the menu when he dramatically asked her, "Are you from America?" "Christ Almighty," Gareth murmured under his breath while listening to their banter. "My name is Andy. I'm sorry; I didn't catch yours." Reaching her hand out she introduced herself. "Kelsey."

Gareth sat back and watched this all unfold in front of him like some bad movie. Watching someone hit on Kelsey wasn't helping his mood, so he took matters into his own hands. "Andy?" Turning to see who called this name he met Gareth's furious gaze. "Now that you've become well acquainted with Kelsey, we are going to need a few moments to discuss the menu. Do I make myself clear?" Kelsey sat back in the booth, completely caught off guard by Gareth's reaction. Andy was a bit confused but carried on. "Right then…here is a menu for you too. I will… be back shortly." The now-deflated waiter walked away as Gareth focused on and perused the menu. Kelsey could only stare at him. Finally looking up at her and making eye contact he let out a "what?" Kelsey continued to stare him down, which made him uncomfortable until he broke again. "Why are you giving me that look?"

"Why in the world did you talk to our waiter like that?"

"Like what?"

"Okay, now you're just being obstinate."

"Kelsey, he was being a typical guy towards you, and I didn't appreciate it."

Confused and getting a little angry, she leaned into the table. "I'm not helpless, and you're not always going to be there to protect me from those guys, so can you bring the testosterone down a notch and let me be an adult." She may as well have just punched Gareth in the gut. He didn't need to be reminded that she'd be gone in less than a week. Her leaving and the gaping wound it was going to create meant that he was just going to have to take matters into his own hands.

Andy approached the table, and before Kelsey could even order, Gareth started barking out instructions. "Bring us two house specials of bangers and mash, an Ale, and water." Grabbing her menu out of her hand he gave them both to Andy who'd caught on that he need not spend any extra time lingering at their table. Embarrassed, Kelsey demanded an answer, "Gareth, what is wrong with you? I mean who are you right now? I asked you earlier if you needed to talk, and you've acted ridiculous ever since."

Reacting strictly out of a place of desperation, he lashed out, "Well apparently you don't appreciate me doing my best to protect you from the duffers who are just looking for a nice piece of ass to tap tonight."

He regretted his words immediately. Kelsey had her hand over her mouth, and tears started to fill her eyes. "Wait. Why...why would you say such an awful thing? Why are you acting this way?" Gareth was ashamed and was at a loss of words. Before he could respond, Kelsey's eyes were large with what seemed to be surprise and a little fear. "Oh my gosh! Oh no?" she said, continuing to hold her hand over her mouth to help choke back a sob. "What?" he shot back in a snarky tone. She stared at him a half a beat longer. "I have to go." Grabbing her purse, she slid out of the booth and ran out through the front door. She walked as quickly as she could, regretting that she didn't bring a jacket, even though Gareth had insisted she needed one, as it was now ten degrees cooler. With a short sleeves and shorts and her emotions at an all time high, she was freezing.

A minute later she heard his voice, "Kelsey, wait!" As his footsteps got closer, she turned to face him. "Why, Gareth? Why me?" He didn't pretend not to know what she was talking about.

"Kelsey, I have so much that I want to say, so much I need to tell you…I just didn't know how because, as much as I wanted you to know the truth, I was desperately trying to respect you and Jason."

In a fury Gareth didn't even think she was capable of, she let started to yell. "You are not allowed to say his name—do you hear me! You leave him out of this. This is between me and you. Do you understand me?" Gareth took two steps back as the fire and anger raged out of her. "How could you do this me? To us? I truly thought after all that we've been through this summer, our friendship meant something to you. God, I am so naive. I need to grow the fuck up," she said, storming off towards the inn. Gareth followed her.

He listened to her sob and watched her use her arm to wipe the tears that were running down her face. She was shivering from the cold, and her feelings were running in overdrive. In an attempt to bring down their emotions, Gareth called out to her in an angry voice that made her stop dead in her tracks. He jumped in front of her, grabbing her shoulders. "Kelsey, stop, just stop it." Without thinking, he pulled her close and let her shiver and weep into him. He immediately took his jacket and wrapped it around her. She didn't fight him. She let him take care of her as he had done the entire summer. "Oh my god, Kelsey. I'm so sorry. I am so so sorry." He could feel and hear his voice breaking as his eyes started to sting. They stood there until they both gained control of themselves. Unwrapping her from the coat, he took it off and put it on over her shoulders. "Are you ready to start walking again?" She nodded her head yes.

They stepped in silence next to one another. Gareth was grateful her teeth had stopped chattering. Once they got to the inn, he went upstairs with her and stopped on the landing as they had done the night before. Her gaze cast down, he carefully used his finger to gently lift her chin. "I need to give you something. Can you give me a second?" Nodding her head yes, she waited while he brought back an envelope with her name on it. Handing it to her, he gave her instructions, "I want you to read this. Once you do, and it still doesn't answer your questions, feel free to ask me whatever you need to ask me. Now I realize after tonight you may want to pack up and go home first thing in the morning. If that is what you want, Kelsey, then I'll certainly honor those wishes. I just ask that you please read this first."

She studied the envelope and then, with red eyes and puffy nose, looked up at him. Gareth thought he was going to die. She looked so defeated, so sad—and he had done this to her. This was the last thing he wanted. In a shaky voice she spoke, "I'll read it." Taking off his jacket, she handed it to him. She turned and opened her door, walked in, and closed it behind her, never letting her gaze travel up to meet his. Gareth walked to her door and gently laid his head against it. He could feel the tears welling back up and the lump sitting heavy in his throat. His only prayer now was that she'd read his letter and give him their last day on the island together. He knew he was asking too much and offered a prayer to the God he never even acknowledged until Kelsey came into his life. Placing his hand on her door, he whispered, "Good night, Lady Kelsey."

At three a.m. Kelsey lay in bed contemplating the contents of the letter. She'd read it at least fifty times. Processing and pondering each line and its meaning. How had she been so naïve? When was she going to grow up and realize that life was never this simple? Gareth wasn't to blame, entirely. She was just as much at fault in this scenario. She saw the signs, she questioned things, but in the end her stupidity won. "Dumb, stupid girl" was all she could mutter.

She had to make a decision: get up and start packing to be ready to go first thing or take his letter at face value and enjoy their last day of this adventure together. She cared for him so deeply. She couldn't give him what he wanted. Her heart was Jason's. What she could give him was one more day together here on the island; and she could make their last few days together free of any awkwardness. She was desperate to keep their friendship intact if at all possible. He made it clear in the letter that, as much as he loved her, he wanted their friendship above everything. The words he wrote her were truly beautiful. Such raw emotion. Kelsey knew that he'd never written another letter like this to anyone. He put his heart on paper knowing that, when she read it, she could pulverize what was remaining once the full gravity of his feelings were revealed. Sitting up on her bed, fighting a headache, she looked over at the writing desk where she saw the stationery. She walked over and grabbed a piece, and with a pen she wrote.

Gareth,

I wish to spend our final day on the island together, if you will still have me?

Kelsey.

She folded it, quietly opened her door, walked over to his, and carefully slid the note under. Going back to her room, she readied herself for bed. Just as she pulled the sheets back, she saw the note sliding across her carpet. She walked over and picked it up. Opening and reading it, she breathed a sigh of relief.

Lady Kelsey,

It would be an honor.

Sir Gareth

She smiled and wiped a couple of stray tears from her eyes. With that, she crawled into bed, her body letting out breathy shutters from all the crying she'd done earlier. Her lids became heavier and heavier, and she finally succumbed to sleep.

APRIL 2014
FULL MOON

"What do you mean I have to answer these questions in order to reset my password?" Kelsey cleared her throat and calmly replied, "Well, when you set up the account, you created the security questions and answers. That's why they're asking you these particular questions right now; these are security measures to protect your information."

"I didn't set up the account; my kids did. I just want to download this book, and it keeps telling me my password is wrong. I hate technology!" Now the customer was on the verge of tears. Taking a calming breath, Kelsey talked the customer back from the brink and reassured her that she would do whatever possible to help get this all figured out. Two hours later, passwords and security questions had been reset, and the customer thanked her profusely for all her help. If Kelsey had known that every customer interaction that day was going to suck on every level, she probably would have called out sick. All the customers she greeted or attempted to help whined or blamed her for their technological woes. She was grateful that her final customer contact for the day ended well, but she was still in a mood.

It didn't help that she was still disappointed with Jason for not sharing with her that Michael had stolen from the company. Trust had never been an issue for them their entire relationship. Maybe that's why Kelsey was taking it so hard. But this occurrence left her feeling like what she thought was a solid foundation was severely cracked. She hadn't made herself available to him all week. Part of her was dying on the inside as making love to her husband was one of her favorite things to do, but she had to make sure he knew how upset she was.

She punched out at six p.m. and looked at her phone to see a text from Jason. *Call me as soon as you get off work. lv u.* She grabbed her bag and called him as she headed to the car.

"Hey, kiddo." That always made her smile. "Hey, yourself."

"Are you on your way home?"

"Yes. It was a stupid long day. I'm pretty sure there's a full moon tonight; it can be the only explanation as to why my customers were such a handful."

Jason laughed, "Well, I have a surprise for you when you arrive. Do me a favor and park in the driveway and call me from the car when you get home."

"Jason Holden, what are you up to?"

"Just do me this favor—and don't ask any more questions and just get home."

"That's three favors. And I'll be there in thirty minutes." She ended the call and hoped that the surprise included a soak in a hot bathtub and a pint of chocolate brownie ice cream.

As she pulled into the driveway she looked to the east and saw the giant orange moon making its way up into the night sky. "Well that explains a lot," she muttered to herself. She grabbed her phone and called Jason. "I'm in the driveway," she announced. "I'm on my way," he answered. When he got to the car, he led her to the front door of the house and gave her instructions, "I want you to go shower, and when you get dressed please clip your hair up, and wear your short, purple satin gown and robe."

"These are a lot of orders, Jason, and I'm not entirely sure I'm in the mood to follow directions," she said with a tired and snarky tone. The look that he gave her was of disappointment, but he quietly responded, "Please, Kels, I just need you to trust me. I know I'm asking a lot, but tonight—just trust and give me tonight."

She could see that he was serious, and she decided not to deny him this. She did exactly as he asked, and twenty minutes later emerged from the bathroom. She threw on her gown and matching robe and cinched the belt around her waist. Jason came into their bedroom with a huge smile on his face. Kelsey's insides melted at the sight of Jason's dark stubbled chin, his button down shirt, unbuttoned, exposing his gorgeous muscled chest that Kelsey loved to lay her head on. Kelsey pulled herself together when she heard his voice. "I need to blindfold you." He held up a satin blindfold. "We're heading outside, but I don't want you to see why."

Though she'd felt so distant from him, in that moment she had no reservations about following his direction. Without a word, Kelsey walked over to Jason and turned her back to him. Jason carefully tied the blindfold on. The soft satin was cool and felt so good on her face. He pulled her back against his bare chest and started to carefully kiss her neck. Reaching around to her breasts, he began to speak with shallow breaths into her ear, "I'm going to pick you up and carry you to the barn." Kelsey nodded her head with a yes. Jason carefully scooped her up. She laid her head against his shoulder.

Once they were in the barn, he kept the blindfold on and carefully whispered into her ear, "I need you to climb the ladder to the loft. I'm going up before you, but you know the ladder. It's only ten steps, and I'll be at the top to grab your hand and pull you to safety." He could tell Kelsey was hesitant. "Please trust me," he asked, and he kissed the corner of her mouth and went ahead of her. Once he got to the top of the loft he spoke reassuringly, "Kelsey, I'm right here waiting for you." Carefully reaching out in front of her, Kelsey put her foot on the first rung and stepped up. "That's my girl; take it slow."

She knew the smell of her barn, but there was something very warm and fragrant that she was smelling as well. It became stronger with each step. As she got to the top, Jason reached for her hand and pulled her up and into his arms where he held her and softly began to kiss her. Kelsey put her arms through his shirt and pulled him in tighter to her. The air was heavy with want. Both their breathing was hitched in anticipation. Jason pulled her away from him. "Not yet, sweetheart."

He took off his shirt and then reached out to her, carefully turned her around and spoke into her ear from behind, "I'm going to take your mask off, and I want you to slowly open your eyes." He removed the blindfold, allowing her to gradually take in her surroundings. Kelsey couldn't believe what she was seeing. She blinked several times. "Jason, how did you? When did you?" He smiled and carefully took her hand. "Let's just say I called in a few favors." He walked her over to a queen size bed made up with oversized pillows, a soft duvet, and Egyptian cotton sheets. It was sitting on a gorgeous red and gold Oriental rug. There must have been fifty, giant, battery-operated candles spread around the bed and on the dresser and chest he'd managed to get up to the loft. The candles flickered as if they were real flames surrounding the barn loft bedroom, giving off a beautifully seductive glow. He'd even gone to the expense of having giant glass globes hung from the beams, filled with soft glimmering lights that completely transformed the space into a sacred room.

Jason walked over and pushed the loft door open. It gave them the perfect view of the moon from their bed. Kelsey stared at Jason with a puzzled look on her face. Coming back over to her, he placed his hand on her face. "Last week when you found out about Michael the way you did, it really hit me how unfair and wrong I was to keep that from you. Kelsey, you've been my best friend for damn near twenty years, and when you walked away angry last week, I became angry with myself because I'd broken a level of trust that we've always held in our marriage. Your opinion and insight will always matter and always come first. You're precious to me, and I'm furious with myself that I took you for granted." Slowly kissing the top of her hand and then each finger, he asked, "Will you forgive me, Kelsey? Will you let me make it up to you tonight so that, going forward, you'll always know that you matter above all others. Let me use tonight to strengthen the vows that I made to keep you first in all things."

He pulled the sash to her robe causing it to fly open as he reached his arms in and slowly began to massage her hips over the silk gown while kissing her neck, her jawline, and landing on her mouth. "Kelsey, will you allow me the honor of worshipping you mind, soul, and body tonight to right this wrong that I've created because of my selfishness?" Her eyes filling with tears from his words, she could only nod her head yes as he pushed the robe off her shoulders.

The spring air was still cool, and when it hit her skin, it created goose bumps all over. Jason laid her on the bed, and she felt as if they were floating on clouds. Firmly he asked her, "Please sit up." Using her elbows to push herself up she found her face against Jason's chest as he straddled her and removed her hair clip and placed the blindfold back on. "That's my girl; now lie back. Tonight is about building trust again. I need to hear you say it, Kels. Do you trust me?" Her breathing heavy, she replied, "Yes. Yes, Jason. I trust you." He kissed her forehead. "Good girl, now lay back."

Kelsey did as she was told as Jason's hands moved down and freed her breasts from her nightgown. He slowly and methodically rolled her pink buds; Kelsey's breath left her body. Pushing her arms above her head, he grabbed a black ribbon and tied her hands together to a spindle in the headboard. Kelsey's entire body was immediately on fire. Jason leaned down and breathed into her ear, "Do. Not. Move." Kelsey began to focus on her breathing. Jason was in total control, something she wasn't used to. Right now, with her hands tied to the bed, she was at his mercy, taking this trust game to a whole new level.

Jason slid her nightgown down, and she felt the slick-smoothness of the satin as it brushed past her belly, over her hips, across her thighs, and then down her calves and feet before he cast it to the ground. She could hear him getting something from the dresser, and soon she felt his return as he slowly poured a soft and fragrant oil up and down her body and began to tenderly massage her. Starting with pressure points in her feet, he pulled and rubbed, working his way up her body. Catching her by surprise, he flipped her over suddenly. Still tied to the post, Kelsey's breathing was now erratic. Jason's large and firm hands massaged and kneaded her calves and then her thighs, making their way up to her backside. "Kelsey, you are so beautiful. Every bit of you."

He allowed his hands to explore, spreading her legs apart and wandering into her heat and massaging until he felt the dampness release around his fingers. Lifting her head, Kelsey was already on the verge of her release when he brought his hands out and began to massage from her lower back up to her shoulders. Jason got up and removed the rest of his clothing and carefully turned Kelsey back to her front. He laid his body over hers, resting his arms on either side of her head. He gently kissed her forehead, nose, and mouth. Kelsey's body was now rippling with desire as she did her best to control her breathing. "Why are your trembling?" Jason asked as he kissed her and allowed his splayed left hand to move down to her side and land on her stomach to feel the tremors. Kelsey was unable to answer as she was shaking with desire and need. Jason smiled and took her in deep, passionate kiss.

When they came back up for air, he slid his body down hers and began to kiss her stomach. As he traveled lower, Kelsey's hips lurched forward, silently bidding Jason's mouth to come closer to her center. Lifting her legs to his shoulders he obliged and ravaged her with his tongue.

Although Kelsey was blindfolded, she saw a burst of colors when she climaxed. Jason quickly untied her arms and carefully turned her back on her stomach and whispered into her ear, "Do you trust me?" Kelsey could only shake her head yes. "No, Kelsey, say it, say you trust me." "Yes. Yes, Jason, I trust you."

Using more oil, he massaged her backside and slowly pressed his finger into her back entrance. Kelsey took in a deep breath as she rose up. Without saying a word, he allowed her body to relax as it became used to his presence. He very carefully but firmly spoke her name and made a request. "Slowly lift to your hands and knees, Kels." Kelsey was still coming down from her first climax and was now hungry for more. As he kept his finger in her back entrance, he plunged his large erection into her front entrance from behind, immediately sending them both over in the most intense and intimate orgasm they had ever experienced in their married life.

Jason held them both there while the aftershocks shook them both to the core.

Sweating profusely and labored in breathing, Jason slowly removed himself and carefully turned Kelsey over to face him. He lay against the giant pillows and headboard and pulled her onto his chest. He kissed her forehead as she could barely move. They held each other and fell asleep on the beautiful bed under the hanging lights and the moon. Trust, on a whole new level, had been restored.

AUGUST 1995
ONE DAY BY THE SEA

Gareth barely slept and knew that he was going to be living on pure adrenaline the whole day. Should he ask her what she thought of the letter? Obviously if it had been that terrible, they'd be going home and not staying the whole day. Should he act as if none of it ever happened? He knew he needed to apologize for his words in the pub last night, but not for the letter. As painfully wrong as the night had gone, she finally knew, and there was some relief in that. Maybe the truth really did set people free.

It was seven forty-five. Gareth showered, dressed, and, taking a last look in the mirror, psyched himself up. *Don't fuck this day up, or you'll regret it for the rest of your life.* With that, he opened his door where he found Kelsey. Locked in each other's gaze, they both began to speak at the same time. When they realized neither of them heard what the other was saying, they both laughed. "You go first, Kelsey."

Pausing to collect her breath and her thoughts, she looked up. "I want you to know that I've never read anything so beautiful in my life. Your honesty and transparency humbled me. With all that said, can we please do our best to try and be who we have been to each other for the past eleven weeks, before last night? I lay in bed and realized that, even though I can't give you what you want, Gareth, I need your friendship. I know that isn't easy to hear, but with all that we've experienced while I've been in England, the depth and value of our friendship counts for something, does it not?" Letting her words go down deep, he nodded his head yes.

They stood there quietly for a few more moments when he finally broke the silence. "May I say something?" he quietly asked. Kelsey looked back up with a small smile. "Of course you can." "I need you to forgive me." Looking confused, she opened her mouth to ask why when he held his hand up. "Let me get this out. I need you to forgive me for not being honest with you about my feelings. I need you to forgive me for being a complete ass last night when I hurled those awful words at you. I need you to forgive me for breaking your trust in our friendship"

Kelsey's eyes began to fill. "Dammit, Gareth, what are you doing to me?"

Throwing back his head, he replied, "Funny, as I've been asking the same question to myself about you for the past eleven weeks." That got him a small laugh. "I forgive you, Gareth, but asking wasn't necessary. You have *not* broken my trust; you've been the truest of friends, and it is *I* who should be asking *you* to forgive me."

Absorbing her words, Gareth said, "You truly aren't like the others, Kelsey." Gareth reached out his hand. When she accepted his hand in hers, he bowed and kissed the top of it. "Lady Kelsey, your carriage awaits." Looking up he saw her big smile. "Ahh, there it is." Letting go of her hand, they walked downstairs to have breakfast and set out on their final day of adventure.

"Look at how gorgeous this is, Gareth." He and Kelsey stood on the side of the bluff overlooking Brook Bay as they headed down the path to the beach. They'd already walked three of the six-mile trail, and Kelsey was determined to get to the water. Taking pictures left and right, she worked really hard to capture the beauty she was experiencing. Kelsey was practically skipping down the path as she spoke, "You know, I read in that book you lent me that General Seeley would ride Warrior into the surf on this beach to build his endurance. I want my feet in the same water Warrior trained in."

"Of course you do; do you want to race to it?" Stopping and putting her hands on her hips with her cream cable knit sweater wrapped around her waist, she pulled the tip of her sunglasses down the edge of her nose. "You can't be serious? You're carrying the picnic basket and blanket."

"I am beyond serious."

"We can't because, if I drop my camera and it breaks, I'll never get some of these pictures back."

He wasn't going to let her get off that easy. "You're scared you'll lose."

Sounding a bit more annoyed, she responded, "No, I don't want to break my camera."

"Okay, sure, whatever you say."

With a huff of air through her nose she yelled, "Fine! On your mark, get set, go!" She wrapped the neck strap from her Nikon around her wrist and took off.

"That is not fair, and you know it." Gareth yelled.

Shouting back over her shoulder, Kelsey taunted, "What? Scared *you're* going to lose?" She dug in deep and prayed she didn't fall and dash her camera against the large rocks that were present all around her. Suddenly the sand and the water were in view, and they reached the edge of the path as it spilled onto the beach. Completely out of fuel, she collapsed on her knees into the sand, trying to find her breath. Gareth was seconds behind when he too collapsed on the sand next to her. She felt some triumph that he, though in excellent shape, was obviously winded. "That…was so unfair, and you know it. I'm completely knackered."

"Hey, it was your idea," she shot back in between breaths. Sitting there for what felt like an eternity, Kelsey put her camera back over her neck and slowly stood up. "Come on. There are some large boulders we can go sit on out there, and I can get more pictures," she said, reaching out her hand to pull him up. He grabbed on, and she anchored herself so that he could stand.

As they approached the middle of the beach, Kelsey turned and noticed the size of the bluffs that perched along the walking trail over the bay. Stunned by the view, she grabbed her camera and started taking pictures of her new perspective. Gareth climbed onto the large rock and watched her. Kelsey kicked off her shoes and socks. "I'm going to get my feet wet and take some pictures." Gareth nodded that he heard her, and she set off.

Surrounded by the sound of the waves hitting the shore, the sea gulls squealing their protest with one another, Kelsey continued to click away. The sun had begun its decent to the west, and the wind was a breeze, not a gale, making the temperature perfect. The water was colder than she was expecting, so she made her way back to the rocks where she dried off her feet with her socks and put her shoes back on.

Gareth clearly recognized this as another moment with Kelsey that he'd treasure. What made it even more meaningful was that this was a moment he didn't feel guilty about, now that she knew how he really felt. A giant weight had been lifted, and he'd never been so grateful. Kelsey came over to the large boulder and leaned against it. If only they'd met before Jason, maybe he would've had a chance. She turned to him. "Do you mind if I come up there and sit with you?" He smiled. "Not at all." Reaching out his hand, he helped her steady herself as she climbed up and sat next to him.

They both looked out over the vast bay. The clouds were the big billowy ones that danced across the horizon. They sat in comfortable silence for a while when Kelsey yawned. "I think last night is catching up with me. The warm sun on this rock and the waves could easily lull me to sleep."

"I know exactly how you feel. Let's hop down and set up our picnic."

"Great idea."

They took their blanket back to the spot near the end of the path that still offered them a great view, but where the sand was a little dryer. They each sat on a corner of the blanket and placed their lunch basket on the opposite corner from where they sat as Gareth organized and handed out the sandwiches. Salivating over the food, Gareth breathed a sigh of relief. "I'm so glad Roger packed these for us. I had no idea that walking three miles would cause me to be this hungry." Kelsey laughed, "Well, don't forget that I did beat you in a race." "Ha ha, you're very funny" sardonically rolled out of his mouth.

They feasted and were quiet once again until Kelsey, finishing her sandwich and taking a drink of her bottled water, lay back on the blanket and looked up at the sky. "Oh, Gareth, look at the view from here." She patted the spot next to her. Finishing his sandwich and water, he lay next to her. Kelsey pointed up. "Look." He was astounded at the perspective. It was truly beautiful. He turned his head to look at her as she gazed up, counting the clouds rolling by and the shape they were in. She smelled of vanilla, and her creamy skin and caramel hair took his breath away. "Gareth?" "Yes, Kelsey?" "I want you to know that if this had been another time… if my life wasn't already on the path that it's on and this summer had happened, I would've given you my heart. I have no doubt." She reached over and placed her hand on top of his. He grabbed it and brought it to his lips, kissing it and placing it back beside them without letting go. "I have no doubt either, my darling."

They lay there for another fifteen minutes when Gareth realized that Kelsey had dozed off. Laying on his side, using his hand to rest his head, he stared at her and the gentle rising of her chest. He let her rest a while longer and moved pieces of hair off her face when the wind blew it across. Knowing it was getting late, he sat up and began to pull their things together. When it was time to pack the blanket, he leaned over her and whispered her name while touching her shoulder. Quietly turning her head, she looked over at him. She could see the sadness on his face when he began to speak, "Regrettably, we must head back. By the time we hike back to the Defender and get back to the inn, it'll be time for our final dinner, leaving us just enough time to pack so we can leave after breakfast tomorrow."

Slowly sitting up, she agreed. "Let's get ready, then." As they made their way back up the path, Kelsey yelled, "Wait! Gareth, let's take a picture of us together. Here! Hold the camera up with your long arms, and snap it with the beach and water in the background. Like we did at the farm a couple of weeks ago." He did as she asked, and they crossed their fingers it would turn out okay.

Handing her camera back to her, he looked at Kelsey and, in a kind and sincere voice, said, "I will never forget this day as long as I live, Kelsey Chapman from America." She kept his gaze and responded with a gentle voice, "Nor I, Gareth Blythe from England."

They were halfway back to the inn when the heaviness of her imminent departure in a week started to creep in. While their trip had gone nothing like he'd expected, he was actually grateful it all occurred the way it did. He was in love with a girl he'd never have the privilege to call his own and was now going to have to navigate through this life without her. It was a bitter pill to swallow.

Once they had breakfast the next morning and said their goodbyes to Pam and Roger, they made it to the first ferry of the day that would return them to the mainland. Kelsey sat over in the passenger seat and finished the book Gareth had given her the day they set out.

"Well, did you like it?" he asked her.

Looking up, she rewarded him with a smile. "What an amazing story. It just confirms that horses are truly the greatest creatures God ever graced this earth with. Well, next to dogs, of course."

They sat in silence together for a moment before Kelsey slipped out, "All in all, this has to have been one of my best birthday weekends ever."

Gareth stuttered in shock, "What? When was your birthday?"

Kelsey calmly answered, "Friday."

"Why didn't you say anything?"

"Because we never really celebrated birthdays growing up."

"But we would have celebrated. So... you're nineteen now?"

"Yes. And we did celebrate! What do you call that incredible trip? I couldn't have planned a better birthday myself."

Gareth pulled the car over on the side of the quiet road.

"What are you doing?" Kelsey asked.

Gareth didn't answer; he just got out and walked to the back of the vehicle, opened the back, and pulled something out of his bag. When he returned to his seat beside her, he handed her a smallish-sized, square parcel, wrapped in brown paper.

"What's this?"

"I'm sorry it's not wrapped better. I was intending for it to be a going away present, but since your birthday deserves real celebrating, we'll say it's a 'happy last year in your teens' gift."

Kelsey stared for a moment at the gift. "Gareth, you didn't have to do anything for me. You've done enough the past eleven weeks."

"Just open it, Kelsey."

As she pulled the paper back, she saw the canvas of the town square she'd admired.

"Gareth! You really really shouldn't have!"

"But do you like it?"

Kelsey unbuckled so that she could lean over and give him a tight hug. "I love it. Thank you. Thank you so much."

Gareth breathed deeply to save the feeling of her embrace in his mind and in his heart. When she finally pulled away, she buckled and sat staring at the canvas as Gareth got them back on the road. Full of sadness and joy, they continued on in silence when he finally asked the question he'd wanted to ask all weekend, "Kelsey, what are you going to miss most about your time here?"

Biting her lip and looking out the front window, she pondered his question for a moment. "The past eleven months of my life have been life-changing. The past eleven weeks have shown me a whole new world that I had no idea existed. The classes have made me a sharper and more focused artist. However, in the end, what I will miss the most are my conversations with Camilla over tea. But mostly

—I'll miss you, Gareth." Turning her head from him, she looked out the passenger window to avoid him seeing the tears. She wanted to toss the question back to him, but he'd already explained everything in the beautiful letter he'd written her.

Shortly there after, they stopped for petrol. Though she was tired, Kelsey asked Gareth to stop periodically so she could take photos of the countryside landscapes. Gareth suggested they break to have lunch at a quaint pub along the way. Neither one seemed in a hurry for the trip to end. They made it home before seven. As they walked into the house, Camilla greeted them both with hugs. "I'll put the kettle on right away; I want to hear all about it."

Quietly Kelsey asked, "Camilla, if you don't mind, I could really use a hot bath and some rest. Can I tell you about it tomorrow after school?" Looking a bit puzzled but understanding, she responded, "Of course, darling. I'm sure you're exhausted after a jam-packed weekend." Kelsey sent her a grateful smile and made her way up the stairs. Camilla looked at her son, sending him a pleading look for that cup of tea. "One cup, and that is all," Gareth told her. Satisfied that a look only a mother could give had just worked on her son, they walked into the kitchen where Gareth sat down as his mother put the kettle on. "When did you tell her?"

Gareth looked up in surprise. "How do you know I told her?"

Camilla shot him a look. "A mum always knows. How did she take it?"

Gareth leaned his arms on the table and looked out the back window into the yard that had a sliver of remaining light cast into the garden. "She took it well, actually. I mean, under the circumstances."

Camilla carefully asked, "What did she say?"

Rubbing his shadowed chin Gareth shared, "At first she was angry, and she cried, a lot. Then she yelled at me for even saying Jason's name when I tried to apologize for not telling her sooner, and then I gave her the letter I wrote her."

Dropping the tea bag to the floor, Camilla quietly croaked out, "You wrote her a letter?"

Nodding his head, Gareth continued, "I did, and I'm very relieved that I did. What was remarkable was that I fully expected her to want to pack up and come home first thing yesterday, but after reading the letter, she very sweetly sent me a note under my door and asked that we spend our last day together as the dear friends that we'd become."

The kettle whistled, and Camilla poured the water in a teapot, placed the pot beside two cups on a tray, and then walked over to the table. Sitting down, she looked at Gareth and placed her hand on his. "I imagine she just needed some time to herself tonight. Surely you can understand?" Nodding his head, he said, "Perhaps." When the tea had steeped, Camilla poured some for each of them. He put in two spoonsful of sugar and stirred. "There will never be another Kelsey Chapman," he said, breathing out as he desperately tried not to choke on the lump wedged in his throat. He and his mother sat at the table and finished up their one cup of tea in the safe and quiet cover of his childhood home.

* * *

The Final Week

Monday greeted Kelsey with the overcast clouds typical of any English day. Camilla had left a note that she had an early board meeting. Kelsey went about making the tea and toast that she'd grown so very comfortable doing in this kitchen. She was trying for a quick breakfast as she was apprehensive to see what her final scores were for her projects. As she finished and grabbed her rain slicker and umbrella, Gareth came down stairs. She smiled when she saw him. "I'm so anxious to see my grades! Do you think you can give me a lift from school today? This weather is not supposed to improve and carrying my artwork home in this could ruin it." Gareth nodded his head yes but remained quiet. Kelsey starred back. She wanted to ask him what was wrong, but deep down she knew. "What time should I look for you?" he asked quietly "Two o'clock." With that she opened the front door. "Thank you, Gareth. See you in a little while." She shut the door behind her, and he knew that staying at his mother's house until Kelsey's departure was no longer an option.

He went upstairs and packed a bag. Coming back downstairs he called his mother's secretary at the school and asked her to pass the message on that Kelsey would need a ride at two p.m. He grabbed his keys and made his way to his on-campus apartment. Four more nights remained; after that, maybe life would return back to normal.

At half past two, Kelsey stood on the sidewalk with the re-wrapped painting of Gareth. She'd gotten an A on both her projects. The stained glasses window she'd created was going to remain in the art department until Thursday when the all of the exchange students would assemble for the big reveal to their host families. She was so thrilled to surprise Gareth when she got home. *Gosh, I hope he likes it*, she thought to herself. It was really unusual for him to be late, she kept thinking. A moment later, she looked at her watch then back up to see Camilla pull up in her Rover. A bit confused but still happy a ride had shown up, she opened the passenger door to the car. "Are you my ride?"

Shaking her head yes, Camilla explained, "I'm so sorry I'm late. Gareth had a message sent to me you needed a ride, and I just got it! I was in meetings all day!"

"Is he okay?" she asked aloud before she could stop herself.

"Why don't you hop in, and we can talk on the way home." As they drove, Camilla asked, "May I speak freely with you?"

Kelsey looked out the window, and she responded quietly, "Did he tell you?"

Waiting for just a moment to answer, Camilla explained, "Actually, I realized it the day he took you riding. It caught me by surprise."

Kelsey could feel the sting of tears in her eyes as she let out a snarky response, "Ha, well that makes two of us." As she used the back of her hand to wipe her eyes, she continued, "I never meant for this to happen. I truly thought we'd become amazing friends. I talk to you and Gareth all the time about Jason. Even when I called home, I'd always give a report or update on my family. I never meant to give the impression I wanted anything more. I care for Gareth so dearly, and I never wanted this to happen."

As they pulled into the driveway, Camilla put the vehicle in park and looked over at Kelsey. "I don't blame you at all, Kelsey, for what's happened. Gareth is my precious son, and he's had a rough year and a half. I think you were the first person to come along and help him realize there was life outside his grief. My word, dear girl, you've helped me more than you will ever know." Kelsey looked up in surprise as Camilla continued, "I won't speak for his heart. I know all too well the heart wants what the heart wants, but hopefully, with time, he'll be able to move on." Kelsey was barely holding it together when Camilla dropped the final bomb on her. "Gareth feels it would be better that he stays at his apartment on campus until Friday. He didn't have the heart to tell you this morning or tell you he wouldn't be picking you up. This doesn't make me happy, as I don't blame you in the least for any of this; however, you and I know that, in the end, this is the best."

Kelsey slumped back in her seat; she could feel the tears and the weeping that needed to come out beating down the wall of her chest. "I understand, Camilla." She opened her door, grabbed her bag and painting out of the back seat, and made her way to her room where she collapsed across the bed and wept until she fell asleep. Sometime around nine, a soft knock on the door and Camilla's voice startled Kelsey out of her sleep. "Kelsey? Darling, I'm just checking on you. May I open the door?" Letting out a soft yes and sitting up, Kelsey watched as Camilla opened the door, letting the light from the hallway bleed in and guide her where she sat on the edge of the bed.

"I made some supper and can reheat it for you."

Clearing her throat, Kelsey responded, "I'm not very hungry."

Camilla nodded her head in understanding "Would you like a cup of tea and maybe a biscuit? Surely that would make you feel better." Kelsey smiled as she realized one of the things she'd come to adore and was going to truly miss about the English culture: there was nothing in this world that a good cup of tea couldn't fix or heal.

"Actually, Camilla, a cup of tea sounds truly perfect right now."

"Wonderful, I'll make my way to the kitchen and have it ready when you come down."

Kelsey walked to the bathroom where the brightness of the light was intolerable. She almost felt as bad as the morning of her first hangover experience. Looking in the mirror, she used cold water on a towel to calm her puffy eyes and nose. Making her way downstairs, she met Camilla in the kitchen. "I'm excited about seeing the student exhibit Thursday night. Professor Jones said that this by far was the most talented group of summer exchange students they've ever hosted." That made Kelsey smile, and she couldn't wait for Camilla to see the coat of arms stained glass window that she'd done for the family. "I know Becs and Ana are coming to see your work."

Kelsey was thrilled to hear this, and it dawned on her that Gareth most likely wouldn't be attending. She could feel her eyes filling with tears and quickly changed the subject. Keeping the conversation going, Camilla asked, "Have you spoken with Jason? I'm sure he and your family are anxious for your return."

"Oh, yes, I spoke with all of them last night before taking my bath. They're all very excited, to say the least. You know, Camilla, my flight leaves very early Friday morning. I'm truly okay if you want to call a cab to get me to the airport."

Camilla sat at the table and looked at her in shock. "I most certainly will not. Kelsey, you've become a dear friend to my family. You being here, the joy you've brought to my home, our conversations we've shared nightly at our table. No, my dear girl, you cannot get rid of me that easily." Kelsey smiled. She truly would never forget the matriarch of the Blythe family. Reaching across the table and grabbing Camilla's hand, she gave a squeeze and said, "Thank you."

Kelsey spent Tuesday and Wednesday taking final exams for her classes in the daytime and packing in the evenings. She'd come with four suitcases and was leaving with those as well as additional carry-ons. Wednesday Camilla held a goodbye dinner for her. Becs, Philip, Ana, and Ollie came. Each sister asked where Gareth was, and both times Camilla stated that he wouldn't be attending but didn't say why.

Dinner was oven-roasted rack of lamb, slathered in olive oil, thyme, garlic, salt, and freshly-ground black pepper. There was fresh asparagus and wild rice pilaf to go with it. Once dinner was done, Camilla served bread and butter pudding with raisins and vanilla custard and, of course, a cup of tea.

Kelsey simply adored this family. Ana looked so radiant pregnant, and it was so sweet watching Ollie place a hand on her belly and leave it there as he continued in his conversation with Philip. Becs could see that Kelsey had grown very quiet and decided to draw her back into the conversation. "Kelsey, are you nearly packed?" Kelsey looked over at her. "Yes, I came with four heavily packed suitcases, and I will leave with four heavily packed suitcases. And then some." Becs chuckled, and Ana chimed in, "Are you excited about revealing your artwork tomorrow night? We're so delighted to attend."

"I'm excited, nervous, and anxious as I hope it will be well received." Camilla came back to the table after retrieving more tea. "You know Pam and Roger called to say that they're receiving many inquiries on the painting you did for them last weekend. They love telling the story of how you did it in one afternoon." All four adults swung their heads in unison as if watching a tennis match at Wimbledon. With a raised eyebrow and suspicious tone Becs came right out with her question to Kelsey, "You drove to Isle of Wight last weekend by yourself?" With eight eyes piercing her, she muttered, "No, Gareth drove me."

There was an awkward silence with puzzled looks. It was all too much. She didn't know what to say; she could feel the tears rising up, and this wasn't how she wanted everyone to remember the dinner. Pushing her chair away from the table, Kelsey excused herself and went straight to her room. Thirty minutes later, there was a knock on her door. She opened it to find Becs and Ana standing there. "May we come in?"

"Yes, of course you can." Opening her door wider, she let them both in and sat on her bed while the very pregnant Ana took the wing back chair by the window and Becs sat at the desk. Ana calmly broke the silence, "Mum filled us in." Kelsey immediately dissolved into tears. Both girls jumped to her side, "Oh, Kelsey, darling don't cry."

"I never meant for this to happen. Gareth has been nothing but a gentleman to me this whole time, and our friendship has been one of the truest friendships that I've ever formed with anyone. I never meant to hurt him, and I certainly never wanted to leave like this."

"Oh, Kelsey, we know. We totally understand."

Trying to catch her breath in between sobs she pleaded, "I do love him and care for him dearly, but I've already given my heart to Jason. I can't give my heart to Gareth as well, not like that."

Becs lightly rubbed her back to console her. "Kelsey, it'll be okay. Please believe me when I say that your time here has helped my mother and my brother heal from losing our father. I hope you know that. Gareth will be okay: we'll see to it. You can leave here knowing that you've made our lives so much better."

Kelsey let those words sink deep into her heart and allowed the silence to help calm her frayed nerves. "Thank you both so very much." She stood and hugged them. "You are coming tomorrow night, right?"

Both girls let out a laugh when Ana responded, "We wouldn't miss it for all the tea in China." Kelsey smiled as that was the same thing that Gareth said to her the day he took her to the farm. If the circumstances had been different, she would've loved to have been sister-in-law to them. As they stepped out, Kelsey decided to take a hot bath to relax so that she could try and get some sleep.

Thursday night arrived, and Kelsey's hands were sweaty and her stomach a jumble of nerves. All the students were there along with their host families. Camilla, Becs, Philip, Ana, and Ollie were present to see the big reveal. Kelsey prayed that Gareth would show at the last minute, but as the assembly started, she knew it wasn't going to happen. Biting her lip to stop the tears from coming, she tried to focus on Professor Jones as he stepped to the podium.

Once he welcomed everyone, each of the twelve students came forward and explained their piece, their inspiration, and then revealed it to the audience. Sitting on the stage, Kelsey knew she was the last to present. After an hour, Professor Jones called her name. She stood and took her place at the podium. Gathering her thoughts, she looked to the back of the room where Gareth was standing in the doorway. She stood in silence for what seemed an eternity, as she couldn't take her eyes off of him. "Ms. Chapman? Kelsey?" She looked at Professor Jones. "Are you ready, Ms. Chapman?"

Nodding her head yes she came back to reality and continued. "When I arrived twelve weeks ago and was given this assignment, I went into total freak-out mode." The small audience laughed. "As an artist, you want to express those things that speak to you, and at the time I had no idea what that would look like. The Blythe family opened their home to a stranger and from day one made me feel like I'd always been a part of their family. One evening before dinner I spent some time looking at all the pictures of their family in the sitting room. It reminded me so much of my own family at home, and while there were days that I'd find myself homesick, looking at these pictures helped alleviate that for me. On one particular evening I noticed a small family coat of arms that was sitting in a curio. Upon further inspection I discovered it was the Blythe Coat of Arms. I spent a few afternoons in the library and did some research."

Looking at Camilla, she continued, "Forgive me if you know this already, but I found this fascinating. Your family name is of Scottish origin, as it was originally found in the Scottish and English borderlands. It's also a name for a happy and cheerful person. After personally spending time with the four of you, this is certainly the truth." The audience gave an appreciative chuckle.

"I spent a lot of time looking at that coat of arms, and I decided that, as a thank you, I'd attempt to do something I've never done. After the couple of weeks that our class spent entrenched in the history of stained glass and the techniques that were used, I thought *how crazy would it be if I attempted something of this magnitude*? To take myself out of my comfort zone and really push my limits. Your family has been through a lot in the past year, all of you have been pushed to your limits, yet the core of what makes your family so wonderful remains intact. It's a shining light to your community.

That was my inspiration. Camilla, Becs, Ana… and Gareth…I hope you will look upon this with fond memories of my time with you."

As she walked over and pulled the cover off for the reveal there was an audible gasp from everyone in the room. At first Kelsey wasn't sure if that was a good thing. Suddenly Camilla, Becs, and Ana got up from their seats and walked up to the podium where the Blythe Coat of Arms sparkled and shined before them, with splendid reds, golds, and whites. How she was able to capture the armor and the crest in the glass so perfectly in such a short amount of time baffled even Professor Jones. Suddenly there was clapping and tears as all three Blythe women tackled Kelsey with hugs and thanks yous.

Professor Jones stood and dismissed the assembly. "Ladies and gentleman, this concludes our program for this evening. Make sure to stop and congratulate each of our guest exchange students on a marvelous job well done." Kelsey looked up to see if Gareth was still there, but he was gone. Camilla had tears steaming down her face. "Oh, my darling girl, you've truly outdone yourself this time." Becs and Ana were delirious with tears and laughter. All three surged into her again and bear-hugged her. Kelsey quipped, "You know that this is very un-English of you!" Phillip retorted, "It must be the American influence." And with that, they all laughed and admired the piece together.

Once she had said her goodbyes to her classmates and professors, Kelsey went to the easel and wrapped up the window to carry back to the Blythe home. As she walked out of the Grace Harding Building for the Arts for the last time, she turned to face the entrance. Closing her eyes, she whispered a prayer of thanks. "I got more than I bargained for on this trip, but I'm a better human because of it. I just wanted to say thank you."

With that she walked to the waiting Rover and celebrated an amazing evening with the Blythe family, minus one. By midnight the house was quiet, and Camilla had long gone to bed, as they had to be on the road to the airport by five-thirty a.m. Kelsey couldn't sleep and found herself staring at the painting she'd done for Gareth. Walking the easel and painting into his room, she realized that she'd never stepped foot in there the past twelve weeks. She set the easel in the corner and then positioned the painting on it so he wouldn't miss it when he came in his room.

As she stepped away to give it one last glance, she decided to look around. She saw all his football medals and trophies. What stood out to her were the dozens of framed photos that he had of he and his father. One was from Halloween. Gareth was dressed as a puppy dog; he couldn't have been more than nine years of age. There was a picture of them snow skiing in the Alps and fly-fishing somewhere in England. Kelsey's heart melted and ached for him. He loved his father so dearly, and to lose him like he had didn't seem fair.

Looking on his desk, she saw a picture of them together from the day at the farm. She studied it for a while and finally sighed, "Oh, Gareth, I so desperately wanted to say goodbye to you." Putting the picture down, she saw stationery and a pen. She knew immediately that she needed to write him a letter just as he had written to her. It was her last chance to give a proper farewell.

Gareth lay awake in his apartment, on his bed facing the ceiling. Suddenly a hand was on his chest, moving down his belly and searching for his cock. This was who he really was. A genuine rake bastard who wasn't looking for anything more than a good romp in bed with pretty girls to release the stress when life was becoming too much. He wasn't committing his life to anyone. Not when he was facing ten more years of medical school. Kelsey was the only one he would've broken this rule for, but she wasn't an option.

He was hard as a rock when Heidi looked up at him. "Do you have another condom?" Reaching to the table next to him, he pulled the last one from the box and handed it to her. Tearing the foil open with her teeth, she rolled the ribbed tip on, slowly pushing out the air. Straddling him, she sank down on him, thrusting her hips forward. He threw back his head and let out a "fuck" as she started to roll her hips slowly.

Gareth closed his eyes and did his best to enjoy it. Sure it felt good, it always did, but the distinct lack of passion and love made this merely a simple, physical act. He didn't care if she came or not; he wanted his release, and then he wanted her gone. As they moved back and forth with each other, Gareth felt the tension building and building until he finally thrust up into her, coming hard as she continued to ride him. He lay there uninterested now as she eventually came and slipped off of him. Lying next to him, she fell asleep without a word.

He took off the condom, tied it, and discarded it. Looking over at the clock, he saw it was five fifteen in the morning. Kelsey would be leaving for the airport in in fifteen minutes. There was still time. He headed into the bathroom and turned on the shower. As the steam started to cover the mirror, he wiped it clear and saw his reflection. *You're a moron if you go to her. A fucking moron.* He jumped in the shower and tried to wash off the dirty, grimy feeling of the past four nights spent with Heidi. It didn't matter how hard he scrubbed—it was still there. Letting the hot water wash over his body, Gareth was reminded of how tired he was, physically and emotionally. Turning off the water and pulling back the curtains, he reached for a towel. As he did, something shiny caught his eye. Leaning in for a closer look, he saw the silver earrings that Kelsey had worn to the party several weeks back. She must have taken them off when she showered that day and forgotten all about them.

Dripping into the tub and gently lifting them as if they were a precious gem, he closed his eyes and muttered, "Time to go be a fucking moron, Gareth." He left a note for Heidi to lock up behind her. He also left one line in there basically saying *it's not you, it's me, and have a nice life.* Yes, it was a dick move, but that's what he'd now been reduced to. He looked at his watch. Six a.m. "Shit!" Thinking, he realized he could still make it to the airport; he had to at least try. He jumped in his Defender and took off in hopes that he hadn't just made a bad situation worse.

Once Camilla was parked, she helped Kelsey carry all her luggage to the airline ticket counter where all bags were checked into Kelsey's final destination. She had a quick flight to Heathrow with a short layover. Then she headed to Atlanta before arriving home at six p.m. Back home.

By the time they'd finished at the ticket counter, it was six forty-five. Her flight departed at eight thirty, and she still had to get through security. Camilla walked with her through security and to her gate. With a little time to spare, they each had a cup of tea as they waited for boarding to begin.

"This is a very surreal moment for me," Kelsey admitted. "Before my senior year, I had to beg my parents to see how beneficial this trip would be to help me as an artist and a teacher later on. Once they were on board, I had no idea about all the life experiences I'd have that final year of high school. Then I get here, and I feel like I've lived two lifetimes in one summer."

Camilla laughed. "I'll miss that wit and so much more being in my home, Kelsey. What are your plans when you return home?"

"I start my college courses in a couple weeks. I can't believe I'll be an art teacher in four years."

"Those kids will be beyond the luckiest to have you as their teacher."

"I appreciate your confidence! Now if I could get my head around it, then maybe it wouldn't feel like such a daunting task." The final boarding call came on the loud speaker, and they stood up. The tears quickly came for both of them.

"Oh, darling girl, always know you have a place here with us."

Kelsey could barely speak as she desperately tried to wipe away the tears flowing down her face. "Thank you so much, Camilla, I hope you know that the same is true for you in Virginia." They hugged and said one final goodbye as Kelsey made her way to the ticket agent to hand her the boarding pass.

Just as she was handing her the ticket, she heard his voice. "Kelsey, please, wait." Kelsey froze in her place and turned to see Gareth standing several feet behind her. Staring at each other for a good thirty seconds, he said her name again, but this time reaching out his hand. "Kelsey?" She jumped out of line, dropping her bags, and ran straight into his arms where she held on for dear life. She was crying so intensely. Gareth just held her and let her cry, tenderly rubbing her back and kissing the top of her head. "Oh my darling, Kelsey, I'm so sorry. I wasn't who you needed me to be the past several days. I'm not a good man. Please forgive me." Kelsey could only nod her head yes as she continued to hold onto him.

When she finally pulled herself together to talk, she spoke from her heart. "Gareth, you are the best kind of man. You have so much to offer this world." The ticket agent approached, cutting Kelsey's words short. "Pardon me, miss, but you must board now, or you'll miss this flight." Reluctantly pulling her away, he kissed the top of her head one last time. Then he gently placed his hands on either side of her face and looked her straight in her red puffy eyes and quietly spoke, "Goodbye, my Lady Kelsey."

Not a half a beat behind him she responded, "Goodbye, my Sir Gareth." He released her as she stepped back. Looking at Camilla one last time, who herself had dissolved, Kelsey gave a final wave. Picking up her bags, she walked onto the jet way and never looked back. Camilla came up behind Gareth and placed a hand on his back. They turned together without a word and headed home.

Two hours later, Gareth stood in front of the painting. He couldn't stop staring at it. He finally worked up the courage to acknowledge the letter. Reaching up, he took it down from the easel, sat down at his desk, and opened it.

Gareth,

I leave for the airport in a couple of hours, and there is so much I wish to say. I just have to trust that, after all that has happened between us this summer, this letter will fill the space between.

As you will know by the time you read this, I came into your room to leave you a gift that I truly hope you like. I so wish I could see your reaction. I'll have to be satisfied with the hope that you will like it and that it'll bring you happy memories. As I sit here and reflect, I cannot help but smile. The awkwardness of that first day. I thought I had you all figured out. Typical young handsome Englishman from a well-to-do, educated family, who was never told no. Always used to getting his way and what he wants. I went to school with many privileged handsome, young men like you. I saw how they treated the quiet, unassuming girls like me. We were a conquest. You were no different, as far as I was concerned. What I didn't have figured out was that you and our friendship would become my most treasured memory to take back home with me.

You have a heart of gold, Gareth. You may not think so, but I know. You are going to change the medical community and save lives because of your golden heart. Time will show you this as you continue your journey. As I close my letter, please believe me when I say that I don't believe that our lives crossed paths by accident. My life is wildly better and more complete because of the summer I spent here with you and your mother. Thank you for proving me wrong for all the right reasons. I wish you nothing but the best in this life, Gareth, and in all that you set out to do.

Yours always,
Kelsey

Gareth got up from the chair and closed his bedroom door. Resting his back to it, he let out an exhausted breath as he slid down to the floor. Staring at the beautiful painting, Gareth finally gave himself permission to let go of all the emotion that he'd been holding back for weeks. Keeping his head between his arms and knees up, he cried himself into oblivion. He remained in his room for the rest of the day, allowing the grief and sadness to wash over him. It would take him weeks to process the reality of losing a friendship that he'd never get back, of missing out on the chance he knew he never really had, and of resolving the regret he felt for not being with Kelsey the final nights that she remained in York.

JUNE 3, 2014
ONE LAST KISS

Another weekend had come and gone. The six o'clock alarm was going off as Kelsey and Jason both chose to groan and turn over. Finally, the dogs began to stir, and they knew that they could no longer ignore the rising sun and all that had to be accomplished. Jason got up, let the dogs out, and promptly crawled back into bed with Kelsey, wrapping himself around her. "Five more minutes," he moaned.

Kelsey didn't argue but turned over to face him. "We really do need to get up, Jason."

"Not yet," he pouted.

Kelsey laughed. "We have so much we need to do before we leave, not to mention the packing."

Keeping his eyes closed, he started to kiss her lightly on the lips. Feeling herself become a little greedy, she began to kiss him back as he started using his thumbs to roll and circle over her nipples. Desperately not wanting to, Kelsey pulled back and rested her forehead on his forehead. "We will never get out of here on time if we don't stop right now."

"Oh, god Kels, are you going to make me wait to finish this tonight?"

"Afraid so, husband."

"Then give me one more kiss to remind me what I have waiting when I come home." She launched into Jason with fire and passion, kissing him with intensity and stroking his already hard cock. Pulling back, she whispered, "We will certainly finish this when you get home tonight." Pushing herself out of the bed, she walked naked into the bathroom, which allowed Jason to enjoy the view.

Jason looked at his list of things that needed to be wrapped up. The remaining obligations of the contract on the new stadium would be finalized today; then he would need to submit the updated permits to the city for the new highway expansion proposal they'd won the bid on. Kelsey was headed in for her last day at work for the month. The time for the trip that Jason had bought her for Christmas was here, and she was finally getting excited.

Jason grabbed a cup of coffee to go, and Kelsey grabbed her packed lunch out of the fridge. As they walked to their cars, Jason set his coffee on the hood of the truck, and before Kelsey could climb in her car, he came up behind her, spun her around, and placed both his hands on her face. "I need one last kiss." He devoured Kelsey, kissing her and leaving her breathless. Softly pulling away, he rested his forehead on hers. "Don't forget that we have unfinished business when we get home." Smiling, he let go of her, stepped backwards to his truck, grabbed the coffee off the hood, climbed in, and pulled out of the driveway. All the while Kelsey watched him as her heart rate finally slowed back down to normal and the throb between her legs stopped long enough for her to get in her car. *God I love that man* was all she could think as she put the car in reverse and made her way to work.

As usual, work was never dull or boring. After lunch the final countdown in her mind was on to get out of there for a whole month. The idea that by this time on Thursday she would be in Italy floored Kelsey. After all these years of talking about it, now they were actually going to see all the beautiful paintings and statues of the Sistine Chapel, the Pieta, and the David. A dream come true.

As she put her purse away, she got a phone call from a number she didn't recognize. She declined the call and figured that, if it were that import, they would leave a message. A minute later the phone rang again. Retrieving the phone out of her back pocket, she saw it was the same number. She again declined the call. A minute later a voice message popped up. Something felt very off. The uneasy sick feeling that had plagued her over the holidays was back with intensity in that moment. She hit play on the voicemail.

"Mrs. B, it's Mac. We can't find Mr. B and were hoping you knew where he was. Will you call me back when you get this message?" A part of Kelsey wanted to panic, but she tried to remain controlled as she immediately called him back. In the conversation she explained that she and Jason left home at the same time that morning. He was going straight into work to tie up loose ends before taking a whole month off. When Mac said that he had not been seen or heard from since nine forty-five, the raw sick feeling in the pit of her stomach intensified.

"I'm on my way." Kelsey hung up with Mac and ran to the closest computer. She logged into the cloud and used the location services feature to find Jason's phone and see if she could locate him. According to location services, he was on company property, but in the back near the giant rock and gravel piles. Those piles were so tall that Kelsey was sure they were just blocking his truck from view. It was also possible that he silenced his phone and forgot he'd done so. She let the managers know that she needed to leave a little earlier than anticipated to help locate her husband and calm concerns. She didn't admit it was to calm the worry *she* was experiencing. Management completely understood and wished her a wonderful time on her trip.

As Kelsey drove to Virginia Beach, she called Jason's number multiple times only to continually get his voicemail. The knot in her belly was so tight that she was nauseated. As she pulled up to the front offices, she was greeted by a police car. She hopped out of her car. As she walked inside, the office manager and Mac were being asked questions. "Oh, there you are, Mrs. B!" said Mac sounding relieved. "Have you been able to reach him?"

"No, I haven't. Bonnie, did he come in this morning?" Bonnie was their front office manager who had been hired by Jason's father. She was a loyal employee and didn't hide the fact that she was very worried as this was not like her boss to go missing in action all day. "He did come in. He took a phone call from Michael Dupree, and then fifteen minutes later said he was going to run some errands but would check back in before heading home. He told me to reach him on his phone if I needed anything. I had a couple of questions for him about an hour after he left but have only been able to reach his voicemail."

Kelsey looked at the clock and saw that it was two thirty. Abruptly leaving the front desk, she walked back to his office where she jumped on his laptop. She logged back into the cloud and looked for his phone. It was in the exact location as forty-five minutes ago. Something clicked in Kelsey, and she knew everything was very wrong. Heading back to the front, she asked Bonnie, "What time did he leave here this morning?"

"Nine thirty."

"When did you try to call him with your questions?"

"Around ten forty-five. He told me he was going to drive back and talk to Mac and the rest of the drivers." Mac nodded and went on to say, "That's exactly what happened. That meeting was over with by nine forty-five, though."

Bonnie then picked back up, "Jason said he was going to the stadium to speak with the manager after seeing Mac, and then heading to the city to drop off paper work for the new highway contract." In her most serious and sullen voice Bonnie also added, "Mrs. Bauer, Michael Dupree didn't come into work today."

Before anyone could blink, Kelsey sprinted to her car. Throwing it in reverse, she sped around the corner, recklessly driving through the gate station. She drove to the very back of the property, bobbing and weaving around the giant gravel and rock mounds. When she got to the fourth one, she hit the breaks, and her heart plummeted. She saw Jason's truck with the driver's side open—but no Jason.

She started to pull the car forward and had to stop as she was trembling too fiercely to drive. She turned the car off and slowly opened her door. As she stepped out and stood up, in a quaking voice she called his name. "Jason? Jason, you answer me right now." The only response she heard were crows fussing above on the power lines. In a voice she didn't recognize as her own, she yelled, "Jason, goddammit you answer me right now!"

Fear completely engulfed her, and she sprinted in utter panic to the truck. As she neared it, she came to an abrupt stop and began to scream. A scream so piercing that the employees on the back of the property heard her. They later explained that the desperate cries they heard would haunt them in their dreams.

Kelsey found his lifeless body slumped over on the seat. Clutching him, she pleaded through her wild tears, "Please, oh god, Jason please don't leave me, not like this." Mac and the police officer and another truck driver came around the corner and were immediately overwhelmed by the sight. Mac pulled Jason's body out of the truck and onto the ground. Kelsey pushed him away and screamed, "Get away from him, and call 911!" Down on the ground, she pulled her husband's body into her lap and was holding him while rocking back and forth and wailing uncontrollably.

Forty minutes later, her screams had dissolved into hiccuped sobs. The ambulance was on scene, more officers arrived, and crime scene investigators were in route. Kelsey's parents had been called but had not yet arrived to help coax their daughter away from his body. Officer Hooper, the young policeman who had been there since she arrived at the office, was now down on the ground, trying to talk to her while she was still holding and rocking Jason's body.

In a complete trance, Kelsey grew eerily quiet and frighteningly still. "Mrs. Bauer, can you look at me?" The shock was still throughout her, and her eyes remained locked on her husband. "Mrs. Bauer, I know you are devastated." As he said that, the news helicopter could be heard overhead, making low wide circles around the property. "Mrs. Bauer, this is a crime scene, and the longer we sit here, the more we contaminate the scene and any evidence that will help capture the person who did this. I know your world is shattered right now, but I also know you want to find out who did this. Let me help you up and get you to your family who…" Before he could finish she muttered a name that Officer Hooper couldn't understand. "Ma'am, I'm sorry. What did you say?"

Kelsey kept her gaze fixed on her husband, brushing his blood-soaked hair back off his face. She finally looked up at the young officer and in a terrifying calm said, "Michael James Dupree. He did this. He's the one that did this to my Jason. He's the man you're looking for."

ABOUT THE AUTHOR

Cobie Daniels lives in the Tidewater region of Virginia with her husband Sam, three Norwich terriers and two miniature donkeys Bob and Bill. When she is not writing, she is doing one of the following three things: hosting The Cobie Daniels Show podcast, training for her next runDisney half marathon or saving the world one password at a time.

For more information visit my website where you can follow me on Twitter or Instagram, like me on Facebook, or listen to my podcast.

Twitter: @cobiedaniels
Facebook: www.facebook.com/CobieDaniels
Website: www.cobiedaniels.com
Email: authorcobiedaniels.com

www.ingramcontent.com/pod-product-compliance
Lightning Source LLC
Chambersburg PA
CBHW030548180626
46816CB00005B/1451